Lethal Voyage

A Mike Stoneman Thriller

Lethal Voyage

A Mike Stoneman Thriller

Kevin G. Chapman

For Sharon, who cares about these characters as much as I do, and without whose constant support and ideas, these books would not be possible. All my love.

Chapter 1 – Hell Hath No Fury

July 16, 2018
Carrboro, North Carolina

A DROP OF BLOOD clung to the tip of the knife. A nasty red stain was forming on the white carpet of Madeline Hawthorne's bedroom. The woman gripping the knife breathed in staccato gasps. The muscles in her right arm twitched from exertion.

Madeline lay on her stomach on the king-sized bed, bathed in moonlight. Blood welled up from the two thin gashes in the back of her silver nightgown and ran down onto the 2,000-thread-count sheet. Madeline groaned and moved her left arm.

"I said die, Bitch!"

The knife plunged into Madeline's back five more times in quick succession. Crimson spatter covered the attacker's face, arms, and blouse. The woman holding the knife was petite, with well-defined muscles in her arms and shoulders, honed by hours in the dance studio. Her lithe calves were visible below a black leather skirt. She tensed for another lunge, but there was no need.

She stood over Madeline's corpse, knife hanging at her side, and breathed deeply. A dark pool spread out on the mattress and ran in two rivulets off the edge. When her pulse steadied, she calmly laid the knife on a clean space near the foot of the bed. She removed her shoes, then tiptoed to the bathroom. Selecting a robin's-egg-blue hand towel from a neat pile on a white wicker credenza, she wiped her hands and face.

She then walked barefoot around the bed, avoiding the patches of blood, until she reached a closet. Inside, she stretched up to a high shelf over a row of dark men's business suits and removed an ornately carved maple box.

John had shown her the box once, when Madeline went away for the weekend. He was unnaturally proud of his Colt Python .357 Magnum with the 4-inch barrel. He had bragged about spending $4,000 for it at a gun show in Charlotte. He once told her he could blow the head off any intruder. He always kept it fully loaded with six bullets. She returned to the bathroom, sat on the edge of the marble bathtub, and waited.

She and John had made love in that spacious tub and on the wide shelf running around its length. She remembered the smooth, cold feeling of the chrome soap dish against the arch of her foot when she had braced herself against it. She could smell the cinnamon candles she lit before their bath. John was more than twenty years her elder, but he kept up fairly well. He enjoyed her flexibility and the taut smoothness of her muscles. He told her what a shrew Madeline was, and said he was going to divorce her as soon as their youngest son graduated from

Chapel Hill.

In John, she had a patron and a lover. He wanted her to be a star someday. He had written to a major talent agent he knew in New York, at the William Morris Agency. John had praised her voice and dancing, her beauty, and her poise. The agent had written back, expressing great interest and asking when she could come to New York for an interview. She smiled at the memory, but then her brows furrowed. John had *lied* to her.

Ten minutes later, she heard the front door open, then close quietly. She heard four faint beeps as John disabled the burglar alarm. She had done the same when she arrived, then re-set it before she came upstairs. She had watched John do it when he brought her home. It was a simple four-digit code, and the numbers were his birthday. It was after midnight and she knew John would be creeping upstairs soon, hoping not to wake his wife. He told her many times how he had perfected the routine. He would go to the bathroom to change into his pajamas, which he kept on a shelf there. Then, he would slip into bed without turning on a light or making a sound.

She waited patiently, the cool wooden butt of the pistol in her hand. With a soft whirr, the air conditioning kicked to life, fluttering the end of a toilet paper roll. She detected a slight creak from a nearby floorboard. The bathroom door crept inward, blocking her view of the threshold. When the door swung shut, she could dimly make out John's silhouette against the soft green glow of his electric razor, charging next to the sink.

"Were you fucking Cheryl tonight?"

Although she whispered, John jumped, then spun around, squinting into the darkness.

His voice came out in a hissing whisper. "Holy shit! Is that you? What the fuck are you doing here? How did – you have to leave. What if Maddy wakes up?" She could hear the panic in his voice and see his head turning quickly from her direction to the bathroom door, listening for movement from the bed. She wasn't worried about Madeline waking up, but she was happy to keep up the charade.

She stood up slowly, keeping perfectly balanced on her bare feet. "Don't worry, I had to be with you, John. I love you. How could you cheat on me?"

"What?" John's eyes were adjusting to the darkness, but he couldn't see any details, except for the reflection of the green charger light off her eyes. "Jesus! No. I told you I needed to work out the details with Maddy. I'm working on it."

"I know you were with Cheryl. I saw you at the motel."

"What?" John tried to control his voice, but failed. "I don't know what you're talking about."

She took two steps forward, until she was inches from John. She smelled his cologne – the one he always put on after having sex with her so his wife wouldn't smell her on his body. She looked up into his shadowy face, the .357 Magnum dangling next to her right thigh. She slid her left arm around his neck, drawing him toward her. Some of Madeline's spattered blood transferred from her blouse to John's white dress shirt.

"Oh, John. I'll go soon. I just had to see you." She pulled against his neck and felt him lean in toward her. As he whispered something she didn't listen to, she brought the gun up until the muzzle touched his chin. At the same instant, she stepped back a half-step and squeezed the trigger.

The explosion was louder than she expected, and the kickback from the discharge jerked the gun out of her hand. John's body slumped forward as she stepped sideways, allowing him to fall with a moist *thwack*. Dark lines quickly formed in the indentations surrounding the 12-inch square ceramic tiles next to what was left of John's head. Bits of bone, blood, and brain matter speckled her face and hair, but the bulk of the tissue covered the far wall and mirror.

She looked down at the gory scene and sighed. It was sad, really. John could have made her so happy, and she would have made him such a good wife. She shook her head and picked up a light blue washcloth, then carefully wiped her hands. She cleaned the butt and the trigger of the gun, removing the spattered blood as well as her fingerprints. She used the cloth to hold the gun and pushed it into John's dead hand, pressing his fingers into the wood and chrome and placing his index finger on the trigger. Lifting the gun and his hand until his arm was fully extended, she pressed his finger into the trigger and squeezed. The bullet burrowed into the ceiling as John's arm dropped back to the floor. The gun skittered across the tiles, settling beneath the waving toilet paper.

She walked carefully back into the bedroom. There, she retrieved the knife and carried it to the bathroom, where she wiped some of the blood from the blade onto John's pants. Then, she repeated the process of wiping away her fingerprints, placing the knife in John's hand, and squeezing his prints onto the hilt. She used the blue cloth to pick up the knife by its blade and tossed it back onto the bed. She retrieved her shoes and tucked the blood-smeared towel and washcloth into the waistband of her skirt.

As she carefully walked toward the door, she passed Madeline's dressing table. She plucked a tissue from its box and used it to remove the top of a small heart-shaped porcelain container. Inside, she saw the glint of a gemstone in the moonlight filtering in through the window. She replaced the lid and picked up the jewelry box, shaking it softly to hear the tinkling sound coming from inside. Then she left the room, leaving no footprints.

As gruesome as the crime scene was, it didn't really present much of a mystery from a police perspective. The official report said the wife was stabbed multiple times, and the husband's prints were on the knife. There was no sign of forced entry. The alarm was engaged. After he killed his wife, the husband retrieved a gun registered to him from a storage box in his closet and went to the bathroom. He fired the gun once into the ceiling, probably trying to work up his courage, then blew his own brains out. He had the appropriate powder residue on his hand and clothes.

Neighbors and friends confirmed that the marriage had been on the rocks. A review of the husband's credit card spending had quickly led them to a mid-level motel on the edge of Durham. There, the night clerk and some low-quality surveillance cameras identified John Hawthorne exiting room 108 an hour before the likely time of death, with a young blonde woman. His Amazon account included sexy lingerie recently shipped to Cheryl Winters, a graduate student at UNC, where Hawthorne was the director of the musical theater program. Ms. Winters was devastated to learn of the man's death and quickly admitted that she had been having an affair with him for the past few weeks. She was not much of a suspect; she had no motive, and her doorbell cam showed her coming home twenty minutes after she left the motel and not leaving again that night.

The forensics unit called in from Durham thought the angle of the gunshot was unusual for one that was self-inflicted. But it was difficult to be sure, since the .357 had blown so much of his head off. They also thought the orientation of the prints on the knife handle was unusual. But the prints were definitely his.

The crime scene was a mess. After a neighbor called in a report of possible gunshots, the officers who responded had not followed precise forensic protocols. The rookie who went into the bedroom first had barfed on the carpet upon viewing the bloody mess. His partner had rushed in to check whether the woman was dead, smearing the blood and leaving his footprints all over the rug. There were no other suspects. There was no robbery. It was obviously a murder/suicide.

John Hawthorne's family had swooped in and tried to convince the insurance adjuster that it could have been a double murder, but the insurance company didn't buy it. Nobody could say for sure if anything was missing, and since the alarm was still engaged when the responding officers arrived, the police dismissed the idea that a burglar was responsible for both deaths. The wife's daughter got paid off on her policy, then accused the husband's son of stealing some of Madeline Hawthorn's jewelry.

Cheryl Winters told the investigating officers she did not believe John Hawthorne would kill himself. She wanted them to investigate a prior mistress, whom Cheryl claimed was "batshit crazy." She had allegedly threatened to kill Cheryl when she found out that John had moved on. The local police tried to find the other woman, but she had left town and nobody knew where she was. Her apartment had been cleaned out. They put out an alert to the state police to be on the lookout for the woman, with information about the car registered to her, but they weren't really concerned. The guy had killed himself. It was his gun. Nobody else had a motive. It was not worth any more resources. They could safely close the case. Nothing to see here. If the other woman ever came back to town, they would question her. If they remembered.

Chapter 2 – The Lullaby of Broadway

Eight months later – March 16, 2019
New York, NY

MAXIMILLIAN HORACIO BLOOM lounged on the king-sized bed, his head nestled in the plush feather pillows. The late afternoon sun peeked through the thin lace curtains of the Milford Plaza Hotel. Turning his head toward the sunbeam, he could barely make out the dark streak of the Hudson River in the distance, between two buildings. The cold March wind whipped the flag atop an office tower across Eighth Avenue. He yawned and stretched his thick arms over his head as the sound of the shower suddenly stopped. Max smiled and rolled ponderously onto his side so he would have a better view.

A few seconds later, he was rewarded when a woman emerged from the bathroom, dabbing at her wet hair. Even in such a mundane act, she looked graceful. She had a white towel wrapped around her slender torso, suspended above her half-exposed breasts. Her fingernails, painted bright red, contrasted against her pale skin. She was not tall, but her long, lithe legs gave the illusion of height. The fresh scent of lavender soap reached Max's nostrils.

"You are amazing," he said softly, admiring her glistening skin and wondering if he could manage another erection so soon. In his younger days, he could always get it up on command, but his younger days were behind him.

The woman lifted her foot onto the corner of the bed and leaned into a deep hamstring stretch. "Did you tell that director friend of yours how amazing I am?" Her fingers reached out beyond her toes and softly stroked the hair on Max's leg, sending a tingle up into his groin. The reaction was immediate, but only momentary.

"Oh, you can be sure I've been singing your praises, Sweetheart. I'm working on several wonderful opportunities for you." Max's baritone was as smooth as a 21-year-old single malt. "I know you're impatient, my dear, but you've been in town barely half a year. These things take time."

The woman pressed her mouth into an exaggerated pout as she switched legs, allowing her towel to fall to the floor. She stretched the other leg, then stood up, ignoring the fallen towel. "Do I really have to go on that stupid boat?"

"It's a ship, my dear, a cruise ship, and a very large one. If you call it a boat, people will think you're a first-timer."

She found her black panties on the nightstand. "It *is* my first time. Are you sure it's really a credit that Broadway producers will care about?"

"Absolutely!" Max swung his legs over the edge of the bed and scanned the floor for his trousers. "This is a Broadway-quality show."

"I'd rather have actual Broadway. I want to stay here – with you. Call them and tell them I got a part here and I can't go."

"Sweetheart, you signed the contract. It's too late to change your mind. Your reputation would be sullied if you didn't fulfill your contractual obligations. You said you performed it in college, right?"

"Sure I did – I played the lead. Well, one of the leads. I love the show; it lets me sing *and* dance." She balanced on her left foot while slowly raising her right leg until it was parallel with the floor. She then reached out to thread the panties over her foot, before returning the leg to the floor in a smooth motion.

"I think I'd be better off staying here with you and auditioning instead." She fastened her black bra and stood with her arms akimbo, staring at Max. "I'm beginning to think that you don't love me as much as you say you do. It's like you're trying to get rid of me for six months by sending me away."

"Nonsense," Max replied quickly. "I love ya, Baby. This gig will be great for your career. The director on board, Brandon Marshall, is a good friend of mine. I've told him you're a tremendous talent. He'll take good care of you."

"Do you promise?"

"Of course. I'm not trying to get rid of you. I'm trying to advance your career. While you're gone, I'll be working on my divorce. With any luck, when you get back, I'll be free of that shrew I'm married to and you'll be able to come to my apartment."

She smiled sweetly, slipping into her heels. "I'd like that." She floated across the floor to where Max was standing and slithered her arms around his neck. With her lips inches from his, she whispered, "When we're married, I'll do things that will make all your producer friends envy you." She pressed her palms against his chest and traced tiny circles in his graying hairs. "I don't see why we have to wait. You can just divorce her now."

Max took a step backwards and gazed out the window. A pigeon perched on the ledge, staring back at him. "I've told you, my pre-nup will make my life very difficult if I leave without her agreement. Her family had money, not that I married her for it. I was successful enough on my own, but I'm stretched thin now and I need her to part amicably. It may take some time, but it will happen, I promise you."

She dropped her chin for a moment, then looked up. "Maybe you can come visit me on the cruise ship. I bet that would be fun, huh?"

Max chuckled nervously. "Well, I'm not sure that would work for me, but I'll see what I can arrange. You do your best and listen to Brandon. He knows what he's doing. I'll make sure that, when you get back, there will be doors open for you here. That's what I do – I open doors."

"I have an idea. Why don't we go shopping for an engagement ring? That way I can show the guys on that . . . ship . . . that I'm off limits. You don't want me to find somebody I like better than you while I'm away, do you, Maxie?"

"My dear, I don't want to undermine my position in the divorce negotiations." He scanned the floor, looking for his socks. "Having another woman going around telling people I've already promised to marry her would not look good. But don't you worry. When you get back, we'll have plenty of time for shopping in the Diamond District."

"You wouldn't lie to me, would you, Maxie?" She looked at him with piercing eyes. "I would be very unhappy if I thought you were deceiving me."

Max wiped a bead of sweat from next to his ear. "Absolutely

not. You can trust me, Honey. I'm going to make you a star."

She sauntered gracefully to the dresser, retrieved her purse, and headed for the door. "I'll hold you to that, Maxie." She blew a kiss in his direction, then turned and walked out of the room, leaving Max holding his pants.

He sat back down on the bed, considering whether he might have any messages important enough to rush back to the office. He reached for his phone on the nightstand. The timer function was displayed on the screen, counting down to the alarm he had set for himself in case he fell asleep after their love-making. He almost regretted that it was time to take a break from her, but it was definitely time. She was resilient and would get over it. They always did.

The good news was that she had talent, so maybe he actually could place her in a show when she got back from her cruise gig. He could use some successful clients.

Max lazily glanced through his unread emails until one caught his eye. It was from Brandon Marshall. The message was cryptic, which was typical for Brandon. "In port with cell service until 5:00. Call me." He put the phone on speaker so he could finish dressing while he talked.

Brandon launched into Max without any pleasantries. "Max. I got your message. What the fuck do you mean you already promised her the gig? You can't just dump all your cast-off women on me! I've got a show to produce and I need talent, not trollops!"

"Easy, Brandon. Don't worry, this one has talent. I'm vouching for her."

"You'd vouch for a porn star if she fucked you good enough."

"Now, now, don't be such a drama queen. You're going to have to trust me on this one. She's good, and she needs some time away from New York."

"I'm about at the end of my rope, Max. I know I owe you, but you're taking advantage of the situation."

"Careful, Brandon. I'm on a speakerphone, and while I doubt there's anyone listening, you wouldn't want to say anything incriminating."

"Fuck you, Max. How long are you going to hold that shit over my head? I think my account is settled by now."

"You're about right on that, my friend. Do me this one and I think we'll be square."

"I'm not your friend."

"Oh, sure you are. And when the time comes that you're back on top, I'm sure you'll give me the inside track on some good gigs. We've been a good team. I wouldn't want anything to jeopardize your future credits."

"This one is the last one, Max. I mean it."

"Fine. Just take good care of her. She might have a future."

"All your girls might have a future in your bed. I'm not so sure about a future on a stage."

"Thanks, Brandon. I'd say I owe you one, but we both know it's the other way around."

"Like I said before, fuck you. Send her details over to Christine at the booking office. We're back next week and I'll have a few slots to fill. Good-bye."

Max sat, staring at the now-silent phone. He sighed and resolved to get back to the office and make some calls before the day was over.

Chapter 3 – Bon Voyage

Wednesday, May 8, 2019

MIKE STONEMAN STARED IN FRUSTRATION at the suitcase on his bed. The flexible sides of the lightweight American Tourister were bulging, but there was still a pile of clothes on his rumpled sheets waiting to be packed. Glancing in the mirror, he sucked in his gut, then held up his swimming suit. He was only ten or fifteen pounds overweight, but most of it accumulated around his waist. Still, it was better than it had been a year earlier. He ran a hand through his brown hair, frowning at the flecks of gray.

His tenth-floor window was open, allowing the warm May air to stream in. Two dogs barked at each other in the plaza across the street. After a winter that seemed to never end, Manhattan was starting to feel like summer. Mike had not realized how much he missed humidity.

He rubbed his chin and pondered whether to unpack

everything and re-evaluate what he absolutely had to have for a six-night cruise. The other option was to buy a second suitcase and admit defeat. He had assured Michelle that, as a man, he only needed one suitcase. He was supposed to be meeting her at Pier 88 in two hours. He sighed and wondered how long it would take him to run out and buy a bigger bag.

Before he could make a decision about a run to the luggage store, his cell phone rang. After glancing at the caller ID reading "Jason Dickson," Mike grunted a greeting at his partner. "Hey."

"How many suits do you think I need to bring along on this thing?" Jason had an uncharacteristic hint of frustration in his voice. He was usually calm and collected, famous for his deep baritone, his perfect diction, and his immaculate wardrobe. A blemish on one of his silk paisley ties or a crease on a shirt collar caused him great embarrassment. Mike, on the other hand, was known for frumpy sports jackets and well-worn slacks. At Mike's age and experience level, he could get away with it. Jason was still dressing to impress around the precinct. Given his six-foot-three frame, athletic build, and chiseled good looks, Jason could pull it off. Mike, on the other hand, would look foolish if he tried.

Mike glanced at his pile of unpacked clothes. "I'm bringing two pairs of slacks and one jacket that goes with both. I figure I can wear each dress shirt twice with a different tie, so three shirts should take care of all our evenings. The rest is casual stuff. It's a cruise, not a wedding."

A siren in the distance began its slow build toward screaming. "If you don't bring a tux for the formal night, then neither will I. It will help with the packing."

"Tux?" Mike shot back incredulously. "Why would you even think about bringing a tux?"

"Rachel says there's a formal night, so she's packing an

evening gown and expects us to pose for photos. You know how she loves pictures. Have you never been on a cruise?"

"No. Never. I have no idea what to expect. I'm certainly not packing a tux. I can barely stuff what I have in my suitcase."

"Oh, I forgot to mention, Rachel says to pack a carry-on bag with a change of clothes and a swimsuit for the first day because we might not get our big suitcases delivered to our rooms until after dinner."

Mike scowled, but then realized that this would actually help him find room for all his clothes. "Thanks, I'll make sure to have plenty for later today that aren't packed away. What time are you planning to get there?"

"Departure is at four o'clock, but I don't want to cut it too close, so Rachel is meeting me here at noon and we'll go right over. She says that she wants to have as much time by the pool as possible before we sail."

"That actually sounds pretty good. I'll see if Michelle wants to move up our arrival time. Either way, keep your cell with you. I'll call you once we're on board and we'll figure out somewhere to meet up before dinner. We'll have cell service as long as we're still inside the harbor."

"Roger that. Once we're out to sea, the phones go into the drawer and we can relax."

Mike smiled at the thought. "Yeah, relaxing sounds like a wonderful idea. I'll be happy not to see Dexter Peacock's name pop up on my phone for a week." Dexter Peacock, City reporter for *The New York Times*, had published a story the prior Sunday that was the impetus for Mike and Jason taking this rather rushed vacation. The front-page article revealed some of the details about a shootout in a Brooklyn hotel in which two cops were killed. The entire affair was a scandal for the NYPD. The fact that Mike and Jason were there without authorization, running an undercover operation that not even their captain knew about, was fuel for the media conflagration. The commissioner had suggested they become unavailable for comment for a while.

"I'll see you on board. And, hey, Jason, how many suitcases are you packing?"

"One. You're not thinking about having more than one, are you, Mike?"

"No. Of course not. I'll see you there."

Mike dug into the bottom of his closet, looking for the small wheeled suitcase that he used for overnight trips. He dragged the little case out with his left hand, then winced as a sharp pain momentarily jabbed at his shoulder. He had technically finished physical therapy a week ago, after having shoulder surgery the prior October. Terry, his therapist, told him he needed to keep up the strengthening exercises. He also told Mike that there would still be pain in the area of the surgery – from time to time. While he was in pretty good shape after spending most of the past several months in the gym and the rehab room, he wasn't getting any younger.

It dawned on him that his 50th birthday would occur during the cruise. He was happy that this would prevent anyone from making a big fuss over it. He wondered whether Michelle would remember the date and embarrass him on the ship. Of course she would remember. She always remembered everything. It was in her nature. Plus, she wrote everything down in her calendar, so it was only a matter of what she would have planned.

He sighed again, and resolved to pretend to be both surprised and happy when it happened. Why spoil Michelle's good time because he didn't want to admit to himself that he was turning fifty? Who knows, maybe he could even enjoy the occasion if it was just him, Michelle, Jason, and Rachel. There would be nobody else on the ship he cared about.

♦♦♦

At the same time, in her apartment at Twenty-Third Street and Second Avenue, Michelle McNeill was humming to herself as she carefully folded a black-and-silver cocktail dress. She slipped it into the pocket of a plastic organizer, perched on the smooth surface of her crisply made bed. She stared into her closet, considering what jewelry and shoes would go best with that dress. Normally, she would choose the three-inch heels, which gave her petite frame a little extra height. But she was worried about walking in heels aboard a ship at sea.

Her wireless personal assistant system pinged. The tinny female voice said, "Incoming text message from Rachel Robinson."

"Read message," Michelle answered, without missing a pleat. Michelle thought about how nice it would be to have Rachel's statuesque body and never have to worry about wearing heels.

The mechanical voice said, "What color are you wearing for formal night?"

Michelle instructed her Alexa system to respond, while she packed her cosmetics. A few moments later, she heard another ping and listened to another text.

"How do you think Jason is going to handle this?"

This time, Michelle told Alexa to dial Rachel. When Rachel picked up, Michelle spoke in the direction of the room's microphone while she counted out twelve Q-tips and zipped them into a plastic bag. "Sweetie, Jason's a great guy, and he agreed to come along. Don't worry about him. He'll be fine."

Rachel Robinson's typical fast chatter came through the speaker. "I know, he's great, and I'm really into him, as if you couldn't tell already. It's just – you know – this is such a *couples* thing and we've only been dating a few months, so I'm worried that he's going to get all freaked out. I want to get closer with him, to find out what he really wants. But I'm worried that I'll push him too much. You know what I mean?"

Michelle sighed. Rachel was twenty years younger, and occasionally she felt like her mother as much as her friend. Imparting wisdom about relationships was not something Michelle felt comfortable doing, given her own tortured history. But Rachel clearly needed a calming influence. "Rachel, this cruise was a sudden thing. It has been pushed on Jason and Mike. And they're both terrible at relaxing. It's great that your aunt was able to get us this deal on the last-minute booking. Now, you and I need to help our men take their minds off the last month. Jason's been through a lot. Give him space and be supportive. Try to relax and take everything slowly."

"Yes. You're right. I know," Rachel said, still speaking twice as fast as Michelle. "I just really, really hope that this can develop into something. He's so great, you know? And we're going to be sharing a cabin for a week, so things can get pretty cramped. What if we have a fight? You may have to swap roommates with me."

"That's not happening, Girl," Michelle said with a light chuckle. "Just stay calm and bring sexy clothes." They both laughed and spent the next ten minutes chatting while Michelle finished packing. Neither of them had been on a cruise ship, but Rachel had spent hours online researching the floorplan and features of the *Colossus of the Ocean*. She knew every bar, pool, club, and restaurant, and she was anxious to share all her knowledge with Michelle, who listened patiently, although not really absorbing the information.

Michelle zipped her suitcase. "OK, Sweetie. I need to finish packing. I'll see you on the ship."

"OK. We'll meet at the Clipper Bar – that's on Deck 6 – toward the back of the ship – that's called 'aft' – at six-fifteen. We have a main dining room reservation at seven o'clock, which will give us time to get a drink before dinner and hang out a little bit. I'm packing a cute red halter top and matching skirt that I can slip on over my swimsuit so I don't need to worry about my luggage until after dinner so you may want to avoid red tonight—"

"Don't worry," Michelle interrupted. "Take a deep breath, try to slow everything down, and have a good time. You and Jason are going over to the pier together, right?"

"Yes," Rachel replied, holding herself back from launching into another monologue.

"Great! I'll see you later." Michelle told Alexa to hang up and resumed humming to herself. She liked Rachel, and she liked Jason. She hoped that they were as right for each other as she thought they were. She was feeling happy herself for the first time in weeks, and was looking forward to a relaxing and much-deserved vacation.

Chapter 4 – Old Friends

MIKE EXTRACTED himself from his taxi in front of a huge blue-and-white sign for Epic Cruise Lines, which was the occupant for the day of the Manhattan passenger ship terminal. The passenger drop-off area was teeming with families and couples trying to get inside as quickly as possible. Michelle was already there, standing off to the side of the very front of the line at the luggage drop-off. Her white tennis skirt and canary-yellow sleeveless top immediately caught Mike's attention. She waved; the sun glinting off her yellow-rimmed sunglasses. She looked like an advertisement for a summer beach vacation.

Mike waved back weakly as he wrangled his heavy suitcase and his roll-away bag over the curb, shooing away a helpful Red Cap who had one hand on the handle of his large bag. When he reached Michelle's position, she explained that she had waited in the line already and the clerk at the front had allowed her to wait there until Mike arrived. They navigated the check-in process for half an hour, politely declining the insistent photographer who wanted to snap a picture of them standing in front of a green screen. Then they dragged their carry-on bags up the long ramp toward the massive ship.

Mike stopped to marvel at the structure in front of them. Ten floors of balconies wrapped around the side of the ship facing the pier, some already populated by smiling cruisers taking photos of the Manhattan skyline. The ship rose out of the water like a wall, towering so high that the upper decks were obscured by the roof of the covered ramp on which they were walking. It was, Mike thought, as if a new apartment building had suddenly appeared in the river.

When they reached the top of the ramp and stepped onto the deck, they joined a line of passengers waiting to show their newly-minted key cards and be allowed to pass through into the inner sanctum. The smell of turpentine from a freshly-painted section of an exterior wall wrinkled Mike's nose.

As they waited their turn, Mike noticed a small group coming down the deck in their direction, featuring a man in a wheelchair being pushed by a uniformed crewmember. The man in the chair had a serious expression on a weathered face beneath a shock of white hair. His eyes were hidden behind dark sunglasses below a baseball-style cap bearing the logo of Epic Cruise Lines. He was dressed in white trousers and slip-on dockers that matched the blue of his sport jacket. Alongside the wheelchair walked a smiling woman wearing a wide-brimmed sun hat, white shorts, and a billowing floral blouse. She seemed to be about the same age as the man in the chair, and Mike immediately figured her for the man's wife. Mike thought the man looked somewhat familiar, but wasn't sure.

Just as he was about to give up wracking his memory, the

man shouted out, "Mike Fucking Stoneman! Well I'll be damned."

Mike instantly recognized the voice. When Mike first made detective, Edwin Ferguson was already a veteran of the NYPD. Ferguson was one of Mike's mentors in his early days at the homicide division. He had been involved in a high-profile shoot-out at the South Street Seaport, a popular destination for summer tourists. Ferguson had saved a group of middle-school students who were caught in the cross-fire. He had taken a bullet in the back, which messed up his spinal cord and left him paralyzed from the waist down. Mike had not seen him in years, but he had a distinctive, high-pitched voice that made him unmistakable.

"Ferguson, you son-of-a-bitch, are you still loafing in that chair?" Mike strode over to his old colleague, leaving Michelle in the line with her mouth agape. Mike grabbed the older man's hand and gave it a solid shake. Ferguson pulled hard on Mike's hand, sending him crashing to the polished wood deck on both knees. Mike let out a groan, while Ferguson laughed.

"You were always off-balance, Stoneman," he taunted good-naturedly.

Mike sprang to his feet and lunged toward the man, wrapping an arm around his neck in a headlock. Michelle dashed from the entry line, shouting, "Mike, what are you doing?" She grabbed his arm and pulled. Mike immediately released Ferguson's head and stepped back, laughing robustly. Michelle just stared.

Mike realized that his behavior must seem bizarre to her. "Doctor Michelle McNeill, please meet Edwin Ferguson – a great cop and an even greater man." He gestured toward the man in the chair, who was smiling up at her with a playful gleam in his blue eyes, now holding his sunglasses in his hand.

Ferguson reached up with his free hand to straighten his hat. "I remember Doctor McNeill, from the ME's office. Am I correct to presume that you are acquainted with this grizzled old bastard?" Ferguson chuckled and winked at Michelle, who was at a total loss for any response.

Fortunately, Mike bailed her out of the awkward spot. "Ferguson, what the hell have you been up to? Last time I saw you, I think, was when you ran your motorized chair over that meter maid out on Ninety-Fourth Street."

"Well, she didn't move fast enough!" Ferguson shot back playfully. "That was after my retirement party, so it's possible that my walking was slightly impaired."

"You weren't walking, you were driving."

"You're wrong about that, Stoneman. My chair is not a vehicle under New York law. It's an appliance, so I can't be accused of drunk driving. Not then, and not now. I gather you and the doctor here are sailing on my ship?"

"Your ship?" Mike raised an eyebrow. "When did you become a ship captain?"

"I'm not the captain, you moron. I'm in charge of security on every ship in the fleet. That's my job now – I'm head of nautical security for Epic Cruise Lines. Been here nearly ten years. So you'll have to behave yourself on my ship or I'll toss you in the brig."

Mike stood frozen for a few moments, staring at his old mentor. "Jesus! Has it really been ten years?"

"It has," Ferguson nodded, "but I'll tell you something; I feel younger and healthier now than I did when I retired from the force. So, you have something good to look forward to when you finally hang up your gun and go private. By the way, do you remember my wife, Millie?" Ferguson motioned to the woman who was still dutifully standing next to the wheelchair, resting one hand on the handle closest to her and allowing her husband to hold court.

"It's nice to meet you, Mrs. Ferguson," Michelle said, extending her hand.

The older woman took it warmly and smiled at Michelle. "Are you cursed to be the wife of a cop?"

Michelle blinked. "Um, I'll say that I'm cursed to be forever subjected to the adolescent behavior of male cops, but we're not married."

"Oh, I'm sorry. I just—"

"Don't worry," Michelle cut her off, seeing her red face. "It's a fair assumption. Mike and I have been together for about nine months."

"Well, I hope you have a wonderful time."

"I plan to," Mike responded, seizing the floor. "We needed a quick vacation."

"So, you retiring soon?" Ferguson asked.

"No, I'm not sure I'm ever going to give up my gun." Mike reflexively patted the side of his jacket, where his holster usually resided. Today, it was missing. "If you're chief of security, don't you have one?"

"Well, I'm head of security at the corporate level. I don't patrol the ships. I'm on vacation, just like you – although I'm probably paying less than you are for this voyage," Ferguson winked and laughed. "I've got my people on the ship handling the day-to-day. They have the guns. I have a cell phone and an attitude, which is all I need," Ferguson finished and grinned up at Mike.

"Pretty good gig, Ferguson. Nicely done. Perhaps we'll have a chance to get a drink during the trip?"

"That would be nice," Millie said. "Ed, you can get your old friend our corporate discount on the drink plan, can't you?"

Ferguson turned to Mike. "You got a drink plan yet?"

Mike turned to Michelle. "Do we have a drink plan?"

Michelle shook her head. "How much do you expect to drink?"

Mike shrugged. "No idea. Hadn't really thought about it." Then, turning back to Ferguson, "I suppose since you asked the question, *you* have a drink plan."

"I never cruise without one. Even if I didn't get the corporate employee discount, I'd highly recommend it. In fact—" Ferguson turned his head around to address the uniformed crewman who was standing silently behind his wheelchair. "Enrique, I want you to consider my old friend, Detective Stoneman, as a part of my party for this sailing. I want him and his party to get my discount on the deluxe drink package. Can you take care of them?"

The man in the white uniform nodded. "I'll take care of it, Mr. Ferguson." Then, turning to Mike, Enrique asked, "What is your stateroom number, sir?"

Mike gave the cabin number printed on his boarding pass, 0931, and Enrique said he would escort them to the table inside where they could sign up for the drink package. He took the handles of Ferguson's wheelchair and pushed it through the doorway, bypassing the growing line of passengers waiting to come aboard, and motioned for Mike and Michelle to follow him in.

"I guess it's nice to have friends in high places," Michelle whispered as they passed their key cards to the attendant at the door, who scanned them and welcomed them aboard.

The interior of the ship was as opulently appointed as any Las

Vegas casino, with glass, gold leaf, and crystal shining on nearly every surface. The gangway funneled arriving guests onto the Deck 5 Promenade, a shopping and dining plaza featuring an atrium rising on both sides, lined with the balconies of interior-facing rooms all the way to the thirteenth level. An enormous artistic mobile hung down several floors from the far-away ceiling, depicting sailing ships from different eras. Natural light streamed down from the skylights, merging with the thousands of bulbs illuminating the Promenade.

Music drifted from hidden speakers all around the space as people circulated between kiosks of jewelry and clothing, storefront eating establishments, and bars. Waiters in white uniforms carried trays of champagne glasses. Next to a bank of glass elevators, two long-legged women in blue sequined costumes with huge peacock feathers posed with arriving guests in front of an image of the ship and two potted palm trees. It was like walking into Wonderland.

Michelle and Mike stood, mesmerized, until Ferguson snapped them out of their bedazzlement. "Well, Stoneman? You gonna stand there like a zombie, or are we going to go get you a drink package?"

Mike turned his head and snapped out of the glitz-induced daze. "Sure. Let's do it."

Ferguson had his attendant wheel him forward across the entrance and up to a table stacked high with liquor bottles and elaborately decorated glasses. He introduced himself to the crew member behind the table, who welcomed Mike and Michelle to the ship and motioned them forward. She explained that, as part of Ferguson's party, they would get the package for $19.99 per day. "You'll break even if you have two drinks," Millie added, smiling at Mike.

"Thanks. That will certainly make it a festive cruise." Then, turning to his old mentor, Mike asked, "Are there any decent single malts included in the package?"

Ferguson shrugged. "Do I look like a fuckin' bartender?"

Mike turned toward the woman behind the table. She glanced down at the bottles in front of her and frowned, as if she didn't know what a single malt was. "Um, I'm not sure which bars have which types available. But I'm sure you'll find whatever you want. We have top-shelf liquor on the plan, including Patron tequila and Gray Goose vodka." She smiled, as if that was all that need be said.

Mike turned to Ferguson. "Say, how 'bout we test out the drink plan at the nearest bar and catch up for a few minutes?"

Michelle tugged on Mike's arm. "Mike, I'd really like to unpack in our stateroom."

"You can't do that yet," Millie said, before Mike could reply. "The guests won't be allowed into the rooms for another half hour or so."

Michelle pouted for a moment at the prospect of not being able to unpack, but she put on a happy face as the group took the elevator up one floor. They went to the back of the ship and through the Clipper Bar, which was bustling with passengers killing time until the staterooms became available. Beyond was a set of closed double doors, above which a sign read "Shangri-La." Inside, an expansive room spread out with a stage and a dance floor. Plush chairs were organized in groups of four around low, circular tables. Beyond the entertainment area, they could see huge windows looking out over the stern of the ship behind a square bar. A smiling bartender wearing a blue-and-gold vest saw the group traversing the empty space between the door and the bar and waved. Ferguson waved back, then motioned to Enrique to wheel him to a cluster of seats next to the giant windows. After he stowed their carry-on bags in a corner, the attendant walked away as the bartender hustled over to the group. A gold nameplate on his vest read "April."

"Mister Ferguson, sir! How nice to have you on board again, sir. Zacapa 23, neat, for you, sir?"

"Folks, meet April, the best bartender in the fleet. He will take good care of you if you treat him right. And yes, April, you remembered my favorite. Please bring one for my very good friend, Detective Stoneman, also." He gave a reassuring nod, letting Mike know to trust him.

April asked Michelle and Millie what they wanted. Michelle asked, "What do you recommend?"

April suggested that they try his specialty – a pina colada martini. Michelle said that sounded good, and Millie agreed. April then scurried back to the bar.

"I've never heard of a Zacapa 23," Mike said to Ferguson. "Is that Islay or Highland?"

"Just wait and see, my friend," was all Ferguson said in response.

"Mike," Michelle interrupted when she recognized the beginning of a lengthy discussion of different types of scotch. "I remember Detective Ferguson vaguely from my early days as medical examiner. When did you two first work together?"

Ferguson responded before Mike could open his mouth. "This greenhorn needed some supervision when he became a detective, so they gave him to me so I could beat some sense into him. That had to be, God, seventeen years ago. He was just a nervous kid who couldn't find a stiff in a swimming pool."

"Hey," Mike shot back, "lay off the swimming pool." He glared at the older man.

"What's the matter, Stoneman – I thought you liked swimming?"

"It's not my favorite memory."

"Not keen on reveling in the misfortune of Susan Fenton, the poor little rich girl?" Ferguson's eyes flashed mischievously.

"I'd rather talk about the Bensonhurst warehouse incident," Mike parried, getting an immediate frown from the older man, which was exactly what he wanted.

"Oh, yeah. Fine. Well, you couldn't find a fingerprint on a mirror."

"That's better," Mike said, nodding.

"What are you guys talking about?" Michelle asked, truly confused. "I recognize the name Susan Fenton. Wasn't she arrested for killing her husband? What does that have to do with—"

"Never mind," Mike said softly. "This old bastard was my mentor for a while. Then I figured out that he was mostly full of shit and I stopped listening to him."

"Only because I retired," Ferguson said.

"Was that because of your injury?" Michelle asked innocently.

"Naw. That happened a few years before. The Department would have kept me around, but I was burned out and needed a change."

They stopped the conversation when April arrived with their drinks. He set down a tumbler with a layer of dark brown liquid in front of Mike and handed one to Ferguson, then set the ladies' drinks down on coasters. Mike picked up his glass and held it up to the light, swirling the liquid in the bottom. "What do we have here?"

"Don't ask stupid questions, Stoneman. Just give it a sniff and a sip and then we'll talk about it." Ferguson took a sip from his glass and stared at Mike.

Mike put his nose into the glass and took a deep breath with his mouth open. He took a sip, letting the liquor sit in his mouth for a few moments before swallowing. He pursed his lips and nodded his head. "Not bad. Very smooth. But not scotch."

"Very good, Sherlock. Not scotch. Better than scotch. It's 23-year-old aged rum. Much better than scotch, and won't give you the same heartburn."

"Scotch doesn't give me heartburn," Mike responded, taking another sip. "But I must say this is tasty. Probably best that a disabled guy like you stick to the soft stuff."

Ferguson's face turned dour. "I most certainly am *not* disabled. I'm as able as any man my age. I'm the head of security for this whole damned cruise line. I've got two hundred and seventy-two people working for me. Sure, I can't get up and chase down a thug, but don't tell me that I'm disabled. There are just some things where other people have a head start on me, or a leg up," He winked at Michelle.

Michelle decided to take the conversation in a different direction. "While we're on the ship together, do you mind if I call you Edwin?"

"Young lady, you can call me anything you'd like. As long as your boyfriend doesn't try it, we'll all be fine."

"Why do you detectives insist on using last names?" Michelle asked both of them.

Neither Mike nor Ferguson answered right away. Finally, Mike gave it a shot. "It's just one of those station things. Some guys like to be referred to by their first names, and some by their last names. It's like, you've never heard me call Sully 'Edward,' have you? It's just not done. We all know his first name, but nobody uses it. Ferguson here's like that. When I was a rookie detective, if I had tried to call him 'Edwin,' he would have slapped me. Am I right?"

Mike turned to Ferguson for confirmation. He nodded firmly. Mike continued, "You see? I've been calling him Ferguson for seventeen years. I can't stop now. If you want to call him 'Edwin' that's fine with me, but I just can't do it."

After an awkward few moments of silence, Millie broke in to change the subject. "Doctor McNeill – may I call you Michelle?"

"Of course," Michelle laughed.

"Well, Michelle, how did you and Mike meet?"

"Oh, we've known each other for years professionally. Mike likes to hang out in the morgue." She raised her eyebrows suggestively. "But we only started dating last summer."

"How lovely," Millie said, smiling and holding up her drink in a silent toast. "I hope you both have a wonderful cruise. You're a cute couple."

Michelle blushed and lowered her head, then said, "Thank you," and flashed her eyes at Mike, who downed the remainder of his drink.

"I think we're going to go see if we can bust into our stateroom," Mike stood up and stretched his left arm above his head. "I hope we get to spend some more time with you during the cruise."

"I tell you what," Ferguson said, "I can arrange for a behind-the-scenes tour of the ship for you. Would you like that?"

Michelle immediately said, "That would be great! Could we bring along Jason and Rachel? The couple cruising with us?"

"Sure," Ferguson said. Then he told them to meet back in Shangri-La at 4:00, shortly before the ship was scheduled to set sail, and he would arrange for the tour before dinner. "You can use the Epic App to send me a text message using the ship's Wi-Fi if you need to get me. Everybody aboard gets to use that for free – no Wi-Fi plan needed. Send to EFerg."

"Look at you, mister high tech telling me how to text."

"Yeah, I'm a regular Bill Gates." The two men shared a laugh, each being notoriously tech-illiterate. Mike and Michelle thanked the Fergusons for their hospitality, made their good-byes, and dragged their carry-on luggage out of the lounge, waving to April the bartender on their way.

Chapter 5 – Troubled Waters

WHILE MIKE AND MICHELLE were finishing up their drinks in the Shangri-La Lounge, Max Bloom and his wife, Shirley, were moving into their stateroom on Deck 9. Shirley had wanted a suite, but Max assured her that their balcony room was a much better value. And, with the money they saved on the room, he had purchased them the deluxe drink package and a specialty dining package for three nights. "We'll be able to eat in the best restaurants on the ship," Max said proudly. "But I'm sure we'll love all the food on board. And I booked you for a three-hour massage, facial, and manicure in the spa for tomorrow afternoon." Max beamed at his wife, despite her sour face.

Shirley Bloom stood like a statue next to the queen-sized bed that took up nearly half the space in their cabin. She held a chrome clothes hanger in her left hand and a black cocktail dress in her right, poised to be draped on the hanger if she ever chose to move. She wore mid-thigh linen shorts with a floral pattern that matched her unbuttoned blouse. White strappy sandals showed off polished toenails at the ends of her long, slim legs. Beneath the floral blouse, a white Lycra tank top hugged her toned upper body. Perfectly applied makeup and lipstick completed the package that made her look like a mature cruise-ship Barbie. At five-nine, she was as tall as Max, even without heels, and her days in the gym left her with only minimal body fat. She stared at Max without expression for ten full seconds before speaking.

"Max, that's sweet of you, but I just had my nails done this morning. I don't need another manicure."

"Well, what about the massage and facial?" Max tried to salvage his gesture. He wanted Shirley to enjoy her cruise. More importantly, he wanted her to be fully occupied somewhere on the ship where he had no chance of running into her for a few hours.

"That would be lovely, Max. Thank you," Shirley said, softening her face and blowing Max a kiss before returning to her unpacking.

"That's it?" Max said, obviously annoyed. "What do I have to do to get a real kiss?"

"Oh, Max, it's sweet that you're trying," Shirley said. "You made it very clear that you didn't want to come on this cruise from the day I booked it. You kept coming up with lame excuses for why we should cancel. I know why, my darling. I'm sure that you had some rendezvous arranged for this week. Don't try to deny it. We're on this ship so I can relax and so I can see my old friend, Brandon. You can chill for a few days without exhausting yourself chasing after your starlet-wannabes. I'm thrilled that we'll eat some decent food while we're here, and I'll certainly enjoy the spa. But if you had been paying attention at all, you'd know that I can't drink while I'm taking my antibiotics. But I'm sure you'll be enjoying the open bar."

Max appeared to be formulating some rebuttal, but before he managed to speak, Shirley continued. "I'll make the dinner reservations. We'll dine together and go to the shows. You know Brandon, too, so maybe we'll hang out with him for a bit. Aside from that, you can do what you want and I'll do the same. I trust that works for you?" She immediately turned back to her suitcase, ignoring her husband.

"It seems that there's nothing I can do to please you anymore," Max said bitterly. "I recall a time when you enjoyed my company."

Shirley calmly tossed a handful of colorful socks onto the bed. "I recall it, too. You're the one who stopped trying."

"I did no such thing," Max snapped.

"I should have known that you would never be able to resist all those pretty young nymphs hanging around you all the time, thinking you could advance their careers. You probably think they're actually attracted to you. Maybe years ago they were. I know I was. You were such a dashing, handsome figure. I guess I might have swooned over you when I was twenty. But you'd think now you'd be satisfied with someone your own age. I've been here all the time, but I'm invisible to you."

"You're not invisible. You're my wife."

"Really? Look at me." Shirley stood with her hands on her shapely hips. "Dammit! Look at me!" Max turned his head. "I'm fucking hot. Most men your age would kill to have me, but all you want are those little girls."

"That's not true!" Max was having trouble keeping his voice down. "Are you saying that you want a divorce?"

"Oh, no," Shirley said, wagging a finger. "You don't get away that easy. You can slink away quietly and bang your little dancers all you want – but you'll have to pay for it all yourself."

Max fumed, then shouted back, "I never should have signed that pre-nup! I've pulled my end of this marriage for the last five years. I brought in plenty of cash flow. It was *my* Amex that paid for all the art auctions and our dinners at the nice restaurants."

"Sure, before you left William Morris. You had a good gig, but you threw it away to open your own office. Great idea, Einstein. Since then you've been nothing but a sponge."

"That's not fair!" Max threw the folder containing the spa gift card onto the bed. "I had a chance to make it big with my own agency and I took it. You didn't think it was such a bad idea at the time."

"I didn't think you'd fail so spectacularly," Shirley retorted.

"I didn't fail! I'm doing fine. I just need some more time to build up my client base."

"It would help if you didn't fuck all of them."

Max froze, his face a mask of rage. "I wouldn't have had to if you didn't turn into an ice princess."

Shirley absorbed the verbal blow, then burst out laughing. "Oh, that's rich. Is that really what you think? Are you that dense? I stopped letting you touch me when you kept coming home smelling of other women's perfume. I wasn't the cause of your philandering. You did that on your own."

Max pursed his lips. "Did you ever even try to forgive me? Did you give me a chance at all? Did you try to win me back? No, you never did. While I've been struggling with the new agency, you've treated me like a homeless bum. You drove me away."

"I drove you away? That's a wonderful rationalization, Max. You keep thinking that if it makes you feel better."

Max's anger exploded beyond his ability to keep his voice

down. "Maybe I should just kill you and take your money when you're dead!"

"You could never do it," Shirley said dismissively. "You don't have the balls. More likely I'd kill you first."

Max smoldered, but said nothing. After a few moments of silence, Shirley said softly, "Just get out. We'll go to dinners together and keep up appearances while we're on the ship. I have a reputation to protect, and I know your reputation is enhanced by being married to me. I'm not trying to sabotage you. Just try to stay out late enough that I'm asleep before you come to bed."

"Fine," Max said after a pause, "Leave my suitcase on the bed and I'll come back later. Leave me a note about what time we should meet for dinner. I'll be in the bar." He turned and stomped out the cabin door, allowing it to slam shut behind him.

As soon as he heard the slam, Max realized that he didn't have his sunglasses or hat, and he was still wearing his loafers, but he was too proud to go back inside to rummage in his carry-on bag for some sandals. He turned left, then right, trying to get his bearings before lumbering down the hallway in search of an elevator bank.

Chapter 6 – In the Wings

IN THE EPIC THEATER, at the aft of the ship, theatrical director Brandon Marshall stood in the middle of the fourth row, arms crossed and frowning at his stage. Under the spotlights, the ship's singers and dancers were running through one of the big dance numbers of *Chicago* while a recording of the Colossus of the Ocean Orchestra blared through the stage monitors.

Three new female and three new male dancers were foundering around the set like rats who had just been put into an unfamiliar maze. Brandon was deciding when to stop the carnage, and how angry he should seem to be when he dressed down the cast. They had to perform the show twice over the course of the six-day cruise, and the audience expected it to be good. Not actual Broadway good, but pretty damned good. This was bad.

Brandon raised his left hand and waved at the sound booth behind him on the balcony level, signaling Emmet to cut the music. One of the new girls had fallen off a table where she was supposed to be lying on her back with one leg straight up. Brandon walked unhurriedly to the aisle and then down to the apron before he spoke. The cast's heavy breathing was the only sound hovering over the stage.

"Children, that was totally unacceptable, which I'm sure you already know." His voice was not raised, but there was an ominous rumble in his tone. He decided that yelling at the new kids wasn't going to help, so he yelled at the cast veterans. "Vicki! You're up there being a diva while the rest of the cast is falling apart around you. Are you doing anything to help them?" Brandon's voice rose with each sentence. "Are you even paying attention to what's happening? You have six new cast members here today trying to learn their blocking and make sure you don't fall on your ass on show night, and you don't seem to give a shit!"

Vicki Nelson, who was playing the part of Roxie Hart, stood in her rehearsal leotard with her blonde hair in a tight ponytail, hands on her hips and panting. She drew her lips into a duck face and looked Brandon in the eyes, but said nothing.

"Donna!" Brandon barked, "you're ten feet off your mark! And you, Derek! Can you tear your eyes off of Malcom's butt long enough to support your partner so she doesn't fall over? You're supposed to be a professional, and a veteran of this cast. Show some leadership!"

Now Brandon was starting to enjoy himself. The veterans looked bored, but the six new cast members were clearly terrified, wondering how badly he was going to rip into them when it was their turn.

"Darci! If you don't stop miming Vicki instead of doing your own moves, I'm going to make one of the new girls the understudy for Roxie and bust you down to cigarette girl. You get me?" Darci, whose black tights, white belt, and gold sequined top made her the flashiest member of the rehearsal group, glared at the director with daggers in her eyes. But she said nothing, knowing better from past experience.

Brandon was the unquestioned Lord of this realm. Each cast member knew that Brandon's recommendation at the end of their tour could mean the difference between getting auditions for real Broadway shows back in New York and settling for an eternal series of road shows and cruise ship gigs. He held all their careers in his hand. He knew it, and he knew that the cast knew it. He smirked slightly, then caught himself and went back into drill sergeant mode.

"Ricky!" A tall, dark-haired dancer spun his head toward the director's voice, an angry frown on his face. He started to say something, but then kept his silence. "Try to keep your hands off Donna's tit during that lift. If she were wearing her costume, we'd be looking at a Janet Jackson wardrobe malfunction. We don't want to give the old folks heart attacks.

"Take it from the top – but without Roxie. Vicki! – come down here and watch with me so you can see what's going on up there." Vicki slumped her shoulders and walked sulkily to the steps on the side of the stage.

Before she reached the bottom, Brandon called out, "Darci! – jump in and block the Roxie part. No singing – just the blocking. Donna, step into Darci's place. Reset to scene start. Emmet! Give me full music from the intro."

Vicki stood with all her weight on her left leg, her right hip pushed out to the side and her arms crossed over her chest, looking bored while she watched the scene play out on the stage. She knew better than to say anything. While they watched, the door in the back of the room opened and the rotund figure of Max Bloom walked through, pausing at the top of the Orchestra level to survey the situation. He proceeded down to the front row, where he took a seat near the aisle. He could see the back of Brandon's head as well as the profile of Vicki standing next to him. This time, the cast made it through the number without anyone falling. When the song finished and silence again washed over the showroom, Brandon glowered at the company on the stage.

"That was acceptable." The players all let out a collective breath. Vicki scowled, but said nothing. "Take ten and re-set for the jailhouse number," Brandon barked out. Immediately, the cast scurried off to the side-stage area to grab a bottle of water or a towel, while the stage crew rushed in to change the sets. Brandon waved in Vicki's direction and she hustled off toward the rest of the cast, in the opposite direction from where Max was sitting.

"What did you think, Max?" Brandon said without turning around.

"I didn't know you saw me come in," Max said, surprised.

"Oh, please," Brandon waved a hand over his shoulder. "Nothing happens in my house that I don't notice. I wasn't expecting you so soon, though. Shouldn't you be in a hot tub somewhere sipping a frozen drink?"

Max stood up slowly and took two steps forward so that he was standing next to Brandon. "I had some time, so I wanted to check in on my stars."

Brandon pursed his lips. "Like I said, I'm at the end of my ability to absorb your – clients – and still produce an adequate show, Max. My debt is long since paid. I'm not going to risk what's left of my career to save you from your wandering dick."

"That's harsh," Max said, without any real anger. "I actually think Vicki is pretty talented, don't you agree?"

Brandon shrugged. "I'm giving her a shot at Roxie. She says her lines and doesn't bump into the furniture. Her voice is decent, and the audiences seem to like her. She's got some work to do, but she's adequate. But the rest? Donna is gorgeous and dances well, but can't sing to save her life and she doesn't want to wait her turn to advance. Darci has potential, but her attitude is awful. She thinks she's already a star."

"I'm sorry about that, Brandon. Just get them through this contract and you won't get them back."

"You're damned right, I won't. I'm serious. That's it. I'm done. Don't ever ask again, or I'll quit and write a tell-all book that will feature you prominently."

"You won't do that, Brandon. Your ego is too big. But I understand your point, and I appreciate it. I won't send you anybody else you don't want."

"See that you don't." Brandon turned towards Max. "You know, your girls don't seem to be missing you that much."

"Oh?"

"They have similar tastes in men. Not that there are many options, since they're not allowed to fuck the guests."

"I'll be heartbroken if any of them find happiness with anyone but me," Max said flatly, then broke into a smile. "But I'll get over it."

Brandon turned away. "I can only imagine," then he walked to the stage left steps and disappeared behind a curtain.

Max took a deep breath, turned, and walked back up to the door at the back of the theater. As Max walked away, a pair of eyes on the edge of the stage followed him until he disappeared through the audience door and into the hallway beyond.

Chapter 7 – Behind the Scenes

MIKE AND MICHELLE TOSSED their carry-on luggage onto the bed in their stateroom. Mike slid open the glass door to their balcony and stepped out, admiring the view of the Manhattan skyline to the east, and the office buildings across the river in Weehawken, New Jersey to the west. He could hear happy laughter and loud voices coming from the adjoining balcony.

He and Michelle only bumped into each other three times as they maneuvered around the cramped space. Mike untucked the sheets on the bed and inspected the pillows, frowning immediately and wishing he had remembered to bring his own feather pillow. As he was staring at the telephone on the nightstand and contemplating how to call for housekeeping, there was a knock on the door.

A rush of wind swept through the room as soon as Mike opened the cabin door because the balcony door was still open. He scuttled outside and allowed the door to slam behind him. A short Latina woman stood in front of him, wearing a blue-and-white uniform with a gold name badge reading "Elisabeth." She was petite, barely five feet tall, with slender arms and legs, short, black hair, and dark eyes. Mike wondered how she managed the heavy chores that no doubt went along with being a cabin attendant.

"Everything OK?" she asked in accented English. "You need anything, you ask me."

Elisabeth immediately turned on her heel and walked away. Then, Mike called out, "Wait!" He realized that he had barked at her a bit more loudly than he intended, and felt embarrassed. "I'm Mike. Nice to meet you. I could really use a feather pillow. I'm still recovering from shoulder surgery and I need to cushion my left side when I sleep. Can you get that for me – maybe two?"

Elisabeth had stopped walking away about halfway through Mike's speech. She nodded and said, "I'll see what I can do," then quickly turned again and rushed away down the narrow hallway. Mike wondered if she was overworked or just surly.

As he stood there in the hallway, a large man emerged from the cabin two doors down. He immediately turned back toward his door as if he was going to go back in, but then he turned and strode down the hallway. Mike smiled and wished him "good afternoon," as he passed by.

Max Bloom nodded and grunted, "I hope it will be."

At the same time, five floors above, Jason Dickson and Rachel Robinson walked slowly down their hallway, counting down the numbers on the staterooms as they approached their junior suite. A small, thin man wearing a gold vest noticed them peering at the room numbers and rushed up to them, a wide smile on his face.

"May I help you find your cabin?" he offered, bowing slightly.

"Why, thank you," Rachel said, happy to have some help. "We're in 14106."

"Very good, madame," the little man said. "I am Sergio and I am your cabin attendant. Anything you need, you ask me anytime, and I will make sure that your cruise is excellent!" He beamed up at Jason, who towered a full foot over him, then turned and extended his hand down the hallway, indicating that they should follow him. He took Jason's key card and showed them how to use it to open the door, and then how to put the card into a slot on the wall inside the door to activate the interior lights. Then, he took out another key card and slid it into the light slot.

"You just leave that one here," he said. Then he showed them through their suite, pointing out all the amenities, where all the hidden drawers were located, and how to open and lock the safe in their closet. They would have figured it all out without him, but they both stood back and watched politely as he explained how to use the knobs in the shower and how to control all the cabin lights from a console next to the bed. He finally bowed again and wished them a wonderful cruise before exiting.

Rachel immediately dug into her bag and retrieved her gold bikini, sandals, and a mesh pool cover-up. "If we hurry, we can still get some time in the hot tub. It's just one deck above us."

Jason sat down on the edge of the bed. "Do we have time? Maybe we should try to link up with Mike and Michelle first."

"We have time. Look, I'm sorry I was late. I told you, my dad insisted on driving me. He's a little, well, protective."

"I noticed. I thought he was going to demand that I show him my I.D. to prove I'm really a cop."

"He means well. I think you'd like him if you got to know him."

Before Jason could respond, Rachel's phone rang. It was Michelle.

"You made it. Great. I hope your room is as wonderful as you expected."

"It's fabulous!" Rachel gushed. "I thought it would be cramped but it's really big. We're going to go up to the hot tub on fifteen next to the main pool. Wanna meet us there?"

"Maybe. But first, I want to make sure you didn't buy a drink package yet."

"No. We decided it wasn't worth it and that we didn't want to drink that much."

"Well," Michelle said enticingly, "you may change your mind. It turns out that Mike ran into an old detective friend who's the head of security for Epic Cruise Lines. He arranged to get us an amazing discount on the ultimate drink package – and you guys get it, too, if you want."

Rachel relayed the news to Jason and they immediately agreed that, for $20 per day, they couldn't turn it down. Michelle said they would meet up at 4:00, right after the mandatory muster drill, back in the Shangri-La Lounge. Rachel was pulling Jason toward the door when it opened and Sergio popped his head in. He called out, "Oh, good, you are still here," then turned around and dragged their large suitcases into the room. "I found your bags and thought you would want them right away."

Jason tried to find a couple of dollars to tip Sergio, but couldn't extract his wallet in time. Their attendant rushed out of the room, leaving them to contemplate whether to unpack now or hit the hot tub first. They had two and a half hours before their 4:00 meet-up with Mike and Michelle. These were the kinds of tough decisions that Jason could handle.

At 4:05, Rachel and Jason ambled into the Shangri-La Lounge. Rachel was wearing a sleeveless pink t-shirt emblazoned with the phrase "Cruisin' & Boozin'" in aquamarine script letters. She told Michelle how she had met three "super-fun" women in the hot tub. Michelle was amused that their names were Peggy Sue, Mary Beth, and Bunny. They were sorority sisters from Texas A&M, here for a five-year reunion vacation. Rachel had instantly befriended them and they all thought Jason was hot. They were supposed to have a fourth friend on the ship, but Nicole broke her leg, so they anointed Rachel as an honorary sister and gave her one of their trip t-shirts. They were going to meet up later that night in the Karaoke Bar.

"That's Rachel – everybody's friend," Michelle said privately to Mike.

Edwin Ferguson was there and introduced the group to one of the ship's assistant activities directors, a perky young man from Tanzania who went by "DJ." He welcomed them all aboard, invited them to grab a drink from April, then ushered them out with the promise of a behind-the-scenes tour of the ship.

For the next ninety minutes, DJ showed them everything there was to see aboard the *Colossus of the Ocean*. He showed them the bakery within the kitchen where all the bread and pastries were made fresh every day. He showed them where the crew quarters were, although they were not allowed inside. He took them to the bridge, where they met the first mate and where Michelle was allowed to push the big black button to sound the ship's incredibly loud horn since it was time for them to cast off and begin their voyage. They finished the tour inside the ship's main theater, where DJ took them backstage and showed them where the actors did their wardrobe changes. Rachel was impressed by the sparkling costumes hanging on neat racks in the cramped space.

They stood in the wings while the production company finished up their rehearsal. Michelle could tell from the body language of the actors that they were tired after a long session. As two of the actresses padded past them, DJ stopped them so they could meet his tour group. Donna and Darci were obviously dying to get out of the theater, but to their credit, they each managed a smile and a friendly greeting and spent five minutes talking with the guests – as they were required to do according to the terms of their contracts.

Rachel told them about how she had been a dancer in her early twenties, and even had dreams of Broadway, but a knee injury put her on the shelf and her life went in a different direction. The performers were impressed that she had become an EMT instead. They joked about which job was more physically demanding. Donna said she was hoping to get a shot to play one of the leads in the ship's production of *Chicago* soon. This prompted a cough and a glare from Darci.

As they finally walked away, DJ called out to the dancers, "Try not to shoot anybody!"

"Don't worry," Donna called over her shoulder, "we leave the guns to Shannon. She's from Wyoming and she's a crack shot."

"Why would they shoot someone?" Mike asked, perplexed by

the comment.

"Oh, it's a joke," DJ explained. "You see, if there's an actual emergency situation where we have to evacuate the ship, members of the entertainment cast are tasked with keeping order at the lifeboats, and they're issued firearms to make sure the guests behave themselves. They're just small-caliber pistols, but a bullet is still a bullet. So, don't ever get on the bad side of one of those dancers – they might have a live weapon."

"Are they trained?" Jason asked skeptically.

"Yes. As soon as they come aboard, they receive safety training and have to be checked out on the guns. But they've never needed to use them, so don't worry too much."

Mike and Jason exchanged a wary glance. "Did you pack your gun, Jason?"

"Hell no," Jason replied. "We're going to be in international waters, and guns are totally banned in Bermuda. I don't want to deal with that shit. This is a vacation."

Mike nodded. "Me neither, although I feel kinda naked without it."

"I like you better naked," Michelle called out playfully.

After leaving the theater, the group headed back to the main Promenade on Deck 5 and finished up at the customer service desk. Before saying good-bye, DJ introduced them to the hotel manager, a woman named Marjorie Barnes, who had recently been promoted to the role and was in charge of all the rooms, the cleaning crews, the attendants, and the room service process. Barnes asked them for their cabin numbers. When Rachel said 14106, she brightened and said they were in one of the best rooms available and that Sergio would take great care of them.

When Mike said 931, Barnes grimaced momentarily, then

regained her composure and said, "I'm sure you will be comfortable there." Mike mentally logged the slight hesitation and wondered what was wrong with their room. He was sure nobody else, except maybe Jason, had noticed.

Michelle turned to Mike and whispered, "Next time we get a suite."

At that point, Edwin Ferguson came rolling up in his wheelchair, self-propelling across the tiled floor with Millie walking alongside. Marjorie Barnes greeted them, but before they could exchange many words, a tall man in a crisp black uniform with white trim strode up and called out, "Mr. Ferguson! So happy that you could join us, sir. I trust that the staff is treating you well?"

Ferguson held out his right hand and shook with the man, then introduced him as Karl Keller, the ship's chief security officer. "Karl here is probably next in line for my job," Ferguson said. "This is the flagship of the fleet, so being chief here is the top of the floating pyramid. Don't you agree, Keller?"

"Of course," the man replied stiffly. "I have a wonderful security staff here, but we always hope that they remain invisible to our guests."

"Just the opposite of the beat cops in New York," Mike said. "There, you want visibility to keep people in line. I guess here, you expect people to stay in line without much motivation."

"You'd be surprised," Keller responded, but did not elaborate. When Ferguson explained that Mike and Jason were homicide detectives, Keller said, "Well, I'm quite sure your professional expertise will not be needed this week."

Mike and Jason nodded their agreement. Then, Ferguson suggested that Mike and his group head up to the sun deck above the pool level, where they would have a great view of the ship passing underneath the Verrazano Bridge.

With the tour group gone, Ferguson turned in his chair toward Karl Keller. "Stoneman is a good cop; make sure you take care of him."

Keller frowned and looked down at his boss. "He's a publicity hound. He's always finding his way into the *Times* or onto the television. I doubt he's that good a cop."

"Now, you listen to me, Keller. I knew the man a long time ago, but I'll vouch for him. He's no grandstander. You could learn a thing or two about detective work if you take the time to talk to him while he's here."

"I don't need his advice," Keller shot back, turning his body so that his back was now toward Ferguson's chair. The older man motioned to Millie that she should push him forward. They left in the direction of the central elevator bank, leaving Keller and Marjorie Barnes standing together.

Marjorie kept her eyes forward and whispered sideways, sounding annoyed. "Why didn't you tell me that Mr. Ferguson would be on this sailing?"

"I only found out an hour ago, Marjorie. I'm sure it won't be a problem. I promise not to push him into the pool, as much as I'd like him to have an accident and step aside so someone competent can take over."

"You have no patience, Karl," she said without looking at her colleague.

"I'm twice as qualified as him to head up fleet security, but the Board is so fixated on having a disabled person in the C-Suite, they can't see he's just an old, washed-up cop and not a real executive."

"Careful, he's still your boss."

"I'm not afraid of him firing me. I'll just try to avoid his insufferable company as much as I can."

"What cabin does he have?"

Keller turned and frowned. "Isn't it your job to know where all the guests are?"

"If I'd known he was going to be on board, then I would have been paying attention. We could have put them in the Stonemans' cabin."

Keller furrowed his brow. "Why?"

"They've got Elisabeth."

"Oh," Keller said, recognition dawning on him. "That's unfortunate."

"Yes, well, it would have been a chance for Ferguson to experience her service level personally. That would have been worth having him on board."

"Marjorie, when are you going to fire her?"

"The wheels are in motion, I assure you," she replied softly.

"It seems like you're being too soft with her."

"I'll deal with it."

"Fine." Keller turned and walked away without another word. They could feel the ship's engines churning as the floating city steamed toward the entrance to New York Harbor.

Chapter 8 – Getting to Know You

BEFORE DINNER, Mike and Michelle returned to their stateroom, hoping that their checked luggage would be there so they could unpack. They had clothes for dinner in their carry-on bags, but Michelle would not feel settled until she had put her things away in the drawers and on the shelves. They were disappointed when their bags were still absent, but they both vowed not to let such small details spoil their good time. Mike meant it. Michelle was lying, but did her best to hide her anxiety. Mike checked the pillows, but they were still the same hard foam.

When they headed out for the main dining room, Mike noticed the large man whom he had seen earlier coming out of the room two doors down. This time, he was accompanied by a woman about his age, whom Mike assumed was his wife. Mike said, "Hello again," as Max and Shirley Bloom walked in his direction. Max stopped, with a puzzled expression that Mike was getting used to. It was possible the man was trying to recall their earlier encounter in the hallway, but more likely he recognized Mike from photos in the New York newspapers and local television.

"You look familiar," Max said, "are you from New York?"

Before Mike could speak, Shirley broke into the conversation. "Max, that's Mike Stoneman. The cop. He's the guy who took down the serial killer last fall – the guy they called the Righteous Assassin. Don't you remember? He got the Mayor's medal at the Hero's Ball a few months ago. We were there with that producer friend of yours." Shirley then turned to Mike. "Don't mind Max. If you're not in the theater business, he doesn't pay any attention."

They all exchanged handshakes and wishes for a good cruise, then Max and Shirley proceeded down the hall, with Mike and Michelle a few paces behind. When they reached the elevator bank, Mike suggested that he and Michelle take the stairs down to Deck 4.

At the entrance to the main dining room, they met up with Jason and Rachel, who were much better dressed. "Must be nice to have your luggage," Mike noted.

They were herded into a small alcove next to the main doors to the dining room, where they were required to wash their hands under the watchful eyes of a female attendant who kept repeating, "Washy-Washy!" as if that were a fun activity.

"They are really obsessive about hand washing," Jason observed.

"They should be," Rachel said, "after that Norovirus problem they had a few months ago."

"This was *that* ship?"

"Oh, sure. How do you think we got such a great last-minute deal?" Rachel finished washing and grabbed a paper towel. "But don't worry, I'm sure this is the cleanest ship in the fleet now."

Jason chose to spend a few more seconds under the soap and water. "I hope so."

As they waited to be shown to their table, Rachel spent two solid minutes extolling the wonders of their cabin attendant, Sergio. The Junior Suite they were in did not seem to impress her as much as Sergio's service. Mike groused about how their housekeeper, Elisabeth, had not come through with a feather pillow for him yet, and was jealous that his partner had his suitcase already. But they were all in a pretty good mood as they stood in a fast-moving line of happy passengers.

They were eventually led to a table set for six next to a floor-to-ceiling window. They could see the distant outline of the New Jersey shoreline as their server and assistant server immediately took their drink orders, provided menus, and laid out a selection of bread in a wicker basket. A few minutes later, two more guests were escorted to the table. Max and Shirley Bloom expressed their pleasant surprise at ending up at the same table as their cabin neighbors.

When the assistant waiter came around for drink orders from the new arrivals, Max loudly ordered a Rusty Nail. When the waiter looked confused, Max bellowed, "Just tell the bartender you want a Rusty Nail. Any decent bartender will know what it is."

When the waiter trotted away, Rachel asked, "What exactly is a Rusty Nail?"

Max was happy to expound on his signature cocktail. "The Rusty Nail was invented at the 21 Club in Manhattan. It was a favorite of Dean Martin and Frank Sinatra, and the rest of the old Rat Pack. Frank himself introduced me to it once. It's Scotch Whisky with a float of Drambuie. If the bartender knows how to make it properly, it's served in an Old Fashioned glass over ice. It's the drink of choice for many of us old guard in the theater industry."

Max surveyed his rapt audience; all but Mike, who viewed the drink as a waste of good scotch.

"You wouldn't add Drambuie to a good single malt, would you?" Mike asked with a raised eyebrow.

"Well, Mike," Max responded, "if you had a bottle of Macallan 25 laying around, I'd certainly take it neat." He winked and raised his glass.

Mike raised his glass in response. "On the drink plan, we have to settle for Johnny Black. I guess that's not good enough to worry about, eh?"

Max laughed. "You should try a Nail, Detective. It might change your preferences."

"I'm too old to change my tastes." Michelle shot him a side glance. "Except where certain beautiful women are concerned." The group all shared a hearty laugh.

Over the next ninety minutes, the three couples chatted pleasantly as they were treated to a sumptuous meal. Max entertained the group with stories of behind-the-scenes Broadway shenanigans, reveling in his status as a theater agent.

While Max was regaling Jason and Mike with another of his stories, Shirley turned to Rachel and Michelle. "Max fancies himself the vanguard of Broadway traditions. He still has his clients refer to him as 'Million.' It was cute when he was at William Morris, but since he started his own agency, not many of his current clients have actually performed in Broadway shows. And I doubt very much that he ever met Frank Sinatra."

"Why 'Million?'" Rachel asked.

"It's his full name. Maximillian Bloom, the Baron of

Broadway." Shirley smiled at her husband, who was seated opposite her. Max was still telling one of his favorite stories and didn't notice his wife's less-than-flattering comments. "We'd be eating at the steakhouse tonight, but Max didn't tell me he had booked us a specialty dining package until it was too late to get a reservation."

"So, it's *my* fault, is it?" Max had finished his story and overheard.

"Yes, Dear, it's most certainly your fault."

"You said you'd take care of the reservations."

Shirley sat calmly, apparently not flustered by her husband's reprobation. "I did, as soon as I knew there were reservations to be made. We'll be eating at the steak house tomorrow night, and at the Italian restaurant on Sunday." Shirley turned to Michelle and Rachel. "I trust you won't miss us at your table while we're checking out the specialty restaurants."

Michelle took a mental inventory of Mrs. Bloom. She was elegant, even wearing relatively casual clothes. Her earrings were large diamond studs. She had a huge emerald ring on her right ring finger, with diamond baguettes all around. The wedding ring on her left hand was a delicate gold band. It seemed like an opportune time to change the subject of the table talk. "Shirley, that's a fabulous emerald."

Shirley's expression became oddly sad. "This ring is the only really nice thing I have that didn't come from my family or from my late husband, Harold."

Michelle decided not to press the point. There was obviously some tension in this marriage, and she didn't want to get in the middle of it.

Rachel chimed in, "And I just *love* that manicure!"

Shirley held up her right hand and fluttered her fingers. Each nail was expertly shaped and coated with a sparkling gold polish. She leaned in toward the other women, as if sharing a secret. "The sparkles are actual gold flakes. I have it done at a place on York Avenue. It costs a fortune, but lasts a month, so I love it, too." Michelle and Rachel nodded appreciatively, hiding their envy.

Michelle then looked intently at Shirley Bloom, as if trying to solve a puzzle. "Wait a minute," she said slowly, her eyes lighting up. "Was your name Shirley Lester?"

Shirley grinned, but her face quickly turned melancholy. "I haven't had anyone call me that in years."

"I thought you looked familiar! I saw you in *Kiss My Face* on Broadway when I was fourteen. You were wonderful!"

Rachel was perplexed. "You were a Broadway actress?"

"It's true," Shirley said softly. "I wasn't a big star, but I worked pretty regularly for a few years."

"You were great. Don't sell yourself short," Michelle then turned to Rachel. "She played the daughter of the leading lady in the musical I saw. She danced and sang a really memorable song. Oh, what was it? Something like, 'I'll Always Be There' or 'I'll always—'"

"'I'll Always Remember You,'" Shirley filled in Michelle's blank.

"That's it! Oh, it was terrific. My mother bought me the soundtrack album on a cassette tape and I wore it out."

"It's sweet that you remember," Shirley said, taking a drink of her seltzer.

"I'm only a little younger than you," Michelle said. "You were an inspiration to me. I followed your career for the next few years, but then I lost track of you."

"What else did you do on Broadway?" Rachel inquired

excitedly.

Shirley hesitantly gave some information about a few other shows she was in, but she seemed reluctant. "I'm afraid my father was not thrilled about my career on the stage. I had a chance to go to Hollywood to do a movie, but he wouldn't allow it. He was extremely old-fashioned and wanted me to settle down and have a family. He used to say, 'Being an actress is not conducive to producing grandchildren.' And he was right about that.

"Eventually I got a little burned out by the grind of performing and then worrying about getting the next job, and he set me up on a date with a man from a wealthy family. Harold was dashing and smart and gorgeous, so we got married. I had a baby within a year, then another after that, and my stage days were over. Not that I'm unhappy about the choice. Harold and I had twenty-two great years together, and we have wonderful children, and now I have two grandchildren of my own, so I kind of understand what my father meant."

Rachel reached out and put her hand on top of Shirley's. "At least you had your moments on the stage. I wanted so badly to be a dancer, but I had an injury that set me back. And it was already tough for me because of my body – too tall and too big-boned for a dancer, they told me. I sometimes wish I had been able to have at least one chance at it. But, that's life, I guess."

"Oh, honey, you have so much life left in front of you," Shirley responded, giving Rachel's hand a squeeze. "There are so many things you can do. Never let an opportunity pass you by. And remember, for every adventure you miss, there's another waiting for you."

Michelle leaned toward Shirley. "Don't you love it when young people like Rachel reminisce about the past – as if they're old, like us?" She chuckled softly and Shirley joined in.

"Rachel, I only wish I had your future."

"And I only wish I had your jewelry!" Rachel responded with a big smile. "I'd kill for an emerald that big." The three ladies all raised their glasses and toasted to the things they wished they had, and that they should all get them.

When nobody could spoon any more dessert into their mouths, they all struggled to their feet and wished each other pleasant evenings. Michelle wanted to see if their luggage had been delivered. Rachel and Jason agreed to meet them in an hour at their stateroom.

An hour later, Mike and Michelle's cabin door was propped open. Jason pushed inside, where Mike was jamming the last of his clothes onto a shelf high up over his side of the bed. "Hey," Mike grunted as he stretched to reach the top corner.

Rachel sauntered over to Mike and handed him two large, fluffy feather pillows. Mike was surprised and thanked her. "Where'd you find these?"

"Sergio brought them to us. I mentioned how you were looking for feather pillows and he just ran out and got them. He's so sweet."

"I haven't seen our attendant since this afternoon," Mike grumbled.

"What was your towel animal?" Rachel asked Michelle.

"What do you mean?"

"Didn't you have a towel animal on your bed when you got back to your room after dinner?" Rachel was reaching into her purse for her phone before she finished the question. She quickly swiped into her photo album and presented the phone to Michelle. "Isn't it so cute?"

Michelle stared at an elaborate sculpture of an elephant made from bath towels, including a pair of black eyes fashioned from chocolate mints. Rachel swiped through six photos of the linen artwork while Michelle gawked. "I hear there's a class on the ship that teaches you how to make them. Won't that be fun?"

Michelle handed back the phone and acknowledged how cute the towel elephant was. "We didn't get a towel elephant."

"Or even a towel squirrel," Mike added. "Although maybe our attendant made one and then moved it."

"What do you mean?" Jason asked.

"Well, when we got back here and started unpacking, some of the stuff we brought on board in our carry-on bags wasn't where we left it. Somebody took Michelle's hairbrush from the counter and put it into a drawer. I found my sports watch that I had left on the shelf under the television in the drawer of my night table. It had to be our cabin attendant, right? Who else would have access to the room?"

"Why would she do that?"

"No idea. Maybe she thinks she's cleaning up by putting things away. I'm going to talk to her, if she ever shows herself again. But who cares for now. Let's have some fun. Where are we going?"

Rachel and Michelle consulted the printed schedule of events and activities on the ship and decided on the Cruise Director's *Welcome to the Ocean* show in the Epic Theater. They gathered their key cards and headed out for an evening of entertainment and unlimited drinks.

Chapter 9 – It's a Small World

NINETY MINUTES LATER, after the singing and dancing show in the Epic Theater, Mike and Michelle walked through the "Central Park" area on Deck 5. Trees and shrubbery that seemed entirely real lined the curving walkways, creating a park-like ambiance. Wrought iron lampposts with glowing gas flames and low iron fences with spikes separated the strolling couples from the manicured flora. There were even recorded sounds of birds and barking dogs to complete the illusion. They held hands and admired the ceiling, which had an image of the night sky projected on the glass eight floors above. It was peaceful and romantic, allowing them to forget about their stress and relax, which was an unusual state for both of them.

The park area ended abruptly as they transitioned from cobblestones to marble tiles and much brighter lights. The Promenade area was lined on both sides with shops selling perfume, jewelry, fashions, and souvenirs. Michelle's attention was drawn to a crowd of people pressing inside the ship's jewelry store. In front, she could see large helium balloons and a sign with oversized letters advertised a FREE GIVEAWAY. She pulled Mike toward the melee and he did not put up a fight. He knew Michelle just liked to window shop and seldom purchased anything on impulse. She was a careful planner and researched any significant purchase for weeks before spending money. Besides, if she bought anything, it came out of her bank account, not Mike's.

As they peered into the crowded shop, they heard a loud male voice calling out for everyone to gather around and to make sure they got a raffle ticket. Two short women who looked like gymnasts, dressed in leotards and tights, were circulating through the crowd handing them out. The tickets were printed with an eight-digit number, awaiting their match to be pulled out of a glass fishbowl displayed prominently on the sparkling counter inside the shop. Mike and Michelle both grabbed tickets. The drawing would happen in five minutes. They didn't bother asking what the prize was.

Behind the counter, the shouting man continued to hawk the jewelry and whip up the crowd over the exciting prize that they should not miss. The man spoke with a heavy accent that sounded eastern European. He seemed tall, but since he was standing on a chair behind the counter to see over everyone's heads, it was hard to be certain. He had a pompadour of wavy black hair, a deep tan, and the chiseled features of a model. His gold silk shirt was unbuttoned halfway down his chest, exposing dark hair and a thick chain with an enormous gold medallion.

"This is a braided gold chain from Spain with charms that are personally selected by you or your loved one, so that every bracelet is unique. This is the most special gift you could ever give – or give to yourself. My beautiful assistant, Helene, is wearing the basic item, adorned with eight unique charms representing cities in the world where she has special memories. I can tell you that some of those memories are very special indeed," he said with a suggestive raise of his brow and a lascivious leer in the direction of the lovely Helene.

The woman was, indeed, stunning, although Mike expected to see someone younger. Helene was decked out in a gold sequined dress matching the host's shirt. Her arms and shoulders were bare except for thin straps that plunged dramatically toward her massive cleavage, which framed a large, sparkling gemstone hanging on a golden filament. The dress ended mid-thigh, exposing long, tanned legs that disappeared behind the display cases. She was also standing on a chair or other platform that Mike couldn't see. She had a bee-hive of blonde hair piled atop her head. Her dark red lipstick matched her long nails, which were dangling below the flashy bracelet she was modeling. Mike's gaze was drawn down her slender arm to the bracelet.

"Is that not the most exquisite thing that has ever adorned your sexy wrist?" the man asked.

"Oh, my goodness, yes!" came Helene's high-pitched voice, followed by a purr of excitement, as if the bracelet were caressing her arm.

It was the voice that sparked Mike's memory. He studied the woman's face, her eyes layered with mascara and shadow. Then he remembered the name Helene, and his mental connections synced up. While Mike was staring at Helene's eyes, she looked straight at him, then winked.

"You see the woman modeling the jewelry?" Mike said to Michelle, tilting his head in her direction. "I know her. I can't imagine what she's doing here, but I last saw her at the Hero's Ball. She was there with her new husband." Michelle had been occupied in another conversation when Helene had accosted Mike and Jason during the gala at the Metropolitan Museum.

She looked quizzically at Mike. "If you say so."

As soon as the drawing (which neither Mike nor Michelle won) was completed, the crowd quickly dissipated. Within five minutes, there were only a few people left browsing the sparkling baubles. While an elderly couple engaged in a detailed conversation with the jewelry hawker, whose name turned out to be Henrik, Mike motioned to the woman. When they first met, she was Mrs. Nick DiVito. Her husband was the first victim of Ronald Randal, dubbed the Righteous Assassin by the New York papers.

"Well, hello, Detective Stoneman. Oh, sure, I remember you. I'm good with faces, you know. I have a photogenic memory."

Michelle flashed a puzzled expression. Mike shook his head subtly. "Let it go." Then he turned back to the woman. "I remember you as well, Helene, but the last time we met you were with a new husband, Mr. . . . ."

"Rosen." Helene's eyes moistened visibly. "Allan took me to the Hero's Ball, I remember. It was only a few weeks later that poor Allan—" Helene brought a hand to her face. After a moment, during which Mike and Michelle stood silently, she choked out, "I'm sorry. It was just so sad. Allan had a heart attack and died so suddenly."

"I'm sorry," Mike said sincerely. "Your husband was a hedge fund manager or something like that? He was on some mayoral commission, I think. How did you end up here working as an assistant for this guy?" Mike jerked his head in the direction of Henrik, who was still locked in a sales pitch.

"Oh, well, Henrik sold my Allan the engagement ring he bought for me." Helene trailed off and fought to maintain control of her voice. "I had to sell it back to him, and he was so nice and he was looking for a salesperson, so he offered me a job."

Michelle then inserted herself into the conversation. "I'm sorry, but if your husband was a hedge fund manager, why did you need to sell your engagement ring? That's awful. Didn't he have insurance or an estate?"

Helene stiffened noticeably, and the emotion in her voice changed from sadness to anger. "You'd think, right? Allan loved me. He really did. And I loved him. He was a good person, which was such a change of pace for me, ya know, after that scumbag, Nick. Well, you see, Allan had kids from his first wife – who got cancer and died a few years ago. It's not like I came along and stole him away. I would never do that." She looked at Mike for confirmation of her honorable motivations.

Mike gave her an acknowledging smile.

"Well, like I said, he had kids, and they convinced him to get a pre-nup before we got married. Can you believe the kids thought *I* was a gold-digger? Me? But I said 'fine.' I didn't care. I knew that Allan loved me and he would take care of me. But the pre-nup said that if we weren't married for five years then I wasn't entitled to anything, and he left his kids as his life insurance beneficiaries. And the lousy kids never liked me, so do you think they were going to give me anything? Ha! They cut me off and threw me out of the house. So, that's when I had to sell the ring."

"That's awful!" Michelle sympathized. "You poor thing."

Mike interrupted the women with a question of his own, unable to contain his investigator's instincts. "If Henrik has a store in New York, why are you both here on the ship?"

"Oh, w–well, you see Henrik was – is – not entirely legally supposed to be working in the U.S. He's applied for a Green Card, but he had to be outside the country while his visa gets processed or something. He booked us on the ship so he can still sell his jewelry while he's waiting. His stuff is so great, don't you think?"

Michelle and Mike both agreed. "I wish you luck," Mike said as he tugged on Michelle's hand, trying to get her to leave the store. Michelle, however, was transfixed by the glamorous woman and her sad story.

"It sounds like you've had some bad breaks, Mrs. . . . Rosen, is it?"

"Sure," she agreed, a tear forming in the corner of her eye.

"Well, Mrs. Rosen, I hope you enjoy the cruise and that you and Henrik sell a lot of jewelry. I may even come back and buy something myself later."

"Thanks," Helene said with a little bit of enthusiasm. "I'll tell you a little secret." She leaned in toward Michelle, as if wanting to say something without Henrik hearing her. "Find something you like, but don't buy it until the last day of the cruise. We always discount everything on the last day. You come see me then and I'll take care of you. Any friend of the detective is someone who deserves special treatment."

"She's more than just my friend," Mike said softly, peeking sideways at Michelle.

"Oh!" Helene said, her voice rising into the high-octave range that Mike remembered. "Well, in that case, I can show you some wonderful engagement rings."

"I don't think that's exactly what we're looking for," Mike said quickly, trying not to sound as though he thought the idea was so far-fetched.

Michelle patted Mike's arm softly. "Don't worry, Mike, I'm not in the market for a ring." Mike breathed an audible sigh of relief. He and Michelle said their goodbyes and left the shop, just as Shirley and Max Bloom walked in. Shirley looked excited. Max looked bored. The two couples exchanged greetings as they passed.

Mike and Michelle searched the Promenade for the location of the Karaoke Bar, where Rachel had suggested they should meet up at 11:00. She wanted to introduce them to her new ship-friends from Texas. They were already a few minutes late, but on the ship, time seemed to have little meaning.

"Are you going to sing me a love song?" Michelle asked suggestively.

"I wouldn't count on it," Mike deadpanned. "Are you going to sing one for me?"

"You'll have to ask me nicely."

"How about if I get you a few more free drinks?" Mike suggested.

"That has some potential, too," Michelle laughed as they walked arm-in-arm down the Promenade.

Chapter 10 – Performance Anxiety

WHILE MIKE AND MICHELLE WALKED from the *Welcome to the Ocean* show to the jewelry store, Max Bloom lingered in the corner of the Epic Theater. Shirley had gone back to their cabin to fetch her antibiotics, which left him just enough time. He pushed through a semi-hidden door leading to the backstage area, then wandered to the edge of the stage and waited. Before long, Vicki Nelson rounded the corner of the plush velvet curtain and walked toward him. She smiled and brushed a blonde hair away from her face.

When she reached him, Max slid his left hand onto Vicki's butt and gave it a soft squeeze, then quickly pulled back. "Looks like Brandon is taking good care of you."

"He hates me," she said, pouting.

"Nonsense!" Max scolded. "He has sent me several reports and says that you are very professional and quite talented, just like I told him."

"I'm glad you're here, Million. I wasn't expecting to see you.

Did you come to get me out of here and into a real show on Broadway?" Vicki looked up hopefully.

"I'm actually here on a vacation," Max said. "So we'll have some time together, if you can squeeze me into your schedule." Max stared down at the shorter woman, making no attempt to hide that his gaze was fixed on her cleavage.

"Careful, Max, you don't want any of the other girls to see that I'm your favorite." She gave him a wink and subtly grabbed his crotch for a moment, before backing away a step. "I have to be poolside in half an hour," she said with a hint of disappointment.

"What about later?" Max inched toward her and slid his right hand around her waist. "I've really missed you."

Vicki allowed herself to move toward Max until he was grinding his hips into her. She batted her lashes, putting both palms flat against his chest. "I tell you what. After midnight, I have no more appearance duty. I could sneak you into the crew quarters. I'm not supposed to be fraternizing with the guests, so we'll have to be careful. But what about your wife?"

Max gaped down at her.

"Oh, Million, you can't keep secrets from the crew on a cruise ship. I asked around and found out that your wife's on board. I even know what cabin you're in."

"Well, don't worry. Shirley never stays up past midnight. I'm sure she'll be off to bed by then. Is there somewhere we can meet?"

Vicki thought about it for a moment. "OK, I'll meet you in the sports bar, next to the casino, at twelve-thirty."

Max leaned down for a kiss and made it linger as he squeezed Vicki and slid his hand down from her waist toward her ass. She disengaged and pushed away. "Careful, you don't want to ruin my makeup while I'm still on duty." She backed up a step, then reached her hand up to Max's cheek and brushed off some body glitter that had transferred from her face to his. "You go have fun and I'll see you later." Max watched her walk away, then returned to the doorway leading back to the theater.

◆◆◆

The Karaoke Bar on the *Colossus of the Ocean* was a horseshoe-shaped space tucked into a corner of the Promenade deck between the 24-hour café and the Irish pub. Mike and Michelle walked in and only had to search for a few moments before spotting Jason, who was standing and waving at them. He and Rachel were sitting in a semi-circular booth in the middle of the room, along with three twenty-something women wearing party dresses. Mike assumed they were the Texas sorority sisters. Mike and Michelle pulled up chairs and spent the next hour listening to a wide variety of talent and musical tastes. Some of the performers were surprisingly good, while others were pathetically bad.

The crowd was supportive and sang along with the guests who were having trouble, while cheering loudly for the better singers. Mary Beth and Betty Sue performed a rousing duet of "Islands in the Sun," then returned to the table sporting huge smiles, waving to the men in the crowd who were hooting loudly at them. After a middle-aged couple struggled through a duet of Johnny Cash and June Carter's "Jackson," Mike was about ready to suggest that they leave. But the host of the event announced over the sound system, "Next up, welcome to the stage Rachel from New York City!"

Rachel was on her feet in a flash and bounced up to the microphone. The sorority sisters, or Rachel's "Squad," as she was now calling them, were right behind her. She whipped up the crowd with her infectious smile and her boundless energy as the first notes of Beyoncé's "Single Ladies" blared out of the speakers. Rachel's performance, with her new friends singing backup and dancing expertly, was amazing. She emphasized the line about putting a ring on it as she waved her left hand toward the audience and danced to the music. The crowd gave her a standing ovation. Michelle and Mike gave her and the Squad high-fives when they returned to the table. Jason gave Rachel a hug and a healthy kiss.

"Your turn, Mike," Rachel called out playfully.

"Not tonight," Mike replied. "I'm not quite relaxed enough to perform. Maybe a different night."

"I'll hold you to that."

"Me, too," Michelle agreed. "What about you, Jason?"

The big man raised an eyebrow and thought about his response. "When Mike sings, I'll sing."

"OK, then," Rachel said as she stood up. "Let's go find someplace quiet so we can wind down before bed. We'll come back tomorrow early and sign up the boys."

Mike opened his mouth to protest, but decided it was not worth saying anything. As the group left the area, other guests shouted out kudos to Rachel and told her she had killed it. The Squad was off to the disco. Jason was happy that Rachel didn't insist on joining them.

The two couples walked up a flight of curving stairs and found seats in the Clipper Bar, where a piano player was entertaining guests at the far end of the space. Mike ordered a scotch – he had to settle for Johnny Walker Black Label – while Jason got a beer and the ladies ordered seltzer. Michelle explained that she was not used to drinking so much and needed to hydrate a little.

They talked about Rachel's aspirations of being a singer and dancer in her younger days and agreed she would have been great. Then Michelle excused herself to use the ladies' room. To Mike's surprise, Rachel did not offer to go with her.

When she had gone, Mike turned to Rachel. "How long have you known Michelle?"

"Oh, a few years now. We've become pretty close. You know, we share all our sob stories and complain about our men to each other."

"Should I be worried?"

"No way!" Rachel said, lightly slapping Mike's shoulder. "She almost never complains about *you*."

"Almost?"

"Uh, I'm not saying anything, Mike – no matter how much you interrogate me."

When Michelle returned, Rachel insisted that they pose for a group selfie in front of the giant wooden steering wheel from an old sailing ship that was mounted on a podium at the entrance to the Clipper Bar.

"You want me to take one of you and Jason?" Michelle asked.

"Sure!" Rachel enthusiastically grabbed Jason by the elbow as Mike escaped from the photo spot.

"I don't think that's necessary," Jason demurred.

"Oh, don't be such a buzzkill," Rachel scolded as she handed Michelle her phone.

"I posed for the group shot, isn't that enough?"

Rachel pouted. "I'm just trying to have fun."

Jason pursed his lips and stood stoically for the photo, despite Rachel's scolding him about needing to smile more.

A few minutes later, they said good night at the elevator as Mike and Michelle exited on Deck 9. It was a little before 1:00

a.m. when they walked down the hallway, which tilted gently as the ship cut through the waves of the North Atlantic. Mike had his arm around Michelle's shoulders as they listed in unison from one side of the hallway to the other. The space was lined with a handrail on each side so guests could grab hold as needed.

When they approached their stateroom, Mike saw Max Bloom walking toward them from the other direction. He waved and whispered a goodnight. Max disappeared into his room, and Mike and Michelle did the same. It had been a remarkably relaxing day for both of them. It hardly seemed possible they had been in their New York apartments earlier that same day. The ship had a way of pulling its guests into another world, where time had no meaning and connections to the real life still going on back in port seemed to fade away.

There was still no towel animal waiting for them, but their bed had been turned down while they were out. As they crawled under the covers a few minutes later, Michelle let out a contented purr. Mike, his head resting comfortably on two feather pillows, instantly fell asleep.

Chapter 11 – Sunrise Surprise

Thursday, May 9

A S THE SUN ROSE OVER THE ATLANTIC on Thursday morning, the guests on the *Colossus of the Ocean* were mostly asleep, the byproduct of over-indulging late into the night on departure day. The crew, including the entertainment staff, took the opportunity to use the ship's facilities and get a jump on the day. Ricky Rosario padded down the stairs from the health club and jogged onto the running track that encircled Deck 5.

The soft dawn light filtered around him as he veered to the side in order to place his plastic water bottle down on a ledge protruding from the wall. He was careful not to step on a canvas drop cloth balled up in the corner, next to some cans of paint, brushes, and other supplies left by the maintenance crew that was repainting the exterior walls during this voyage. He ramped up his pace as he rounded the corner and headed into the wind.

Far ahead, he saw another early riser striding in tight black Lycra pants. Ricky was pretty sure he knew who it was, and picked up his pace.

When he rounded the prow and headed back aft, the wind was at his back and his quarry was only thirty yards ahead. He could see the red headband holding back her short black hair. Before she reached the end of the long straightaway, Ricky pulled alongside and slowed to match her pace.

"Hey, Sweetcakes," he panted, working hard to be suave despite the heavy breathing.

"Hey," the woman responded flatly, keeping her gaze fixed on the track ahead.

"I missed you last night," Ricky pressed.

"No, you didn't. I wasn't there. I told you, we're done."

"Done?" Ricky reached out to touch her shoulder. She stopped running halfway around the corner curve, near the glass doors leading back to the health club. Ricky took two more strides before realizing that he was pulling ahead, then slammed on the brakes and turned around. "Whadaya mean, done?" he yelled, his native Brooklyn accent coming through.

"It's not complicated, Ricky. I have more important fish to catch. I'm off limits, so we're over. You were a nice distraction for a few months, but it's time to move on."

Ricky stood in the center of the track with a dumbfounded expression, panting. He was not accustomed to women rejecting him. He was talented, a great dancer, and heterosexual, making him greatly in demand among the women in the ship's performance cast. The entertainers were not permitted to fraternize with the guests, leaving them only the other performers with whom to socialize during the long stretch of their contracts. Available straight men were scarce, and Ricky had no shortage of conquests. He could easily move on to one of the newer members of the theater company, but he had not yet fully satisfied his desires with this one.

"C'mon, Babe. We still have some unfinished business." He walked to her and put his arms around her shoulders. She was eight inches shorter than him, and eighty pounds lighter. As his arms pulled her toward him, she lifted her right knee and planted it squarely into his balls. He squealed and dropped to a knee, releasing his grip.

"When I say we're done, I mean it."

As she walked past him, Ricky reached out and grabbed her arm. "That was not fucking necessary," he huffed out as he regained his equilibrium.

"Let go of me!" She jerked her arm from his grip.

Ricky stayed on the ground. As she walked away, he called out, "You still owe me. I did what you wanted. I kinda like Vicki, but tonight her shoes are gonna kill her feet, just like you wanted. Of course, I could go take those inserts out before the show. And I could tell her, and Mr. Marshall, it was you who put 'em there in the first place. You wouldn't want that, would you?"

She stopped and turned to face him. To her left, on the deck, she saw the canvas drop cloth and the paint cans. She reached down to grab the thin metal handle of the nearest can.

Ricky had struggled to his feet, but stood gingerly with his legs pressed together. She covered the space between them in three strides. Then, she tensed her arm against the weight of the paint can and pulled.

The metal can, about three-fourths full, whipped through the air with surprising speed toward the side of Ricky's head. He tried to raise an arm when he saw what was happening, but he was too slow. The bottom rim of the can hit his left ear, indenting his skull and sending him toppling over onto the maroon running track. She stood over his crumpled body and whirled the can around again in a circular motion like a softball pitcher wind-milling the ball over her head. The can crashed down again on Ricky's skull with a squishy *thud*.

She glanced around at the deserted track, taking note of the increasing brightness as the sun rose out of the ocean. She walked quickly to the rail beyond the curve of the track, where a water bottle stood on a protruding ledge. She peered over the side and saw the whitecaps lapping at the ship as it cut through the gentle swells. She heaved the paint can, then turned before seeing it impact the water.

She rushed back to Ricky's prone form and grabbed his ankles, dragging him across the smooth deck. She wedged both his feet under the lowest of the steel bars that composed the ship's rail. Each bar was about one foot apart, making the spaces too narrow for a person to slide through. She grabbed an arm and pulled the limp body up until his abdomen sagged against the polished wooden top and his torso leaned over it. Then, she gripped the two ankles, jerked them out from under the bar, and flipped Ricky over the rail, where he dropped into the sea. The noise of the body's impact barely registered above the sound of the ship cutting through the waves.

Looking around at the quiet, empty space, she grabbed Ricky's bottle of water and splashed it on the patches of blood on the deck. She used the corner of the drop cloth to dab up the liquid, then returned the cloth to its disheveled pile. The daily cleaning crew would take care of any remnants. She drained the final ounce of water into her mouth, tossed the plastic bottle into a recycling container on the deck, and then resumed her morning run.

Chapter 12 – Card Shark

EARLY THURSDAY MORNING, Mike and Michelle had been awakened by cracks of thunder and flashes of lightning through the glass balcony door. The storm had come up quickly, and passed just as fast. Michelle marveled at how little motion they felt on the huge ship, even as it crashed through the stormy sea. By morning, the sun was out again and the ocean was quiet.

After sleeping late and then eating a much larger breakfast than usual at the Spinnaker Buffet, Mike and Michelle spent the rest of the morning alternating between the hot tub and the swimming pool. After lunch, where they both made a conscious effort to stick with salad, they met up with Rachel and Jason in one of the performance venues and participated in a music trivia game.

Twenty or so teams hotly competed in the genre of classic rock. Michelle and Mike were far more familiar with the era, but Rachel's deep knowledge of Motown and Jason's surprising familiarity with Led Zeppelin got them all the way to the final two before they fell just short of winning the coveted Epic Cruise Lines lanyards.

Michelle and Rachel then set off to find the rock climbing wall. Mike and Jason adjourned to the ship's casino. Mike wanted to play in the preliminary round of the cruise's poker tournament; Jason wanted to watch.

The poker tournament was set up with five preliminary rounds and then a final table populated by the five winners. The winner of the final table would receive a free cruise for two. Jason, who was not a card player, had heard Mike talk about the strategic elements of poker and wanted to see if Mike was really as good as he claimed to be.

After using his key card to pay the $100 entry fee, Mike commented on how easily the ship was able to separate him from his money without ever having to open his wallet. He took his place at the single poker table inside the tightly packed casino floor, while Jason found a stool at the nearby bar where he would have a good view. Five minutes later, there were eight players around the table, including two women, one young man who seemed barely eighteen, one elderly gentleman, and four middle-aged men. Almost everyone had a drink in front of them, including the elderly man. Mike had a Diet Coke.

Mike introduced himself to the man next to him, Quentin Richardson from Huron, South Dakota. Quentin was a big man, at least 300 pounds, with large hands, a round face that was perpetually smiling, and a mop of blond hair. He was a talker. He reminded Mike of Tom Tuttle from Tacoma, the John Candy character from *Planes, Trains, and Automobiles*. They quickly determined that Quentin and his wife were the occupants of the cabin directly next to Mike and Michelle. Quentin promised to keep the noise down on the balcony, and mentioned that he felt like he already knew the couple in the other neighboring cabin from overhearing their conversations.

"You mean the Blooms?" Mike asked.

"I don't know that I ever heard their names, but I tell ya they sure do have loud voices."

At that moment, the casino host announced that the poker tournament qualifier would be starting.

The game began while there was still one empty seat. After the second hand, the last player rumbled in. The man was rather short, but had bulging muscles around his neck and shoulders and oversized biceps that pressed against a tight t-shirt. He had a weathered face, with a scraggly goatee but clear, bright eyes under a baseball cap, pulled down low over his forehead. The man was accompanied by two large bodyguard-types, who stood several steps behind him. He carried a tumbler with ice and a golden liquid that Mike guessed was whisky. As soon as he sat down, he drained the glass, letting the ice cubes rattle against his mouth. Then, he held up his glass. One of his companions immediately grabbed it and headed toward the bar, presumably to fetch a refill.

Under any circumstances, Mike would have pegged this guy as a loose and likely aggressive player, whose alcohol consumption would make him unpredictable. In this case, Mike also thought he looked familiar. Mike scanned his face, then noticed that he had a thick gold necklace. Dangling from the braided gold was a charm of gold script letters reading "Nails."

Mike then saw the ring. It was oversized and square, with a large diamond in the center, set on a diamond-shaped field on a blue background. A circle of smaller diamonds surrounded the center stone. The border of the square was made up of words that Mike could not read from across the table. But he knew what they were. They read "WORLD CHAMPIONS" and had the number "19" on one side and "86" on the other. Mike had seen pictures of that ring, given out to members of the World Series-winning 1986 New York Mets. The man sitting across the table was Lenny Dykstra.

Mike played the next few hands while watching Dykstra carefully, trying to gauge how skilled a player he was. He knew that Lenny had a reputation as a gambler, but he wasn't sure if poker was his game. Mike didn't give away the identity of his celebrity table-mate to the other players.

After thirty minutes, three of the original nine players had busted out of the game. Mike watched Dykstra play aggressively, shoving all-in repeatedly to put pressure on the other players. The ex-ballplayer had amassed a stack of chips equal to Mike's, without showing his cards once. But Lenny was savvy enough not to try to bully Mike. This may have been because Mike had a big chip stack, or it may have been that Mike obviously knew what he was doing.

Mike made a flush and knocked out his neighbor, Mr. Richardson. Then Dykstra showed a hand that turned out to be pocket aces to knock out two players. Now there were three – Mike, Lenny, and the elderly man, who had not introduced himself. Mike took the old guy out with a flopped two pair that beat his pocket tens. That left only Mike and Lenny, who was on his third Jack Daniels.

At this point, Mike decided to pull out the Mets fan card. "Nails, I just want to say that I always appreciated your hustle on the field. When you hit that home run off Houston in game 3, I jumped three feet off my bar stool."

Dykstra shrugged, apparently not wanting to talk about his

baseball days. He looked down at the two cards that had just been dealt to him, then up at Mike.

Mike peeked at his cards: two sixes. "Hey, c'mon, Lenny. You can't walk around wearing that ring and that necklace and expect that fans won't recognize you. I was there when they brought back the '86 championship team at Shea. A great day. I remember when you came out, you couldn't find your way out to the big cardboard placard with your number on it in the outfield. We all thought you were drunk. Were you?"

Dykstra glared at Mike. He picked up his glass, but changed his mind about taking another drink and set it back down. Lenny was first to act in this heads-up battle. He reached with his left hand and fondled his championship ring, then pushed out a bet of four times the amount of the big blind. At this point in the tournament, the blind levels, which were going up every ten minutes, would soon leave them both with relatively short chip stacks, even though they now had all the chips between them. Lenny had a slightly smaller pile. Mike took his time, then slid out a call.

The cards in the middle of the green felt on the flop were 5-7-9, with three different suits – a terrible flop for most of the cards that Lenny should have been making such a big pre-flop raise with. Lenny checked. Mike checked back, figuring that he likely had the better hand, plus a draw to a straight. The fourth card on the board, the "turn" card, was the queen of hearts. Lenny stared at Mike, then announced, "All in."

Mike stared back at Lenny, thought about it, then said, "Call."

Dykstra grimaced, then tossed his two cards face-up on the table, showing jack-ten of hearts. Mike had been correct: Dykstra was bluffing when the queen hit the board. Lenny still had two overcards to Mike's pair of sixes, but when the eight of spades came on the river, Mike scooped up all the chips. Mike accepted congratulations from all the folks who had gathered around the table to watch the ending. Several guests crowded around Lenny, now that his identity had been revealed. Mike joined Jason at the casino bar.

"How did you know he was bluffing?" Jason inquired.

"I didn't know for sure, but I knew he was a bully at the table and he was annoyed with me for talking about the Mets, so he wanted to end the game quickly. Now we'll see if he can play his way to the final table by winning one of the other preliminaries so I can do it to him again."

"I have to hand it to you, Mike, that was damned impressive. When did you learn to play poker so well?"

"I picked it up as a teenager, when I worked for the Long Island Rail Road after high school. The crew used to play poker to pass the downtime. Then I started watching on television when it hit the big time on ESPN. I figure that poker is just like interrogating a suspect. You have some of the information, but not all of it. Sometimes you know things the suspect doesn't know. You have to know when to bluff, and you have to know when the other guy is bullshitting you. It's the same game, really."

Jason turned back to the bar as Mike hopped onto the stool next to him. "I'm not sure I agree with all of that, but I'll come watch you at the final table on the last day."

Mike smiled and ordered a scotch, now that the poker was done.

♦♦♦

While Mike was at the poker table, Shirley Bloom was in the

Solarium on Deck 13, sitting alone in a swinging seat. After waiting for five minutes, she was rewarded by the appearance of the man she had been waiting for.

"Brandon!" she exclaimed when he rounded the corner past the hot tubs lining the adults-only area, walking carefully on the wet, slippery hardwood. It was hot and humid inside the windowed enclosure, but Shirley looked fresh in a sleeveless top and a pink skirt. She hopped off the swing and waited for Brandon Marshall to reach her. They exchanged a warm hug and a double cheek-kiss, then sat down together on the swinging chair.

"You look wonderful, Shirley," Brandon said as he waved his hands toward her. "Your legs were always amazing and they haven't aged a day since the last time you were on my stage."

"Oh, you're such a suck-up," Shirley said with a beaming smile. "You'd say anything if you thought it would get you a donation to your charity. I remember your last Broadway Cares gala. You told me you'd cast me as an extra for one night for a ten-thousand-dollar check."

"I meant it!" Brandon said with a laugh. "You were always one of my favorites. It's such a shame you hung up your tap shoes."

"Well, it was the right choice. I did alright with Harold. We had two beautiful kids, and twenty-two years that were as wonderful as being on the stage – well, almost."

"You'll never know. But most of my actors these days are more unhappy than they are happy, so you probably made the right choice. Broadway isn't what it used to be. Look at me. I'm happy enough here on the ship, which is a pretty good gig, but I'm only here because nobody on Broadway would hire me."

"Oh, Brandon, you were the best director I ever had. They're stupid if they can't see that."

"Will you tell them the next time you see them?" he chuckled.

"Sure. The next time Max takes me to some bullshit fundraiser social, I'll be sure to tell every producer we meet that they are crazy to be using anyone else."

"I'll hold you to that, my darling." Brandon's face then got serious. "I'm really happy that you came to visit, Shirley."

"It's my pleasure. I've been nagging Max for months and he kept putting me off. I finally booked it on my own and told him we were going whether he liked it or not." They shared a chuckle. "I wanted to let you know I still think about you, and I'm looking forward to seeing your onboard shows. For some reason, Max seems to be avoiding you. It feels like we've barely seen each other since I've been married to him."

"I know," Brandon said, averting his eyes. "I'm not sure why Max would want to avoid me."

"It doesn't matter," Shirley said, slipping her arm through Brandon's and leaning her head onto his shoulder as the swing slowly rocked them. "I just want the world to stop for a few days while we're here so I can relax. Thanks for meeting me. It's so good to see you."

"You want to take a walk?"

"Sure." Shirley sat up and hopped off the swing. "You lead and I'll follow you anywhere."

Brandon took her hand and they walked out the back of the Solarium, through the automatic sliding doors, and past the main pool. They talked about Shirley's days on Broadway and Brandon's two Tony nominations. He didn't win either time, which Shirley said was a great injustice.

They circumnavigated Deck 13, then walked up to Deck 14 and stood on the ship's prow with the wind in their faces. Eventually, Brandon said he had to get back to the theater, because he had some new actors who he needed to put through their paces.

"It's like herding cats."

"It could be worse; it could be *Cats*." They both laughed at the prospect of staging *Cats* on a cruise ship.

They exchanged a long hug. When they disengaged, Brandon had an excited expression. "I have a wonderful idea."

"What?"

"A friend of mine is putting together a cast for his new show. There's a part in it you would be perfect for. It's a sexy older woman, a little like Joan Collins from *Dynasty*. It has comedy and tragedy. He asked me to recommend some potential actors. I didn't think of you then. But, now that I've seen you here, do you think I could entice you back, now that your kids are all grown?"

Shirley stared out over the placid ocean. The sounds of playful children on the pool deck below made her think of her own kids when they were young and carefree. "You said your actors were unhappy and that Broadway isn't what it used to be."

"I lied. I'd kill to be back on Broadway."

"Brandon, it's a tempting offer, but I don't think I—"

"Stop," he said, putting a finger to her lips. "Don't make a decision now. Sleep on it. Think about it. Meet me for breakfast tomorrow at nine o'clock in the main dining room. We'll talk more about it then."

"I must admit it's an exciting idea."

"Great! So, you'll keep an open mind?"

"I will. I promise." Shirley took Brandon's arm and they walked to the elevator lobby. They waved goodbye and Shirley blew him a kiss.

Chapter 13 – A Little Less Conversation

THAT EVENING, Mike and his group attended the ship's musical revue. Thanks to Edwin Ferguson's influence, they got reserved seats in a raised section in the middle of the theater. Ferguson and Millie were seated next to them, with Ferguson in the space reserved for wheelchair-using guests.

The performers sang and danced their way through the show to enthusiastic applause. Several of the numbers were Broadway standards, while others were Motown and pop classics. Rachel was impressed with the singers and the backup dancers. She whispered to Michelle how unique it was when one of the women kicked off her shoes at the start of one number and finished dancing barefoot.

"I've never seen that happen outside of *Pippin,*" she said.

"Maybe she was losing her balance in those heels," came Michelle's hushed reply.

Rachel rushed down to the front of the house during the curtain call to congratulate the cast. She waved at Donna and

Darci – the actors they met during their backstage tour the day before.

As they left the theater, Mike acknowledged that the show was nearly up to Broadway standards. Rachel thought it was better than some things she had seen in New York. Jason had no opinion; he had not seen many Broadway musicals.

Rachel announced that she wanted to go back to the Karaoke Bar and reminded Mike and Jason that they had agreed to sing. Before Mike could dispute having agreed to any such thing, Ferguson challenged him to get on the stage. "If you're not a pussy, you'll do it."

"What if we wheel *you* up there?" Mike retorted.

"There's no ramp," Ferguson snapped back quickly.

Mike figured he had used the excuse before. Since the old man had backed him into a virtual corner, he shut up and followed Rachel out of the theater.

When they arrived in the Karaoke Bar, the couple who had butchered "Jackson" the night before was on stage trying to sing "Your Cheatin' Heart." Their names were Alex and Suzie. Mike had noticed Alex walking around the ship earlier wearing his cowboy hat. It seemed that he wore it constantly, even in the hot tub.

Michelle turned to Mike and spoke into his ear. "Mike, you have to sing, if only to keep Alex and Suzie off the stage."

Mike laughed and looked at Jason. "I'll do it if you do it."

Rachel heard the comment and jumped up, shouting, "Yes, he will!" She grabbed Jason's arm and hauled him out of his chair.

Jason motioned for Mike to come along and the three of them walked to the podium, where there were several large binders with laminated pages listing the songs available to be performed. The three of them traded binders, then each wrote down the title and number of their selection, along with their name and where they were from. When Mike turned around to walk back to their table, he saw Alex and Suzie pressing forward, reaching for the clipboard. He grimaced and hoped his group would leave the venue before they took the stage again.

Twenty minutes later, the cruise director called Rachel's name. She provided a high-energy rendition of "Respect" and the crowd roared with approval. Mike noticed that several people had applauded and yelled loudly for Rachel before she even began, apparently remembering her from the night before. She did a circuit around the room afterward, giving high-fives and fist bumps to her adoring crowd. She was glowing.

Then it was Jason's turn. The room erupted into hoots and applause as the initial strains of "Can't Get Enough of Your Love, Babe" wafted through the room. Jason's deep bass voice was a dead ringer for Barry White. Everyone loved the performance, which featured Jason jumping down from the stage to sing the sexy lines directly to Rachel, who was the first one on her feet cheering when the song ended.

As Jason was coming down from the stage, Mike turned to Rachel and asked her to give up her cell phone. He held out his hand, with a stern expression on his face. She was confused for a moment, but then relented and handed Mike her phone in its pink case. He then gathered up Michelle's phone and, when he reached the table, Jason's phone. He shoved them all into the pockets of his jacket, then took off to the stage. Michelle was surprised at Mike's stage moves as he pumped out Elvis Presley's "A Little Less Conversation."

After taking his bow and returning to the table, Mike handed back the cell phones. Michelle pouted and said she really would have loved to have a video of the performance.

"Exactly why you can't have one," Mike said. "You wouldn't be able to keep it to yourself."

"I resent the implications of that statement," Michelle said with a laugh.

"Look me in the eye and tell me you would not send a copy of that video to Rachel if you had it on your phone." Michelle didn't say anything. "Case closed." Mike smiled and gave her a hip shimmy before sitting back down.

Two songs later, the karaoke host announced that the session was concluding after the next song. When the group got up to leave, they all waved to various strangers who were calling out "great job!" and similar well-wishes.

As soon as they got to the Promenade, Rachel and Michelle excused themselves to use the restroom. Mike and Jason started back toward the casino so Mike could teach Jason how to shoot craps.

When Michelle and Rachel reached the restroom, they saw Shirley Bloom standing at the sink, adjusting her makeup.

"Oh, hello, Mrs. Bloom," Michelle said warmly.

"Call me Shirley. I don't want to be reminded that I'm Mrs. Maximillian Bloom."

"Oh, I'm sorry," Michelle stammered. "Did something happen?"

"No. . . . Yes. . . . It's complicated." Shirley threw a hand into the air. "I wanted to take this cruise to have some fun and relax. You don't need to hear about my marital problems. I'm sorry, I'm just frustrated. I got sick last week, so I'm on antibiotics and can't even fucking drink."

"Do you need a doctor?" Michelle asked.

"No. I'm fine. But I'm supposed to finish all ten days of

antibiotics. I'd like to make Max take them, too, so he'd stay sober for more than half an hour at a time."

Rachel stepped forward and handed Shirley a tissue. "If you're not happy being with Max, why don't you just divorce him? Life's too short to be unhappy in a relationship."

Shirley's face softened. "Thanks, Sweetie. I love how you still think marriage is romantic. I've gotten over that. I'd throw the bum out but I have a pre-nup to make sure he can't take my money if he dumps me. If I divorce him, he gets a pretty big payment. I don't want to give him the money, so I'm waiting for him to divorce me, or die of a heart attack. Unless I throw him overboard first."

"Be careful saying things like that," Michelle said. "You never know who might take it the wrong way."

They exchanged a laugh. Shirley thanked them both for being so supportive.

Later, Rachel and Michelle found a quiet seat in the Champagne Bar. Rachel said, "Just tell me that not all men are scum. Like Mike, right? He's a nice guy, isn't he? He's never going to treat you like Max Bloom treats Shirley, right?"

"I certainly hope not." Michelle took a sip from her crystal flute. "He's never given me any indication that he's really a creep and he's pretending to be a gentleman in order to hook up with me."

Rachel laughed. "Yeah, I know what you mean. I feel the same way about Jason. He seems nice and sweet. But, I'm worried that I'm going to end up wanting more from the relationship than he does."

"Why?"

"Because he's devoted to his job, like Mike. He is so intense about finding the next killer and getting justice for the victims and their families. Don't get me wrong, I love that about him. He's so passionate and dedicated. I worry that he's not able to be as dedicated to anything else, or anyone else."

"What about you? Don't you feel the same way about your job? You do such wonderful work as an EMT."

"I like my job, but it's not a calling. I could give it up tomorrow if there was something more important to me. I'm not obsessed with my work."

"OK, fair enough. I feel the same way about my job as Mike feels about his. Maybe that's why we're so compatible."

"I see that," Rachel agreed. "I'm really loving being with Jason. I'm just not sure that he's *the one* for me. I need a little more time with him, but he's kind of, I don't know, distant. Like he doesn't want me to get too close. He doesn't like talking about his childhood or his family with me. Like he's holding back. You know what I mean?"

"I do. Mike's the same way. It may just be a man thing, or a cop thing."

"Or a male cop thing," Rachel suggested. They both laughed. "It's just that, I'm not getting any younger, and I don't have time to waste." Rachel held up her empty champagne glass and motioned toward their waiter for another round. "I'm just saying that I'm going to give Jason some more time, but I'm not going to wait around forever."

"You're not going to find many better men than Jason," Michelle said.

"I know. That's what I'm worried about."

Chapter 14 – Rushed Reunion

WHILE MIKE AND JASON were an hour into rolling dice at the craps table, Max Bloom was sitting uncomfortably with Shirley, listening to the piano player in the Clipper Bar. She had insisted that they make an appearance and at least give the impression of being a married couple. He had balked, but agreed rather than getting into a loud argument in a public place. Now, he was sweating as the clock inched toward midnight. He had arranged to meet up with Vicki again at 12:30, and he needed his wife to be gone before then.

At 11:45, their waiter came by and asked Shirley if she wanted a drink. She declined and announced that she was tired and ready for bed. Max said he was going to stay awhile and ordered a Rusty Nail. The waiter was puzzled, but Max waved him away after handing over his key card. Then, he stood politely and gave Shirley a kiss on the cheek as she walked away toward the elevator.

As soon as Shirley disappeared around the corner, Max sat

back down, then felt a hand on the back of his neck, massaging his hairline with long-nailed fingers. He leaned back into the pressure, then turned his head and saw a face he wasn't expecting.

"Oh!" Max exclaimed, pulling forward, away from her hand. "My, I – I wasn't expecting to see you."

"Don't worry, Maxie, your bitch wife is gone already. I've been watching you." She flashed a devilish smile and put her hand back on his neck, leaning in to whisper, "I've really missed you. How about we go somewhere and I can show you how much?"

Max turned and grabbed her wrist. "Look, this is not a good time. I told Shirley that I'd meet her in our room in ten minutes, as soon as I finish my last drink. She's going to be expecting me. I can't just slip away. I tell you what, we can set up a place and time tomorrow, how about that?"

At that moment, the waiter came by with Max's Rusty Nail on a tray. She reached for the glass and took it, along with the receipt and Max's room key. She took the ballpoint pen from the tray and wrote in a nice tip from Max. "What's the room number, Maxie?"

Max looked around to see who was possibly listening to the conversation, then said softly, "Nine thirty-five." She wrote in the name and room number, then handed the receipt and glass to Max.

"Don't worry, lover, I won't do anything to embarrass you here. I need to keep a low profile myself, or the crew will bust me for inappropriate contact with the guests."

Max let out a sigh of relief. "That's good. That's really good. I tell you what, why don't we meet up tomorrow when you have some free time? When would that be?"

"I'm off-duty tomorrow between two and four. Meet me in the

health club a little after two. You can pretend to exercise while I work out, and then we can find somewhere to shower together." She reached down and squeezed Max's crotch, then licked his ear and breathed heavily into it.

Max couldn't help himself; he melted and let out a low moan.

"I'll see you tomorrow," she purred into his ear, then turned and sauntered away, out of the bar and out of sight. Max slumped back into his seat and drained his glass in two gulps. He surveyed the room as subtly as he could, but nobody was paying him any attention. He raked his fingers through his hair and tried to regroup. Vicki would be there soon.

Chapter 15 – Paradise Lost

MIKE AND JASON FINALLY called it quits at the casino when Jason noticed that it was 1:00 a.m. As Mike headed back to his cabin, he was amused to find Max Bloom already in the upward-bound elevator car. Max appeared a bit disheveled. The casino was on Deck 4, the lowest deck with entertainment venues. Mike wondered where Max was coming from on a lower deck, but he shook off his investigator brain. It was none of his business. The two men greeted each other politely. When they arrived on Deck 9, they walked together down the hallway toward their cabins.

As Mike stopped at his room and fished out his key card, Max passed behind him. Then Mike heard a voice call out, "Mister Bloom?" Mike turned his head and saw a uniformed security officer standing in the hall, motioning toward Max. Mike had not seen such uniforms anywhere aboard. The security team usually stayed out of sight.

"Yes?" Max said.

"I'm going to need you to come here," the officer said in a tone of voice Mike recognized as a precursor to either an arrest or an interrogation. He put his key back in his pocket and turned to walk along behind Max. The security officer took Max by the elbow and directed him inside his propped-open cabin door as Mike reached the threshold and looked inside.

He sized up the situation instantly. There were four people in the cabin, none of whom was Max's wife, Shirley. Mike recognized Karl Keller, the ship's chief of security, whom he had met briefly the day before at the end of their VIP tour. There was one other uniformed security officer inside the room wearing blue latex gloves, indicating that there was some kind of search happening. The balcony door was wide open. Mike could see a female figure, shorter and stockier than Shirley Bloom, standing next to the railing.

Mike put his hand on the door and prevented it from closing after Max walked through. The security guard immediately confronted him. "Who are you?"

"NYPD Detective Mike Stoneman. I'm . . . a friend of Mr. Bloom."

"I'm going to have to ask you to leave this room," the officer said firmly, but politely.

Mike held up his arm and waved. "Hey, Keller, what's going on here?"

Keller frowned, and Mike could see him mentally running through his options. After a pause, he called out, "Let him in, Stan." The officer stepped aside so Mike could walk in, squeezing past in the narrow space.

Max had stopped in the middle of the room, looking around in confusion. "Where's Shirley?" he asked Keller.

"You're telling me you don't know?"

"No. Who are you?" Max asked back.

"I'm the chief of security, Mr. Bloom. Can you tell me where you've been for the past hour?"

"I – I was in the Clipper Bar – then I took a walk, out on the deck. I sat in a lounge chair to look at the stars. I guess I – I must have fallen asleep, and then when I woke up I came here."

Mike watched Max as he stammered his way through this explanation. He had seen suspects answer such questions for nearly a quarter-century, and he could tell immediately that Max was not telling the truth. It may not mean anything, of course. People lie for many reasons, but he was sure Max was lying, and he was pretty sure Keller would be able to tell.

"Is that right?" Keller said doubtfully. "Then I guess you weren't here when your wife fell off your balcony?"

Max's face turned ashen. "What?" he gasped. This time, Mike thought that the man's reaction seemed genuine.

"Your wife, Shirley Bloom, fell from this balcony and landed on top of a lifeboat on Deck 5. The ship's doctor pronounced her dead half an hour ago." He stopped talking and watched Max's reaction, as did Mike. Max seemed shocked, but not particularly upset.

"What?" was all Max could say. He looked like a fish out of water, struggling to breathe. "But, she was just with me downstairs. She went – she was going to bed. I was coming up to meet her."

Keller stepped forward to get right in Max's face. "When you last saw your wife, Mr. Bloom, what was her mood? How did she seem to you?"

Max stared at Keller, unable to speak. All the eyes in the room were fixed on him. Finally, he said softly, "She – she was, um, tired. She, er, had a busy day, I think, and so she was, um, like I said – tired. That's all I can tell you, Officer."

Keller scrutinized Max carefully, allowing the silence to linger before he asked his next question. Mike was impressed by the technique. "Do you know of any reason why your wife would want to end her life?"

"End her – huh? – you mean kill herself? What? I can't – No. I mean, she wasn't the happiest person in the world, but . . . well, on the other hand, I guess she had been a bit depressed lately, and, you know, she had been ill and she was on antibiotics. She wasn't allowed to drink alcohol, so, maybe she forgot and had something to drink, which, you know, might have had a bad reaction, or something." Max seemed to gain steam as he kept talking, almost as if he were figuring something out. Mike was skeptical. Max's initial reaction to the news of his wife's death seemed genuine, but the more he talked, the more the story became speculative and contrived.

"Is that so," Keller pressed. "So, you think it's more likely that she fell than that she jumped?"

"I think—" Max paused. "I think I don't really know." Max slumped down onto the sofa.

"Sir, I'm going to need you to gather up what you need for the night. We'll escort you to a different stateroom. Hopefully by tomorrow, you'll be able to come back to collect the rest of your belongings." He turned to the balcony and said, "Marjorie, do we have a cabin for Mr. Bloom for tonight?"

The woman emerged from the balcony and Mike recognized her as the hotel manager, whom they had met the day before at the same time as Keller. Mike wondered why she was there, but perhaps anything that happened inside a stateroom was her jurisdiction. She said she had a vacant cabin for Max, and waited while he tossed his pajamas, his toothbrush, and a pair of slippers into a canvas pool bag.

"Mr. Bloom," Keller said as Max was walking toward the door, "please don't talk about this to anyone. We would like to keep this terrible situation quiet and not ruin the cruise for the other guests. Do you understand?"

"Sure," Max said vacantly, then he followed Marjorie Barnes out the door.

"Who reported the death?" Mike asked, as if he had a right to know.

Keller responded without any hesitation. "The impact of the body hitting the top of the lifeboat attracted the attention of a couple on their balcony. They say they didn't actually see the body falling, and didn't hear anything before the bang. They called security. It only took us a few minutes to trace her back to this room."

"Did you get photos of the body?"

"No," Keller answered quickly. "In situations such as this, we try to avoid photos. We want to remove the body as quickly as possible so it doesn't upset the guests. We're pretty sure nobody got any photos."

Mike frowned at the absence of proper crime scene protocol in dealing with a dead body. "Was there a suicide note?"

"No. At least not one we could find. She could have sent a text or email, but no paper here in the room that we saw."

"Any sign of a struggle?"

"Detective, I appreciate your interest, but it's really not something you should be concerned about."

"I guess it's just a cop's instincts."

Keller called out to the two security officers who were still in the room. "OK, let's lock this room down."

Mike raised an eyebrow. "Aren't you going to do a sweep of

the room for evidence?"

"Detective, we reviewed the scene when we got here. This is probably a suicide, and possibly an accident, but those are the only two options."

"Did you get pictures of the room?"

"I got a set on my cell phone," Keller said as if that were standard protocol.

Mike thought about asking whether one of the ship's official photographers could be brought in to take some proper photos, but he begrudgingly recognized that this wasn't his crime scene. "What about an inventory? Do you have a complete accounting of everything in the room? What about the body? Where is that?"

Keller was obviously annoyed. "I appreciate your interest, Detective, but I assure you that we have the situation under control. The body has been taken to the infirmary, where we have appropriate storage facilities."

"You have a morgue on the ship?" Mike asked, but then he thought about it for a second. "Of course you do. Lots of elderly passengers on a week-long cruise. I guess sometimes the cruises are even longer, right? So the law of averages says that every once in a while, somebody's going to have a heart attack or a stroke."

"Right," Keller said. "We deal with these situations from time to time. I'm afraid that someone throwing themselves off a balcony is not unheard of, either."

"You've already got it pegged as a suicide and not an accident?"

"Well, it is extraordinarily difficult to fall accidentally from a balcony, so a leap is much more likely." Keller motioned for his security men to exit the room. "I'm going to seal up the room until tomorrow, so I'll have to ask you to step into the hallway."

Mike exited and watched over Keller's shoulder as he placed a security seal on the door. "Are you going to sign the seal?"

"No, Detective. That's not necessary."

"If you say so. If you need any assistance—"

"No, thank you, Detective. I have this under control and I have a very well trained staff to handle it. You should go back to enjoying your cruise and try to forget about this tragedy. And I'd appreciate it if you would also keep this matter to yourself. There's no need for the other guests to be gossiping about the poor woman. Good night." He nodded toward Mike, then walked away in the opposite direction from Mike's room.

Mike stood in the hallway, watching him go with his two officers chugging along behind him. Mike inspected the seal on the door, which seemed to be standard tamper-proof tape. There was nothing he could do, so he walked back to his own cabin, thinking about what he was going to tell Michelle about what had just happened.

Chapter 16 – Everyone's a Skeptic

MICHELLE WASN'T BUYING IT. "Mike, I spoke to her tonight. She was pissed off at Max and told me she wasn't going to divorce him because she'd have to pay him according to the terms of their prenuptial agreement. She was willing to put up with his philandering rather than give him that money. There's no way on Earth that she would then kill herself. It's simply impossible."

They had been up since Mike came into the stateroom, trying to be quiet. Michelle had sleepily asked him what was going on out in the hallway. When he tried to give her an abbreviated version of the story, she ended up wide awake and insisted on hearing all the details.

"Maybe it was just an accident," Mike said.

"How would that be possible?"

"Well," Mike sat up in the bed, thinking carefully. "If she had been drinking, she might have lost her balance when the ship hit a big wave and toppled over the railing."

"Except she was not drinking," Michelle responded sharply – more argumentative than she intended. "She was taking antibiotics and couldn't have alcohol with her drugs. I bet if you look in her bathroom, you'll find the pill bottle with a big warning about not drinking."

"Well, she might still lose her balance and fall, even if she wasn't drunk."

Michelle paused to think. "I doubt that happens very often, but I guess we can't totally rule it out. Of course, I didn't feel any rocking tonight. Was she wearing her high heels when she fell?"

"I don't know. I never saw the body. They whisked it away before the guests could gawk at it and take selfies with the corpse. Keller said he didn't even get photos. You think if she was barefoot she'd be less likely to lose her balance?"

"Oh, God, yes," Michelle responded, as if it were the most obvious thing in the world. "Plus, her center of gravity would be lower, so it would be harder for her to accidentally fall over the railing. The question really is whether she went out onto the balcony on her own to get a little air, or if somebody carried or pushed her out there."

"What if she was already out there getting some air when the other person came in?"

Michelle smiled. "Then we agree that there was probably another person involved?"

"Well, I'm not ruling it out. But I watched Max's reaction when Keller told him his wife took the dive, and he seemed genuinely surprised."

"Do you think he could have been acting?"

Mike took a few moments to think before responding. "I don't think so, but I've been fooled before. Let's say that it's not impossible, but my gut isn't pegging him as a killer here. Plus, I think Shirley was more likely to send him over the rail in a struggle."

Michelle laughed and had to agree.

"Of course, if he caught her by surprise, you never know. He could have taken her in his arms for a kiss, dipped her across his knee, and then hefted her over the side."

"I can't see her letting him kiss her like that," Michelle scoffed. She stood up and walked to the door of their balcony. She slid the door open and stepped out into the warm, humid air, then measured the distance from the door to the polished wooden rail, which stood about four feet off the balcony floor. A small, circular metal table and two mesh deck chairs took up a good percentage of the floor space. She pressed her back up against the rail and pushed up onto her toes to see where her center of gravity was. She could not have levered herself over the side easily even if she tried.

"There's not a lot of room out here to have a struggle. Any kind of wrestling match and you would start banging into the metal furniture. That would make a huge racket. It was after midnight, so if the passengers in the adjoining cabins were in their rooms, they would have heard that kind of noise."

"Well, I'm sure Keller – the security chief – or somebody from his team will speak to the passengers in those rooms. Were you here then?"

"Probably not. I didn't get in until after twelve-thirty. But no, I didn't hear anything."

"Figured I'd ask."

"When can I get a look at the body?" Michelle asked with a tone of not whether it would happen, but merely when.

"It's not your jurisdiction, Doctor McNeill. It's not mine either. We're guests on the ship. We're not involved. We should let Keller and the ship's security team handle it, try to forget it, and enjoy our vacation." Mike said this with as much sincerity as he could manage while he looked into Michelle's eyes.

She stared back at him, determined. "All I need is five minutes with that corpse, and I'll be able to tell you whether she was in a fight and went over the rail involuntarily."

"OK, let's say, hypothetically, that you could somehow get permission to examine the body. And let's say you form an opinion that her death was not an accident or a suicide. What would we do with that information? I can't direct the ship's officers about how to handle their investigation. The crime – if there was one – happened on the high seas and outside my jurisdiction, so it's really—"

Mike stopped talking as he saw the expression on Michelle's face and realized there was no chance she would give up on the idea of examining Shirley Bloom. He sat down on the deck chair, breathing in the salty air and listening to the soft crash of the waves as the bulk of the huge ship cut through the Atlantic Ocean. "Alright, I'll see what I can do."

"Your old buddy Ferguson is the head of security for the whole cruise line. I'm sure if you asked him, he would help."

"OK, I'll ask him in the morning."

Michelle looked up hopefully. "Why not ask him now?"

"It's a little late, isn't it?"

"Ferguson told you to text him if you needed anything. You can send him a text now and he'll get it as soon as he wakes up."

Mike knew better than to argue with her logic, so he grabbed his phone. Two minutes later, after sending the text message, he and Michelle finally crawled into bed. But, of course, neither one could fall asleep. After twenty minutes of playing the game of who could pretend to be sleeping the longest, Michelle gave up.

"What if it really was just an accident?" she said quietly.

Mike rolled onto his back. "We'll find out tomorrow. I was kinda looking forward to touring Bermuda. But perhaps we'll take care of this little bit of business before lunch, and then we'll do some sight-seeing in the afternoon, eh?"

Michelle snuggled into the crook of Mike's arm. "Let's hope."

Chapter 17 – Trouble in Paradise

Friday, May 10

THE NEXT MORNING, Karl Keller read his morning report and frowned. Aside from the highly unusual death of a passenger by accidental fall from her cabin balcony, the rest of the report was fairly standard for the second night of a Bermuda cruise. Two drunk passengers had to be escorted out of the disco after groping two women. One passenger and his two cohorts got into a screaming match with the pit boss in the casino, but the two security guards who responded convinced them to go quietly. One couple having sex in a lounge chair on the helipad were each issued a warning. Other than the death of Shirley Bloom, it had been a quiet night.

He had already written his report and concluded that the local authorities in Bermuda need not be notified about a crime. His boss should be happy about that. Reporting a homicide would create an amazing amount of paperwork and would prompt an onboard investigation by the local police. Neither Epic Cruise Lines nor the *Colossus of the Ocean* needed that kind of publicity.

He noted that there was no mention of the whereabouts of Ricky Rosario. He had been reported missing from his assignment at a salsa dancing demonstration at 11:30 a.m. the day before and had not been seen since. The security officers who went to his cabin reported nothing out of place. His roommate had not seen him since they both went to sleep. The roommate thought he heard Ricky leave early in the morning, which was not unusual since they both often worked out before things got crowded. But he was not sure what time that might have been, since he was sleeping off a late-night encounter with someone he declined to name.

When Ricky was a no-show for the evening stage show, Keller had put out a low-level alert. From the lack of any mention of him in the morning report, none of the security officers had seen him. It wasn't as if there were many places for Ricky to hide. It was a puzzle, but not one Keller was going to spend much mental energy on. The kid could be shacked up in some guest's stateroom having a day-long orgy.

Keller had a body in his morgue. That, by itself, was going to create rumors and agitation among the passengers and crew. A missing person would only add to the general anxiety level. He didn't need that, especially with Ferguson on the ship. Things needed to stay calm. That was job one. If Ferguson was reading the daily reports while on vacation, he would see the reference to the alert. There was no need to bring it up.

Keller closed the report on his computer and sat back in his chair. He'd let Brandon Marshall deal with his wayward actor.

Michelle awoke as the sun was rising over the ocean. She was too agitated to sleep and so she grabbed a terrycloth robe, generously supplied by Epic Cruise Lines, and stepped as quietly as she could onto the balcony. She immediately noticed the color of the ocean, a tapestry of aqua, turquoise, emerald, and brown. She realized they were nearing Bermuda, and shortly figured out that the patches of brown in the water were clumps of coral reef, so close to the surface that they were visible through the clear water. She saw bright green buoys secured to the sea bed, which marked the contours of the shipping channel through which the giant craft was navigating. The water in places was no more than a few feet above the jagged coral. Michelle had heard that many sailing ships had wrecked in the waters around the island, and she could now understand how.

A few minutes later, the ship turned and Michelle could see the tip of the island coming into view. A stone battlement stood a silent sentry, armed with a row of black iron cannons pointed at the brilliant, sparkling sea. At that moment, she felt Mike's arms slipping around her waist and the stubble of his unshaven face kissing the back of her neck.

"Good morning," Mike said, squeezing her backside into his groin.

"Are you dressed?"

"I'm wearing pajamas."

Michelle enjoyed the thought of Mike's bare upper body being on full display, except that nobody from the adjoining balconies could see him. "It's really beautiful, isn't it?"

Mike surveyed the view as they steamed toward the extreme west end of the fish-hook-shaped island. "It's gorgeous."

"Did you check your text messages yet?"

Mike broke out into a full belly laugh, which he quickly suppressed. Quentin Richardson, in the next cabin, might still be trying to sleep. "I figured I would come kiss you first, but if you'd prefer me to check my phone, I'll keep that in mind for future reference."

Michelle spun around to face Mike and gave him a pantomime punch to the chest. Then she raised her eyes and asked a question that Mike had been thinking about himself. "Should we tell Jason and Rachel?"

Mike lowered his eyes as he thought. "What were we supposed to be doing with them today?"

"They're going on a jet ski tour, so they're leaving the ship as soon as we're docked. They get back at noon. We were going to meet back on the ship for lunch and then go out together to the beach."

"OK. Well, there's no need to ruin their morning, so let's not tell them until lunch. Keller wants me to keep it all to myself anyway, so I'll be able to tell him I'm following his instruction and not be lying about it."

"I agree. Maybe I'll find nothing and we can forget about it and enjoy our vacation."

Mike didn't respond, but turned to retrieve his phone.

Chapter 18 – Cold Storage

MICHELLE WAVED GOOD-BYE to Jason and Rachel as they queued up with the mass of other passengers trying to disembark as soon as the ship was cleared by the local authorities. The central staircase was backed up from the gangway on the second level all the way to the Promenade on Deck 5. Mike was having breakfast in the Epic Lounge with Ferguson, and Michelle was anxious to join them.

When she exited the elevator on Deck 13, she walked to the rail and peered over at the stream of guests walking down the long pier toward the clump of tour buses and guides holding up colorful balloons and signs. She wondered how many of the 5,000 guests would be leaving the ship in the next hour.

She walked along the open deck in the morning sunshine until she reached the main buffet dining room, sprawled across the ship's midsection near the stern. Instead of entering the Spinnaker Buffet, however, she veered off to an understated glass door: the entrance to the exclusive dining room reserved for suite passengers and Diamond-level cruisers.

She immediately spotted Mike sitting at a table for four with Ed and Millie Ferguson. Ferguson was wearing a captain's hat and navy blue sport jacket. Mike had on a powder blue polo shirt and khaki slacks with no jacket – as casual as he ever got. Michelle could tell from their body language that the two men were engaged in a serious discussion. She walked purposefully to the table and seated herself, before the hostess by the door could ask her for her suite number.

When she reached the table, the men stopped talking. "I hope I didn't miss anything important," Michelle said brightly as she fluffed her napkin onto her lap, covering the bare thighs below her white shorts.

"The detective here was trying to convince me that we have a possible homicide that needs an investigation," Ferguson said skeptically.

Mike passed Michelle a basket of pastries. "The key word here is 'possible.' Your head of security wants to call it a suicide, but we're pretty sure that's bullshit."

"That seems like speculation," Ferguson retorted, quite unwilling to entertain the notion that a serious crime could have been committed on one of his ships.

Michelle then walked Ferguson through all the reasons why she was convinced that suicide was out of the question. Ferguson had to acknowledge that the facts very much seemed contrary to the suicide theory.

"It still could have been an accident," he offered, without conviction.

"Sure. I hope it was. Really. I'll be the happiest person on the ship – well the happiest after Max Bloom – if I can rule out foul play here and let you chalk it up to a tragic accident. But I rather doubt it."

Mike jumped in to support Michelle. "In any case, it happens that you have a qualified ME on board. That gives you the unique opportunity to immediately determine whether you need a further investigation or not. Hopefully not. But you know as well as I do that if we have a problem, our window of time to catch a killer is tight. If you wait to get back to New York, after everyone leaves the ship and scatters, solving the case will be pretty much impossible. You know that."

Ferguson pursed his lips, then sighed. "Mike, the thing you don't understand is that it's not my ship. Keller is the head of security and the officers on board report to him. It's his call."

"Doesn't he report to you?"

"Sure he does, but company policy is to not interfere in the operation of ships at sea. If I start second-guessing my chiefs, I won't have much of a force. I have to let him make the decisions."

Mike dropped a fork onto his plate, which made a louder *clang* than he expected. Several diners at nearby tables turned to see what happened. Mike waved an apology, then lowered his voice. "Fine. You can let Keller make all the calls and all the decisions. But he needs information to make decisions, so after Michelle takes a quick look at the body, we'll make a report to him and let him take it from there."

Ferguson bristled. "How 'bout I call him and have him make the decision about letting you see the body?"

"How about you exercise a little authority here? Call Keller and tell him to meet us in the morgue. We'll roll you down there. He can say it's his gig all he wants, but we'll make sure this gets done and done right. You know that it's critical."

Ferguson's face hardened. Mike knew how to push his ex-cop

buttons.

Millie then spoke up for the first time since Michelle arrived. "Dear, I thought we were on vacation and you weren't working." She directed a pleading look toward her husband.

Ferguson picked up his napkin, dabbed his mouth, then threw the linen down onto his plate – still half-filled with eggs and toast. When he pushed himself back from the table, the wheels on his chair did a half-turn before he stopped. "OK, Stoneman. I'll text Keller and tell him to meet us there."

Millie gave a resigned sigh, then reached to take the handles of the wheelchair, but Mike put up his hand and intervened. He took charge of pushing his old mentor, who gave directions to the ship's infirmary on the second deck. Michelle and Millie walked behind them.

"Is he always like that?" Michelle asked.

"Always."

"I know the behavior. Mike's the same way. Do you think it's something in the water at the police precinct?"

"Well, my Edwin's been away from the police department for ten years, so I guess it never wears off. The truth is that he misses the excitement of being a cop."

Michelle was confused. "He said it was the best thing that ever happened to him."

"Sure. He says that. And sometimes he even means it. But, when he got injured, he felt like he was forced to retire. He couldn't handle the physical aspects of being a detective. He tells me sometimes that he wanted to go out on top, not be rolled out because he couldn't cut it."

"Mike would probably feel the same way," Michelle mused. She put her arm around the older woman as they walked to the elevator.

When they arrived on Deck 2, Michelle scampered ahead to open the door, marked with the classic red cross symbol, so Mike could roll Ferguson in. The nurse, wearing a crew uniform but with a white arm-band, jumped to her feet. Ferguson raised a hand and introduced himself. The young South Asian woman, whose gold nameplate read "Esmerelda," looked at him quizzically, trying to recall whether she should know his name. Ferguson dragged his wallet out of his jacket pocket and showed her his corporate identification, after which she took on a more formal state of attention.

"We're investigating the circumstances of the death of a guest last night. This young lady here," he motioned toward Michelle, "is the medical examiner for New York County and needs to see the body. Karl Keller will be along in a moment. Please take her into the morgue."

Ferguson spoke with an attitude of ultimate authority. The nurse dared not question him, although she turned her head around as if searching for a superior to give her permission. "The doctor is with a guest," she said hesitantly.

"We don't need the doctor. The lady is dead – there's nothing the doctor can do for her. We just need to examine the body. Please, lead on."

The nurse hesitated, but then ran out of reasons for not complying with the instruction. She turned and walked to the back of the small antechamber, then keyed in a code on a pad next to a large door that looked exactly like the entrance to an industrial refrigeration unit. It had a large, lever-like chrome handle and a red lightbulb, not illuminated, set into the wall overhead. When the nurse pressed the ENTER button on the pad and pulled on the big handle, the red light glowed. The door swung open and a puff of fog spilled out as if a witch's cauldron were being revealed. A fluorescent light sprang to life inside the room and flickered a few times before stabilizing. The nurse stood aside as if Mike were going to roll Ferguson inside, but instead the older man motioned to Michelle.

"Doctor, you will find the body in one of the units on the right wall. Nurse, do you know which drawer?"

Esmerelda shook her head, looking somewhat squeamish about opening up the cold storage compartment and seeing the dead woman.

Michelle asked the nurse for a pair of latex gloves, which she produced from a nearby drawer. "And a pair for Mike," she added.

Michelle put on the gloves, then slipped past the wheelchair and entered the cold room. Mike followed, snapping on his own gloves. There were four square doors, each with a small handle, lined up at about waist level. They all looked the same to Mike. Michelle surveyed them for signs of entry, then grasped the handle of the second unit in from the door and pulled it open. Mike immediately saw cold feet sticking up from the end of the slab. Michelle grabbed the end of the plank in between the two feet and pulled, causing the slab to roll out of its enclosure toward her. A black plastic sheet covered the body, except for the feet. By the time the drawer was fully extended, the feet were nearly touching the far wall of the refrigerator.

Michelle took out her cell phone, swiped a few times, punched an icon, and handed the phone to Mike. "Please hold this up while I speak." She ignored Mike and carefully removed the cover, starting her examination. Shirley Bloom's stiff body, still wearing the red dress from the night before, stared up from the slab. Michelle meticulously examined the exposed portions of the corpse, pulling the dress up above the knees as she dictated into the phone in Mike's hand.

"Deceased displays an expected level of lividity. Time of death is known to be approximately nine hours ago. Left tibia has a compound fracture consistent with the known fall of five floors from a balcony. Right ankle is displaced and right foot shows signs of impact fractures." She leaned down to peer at the dead woman's foot. "Mike, can you turn on the flashlight and shine it down here?" she said, pointing at the foot.

Mike fumbled through the controls on Michelle's phone to find the flashlight icon, which then brightly illuminated the area. "What have you got?"

"Shhh," Michelle scolded. She reached out and moved Shirley's foot to the side so that the light could shine on the place she was examining. "Right foot shows a shallow laceration running from the instep toward the little toe, consistent with a scrape on a sharp surface. Big toe shows a deep bruise, with some discoloration around the nail and indications of bleeding before death, with stains across the digit and onto the sole."

Michelle stopped examining the foot and worked her way up the legs toward the body's midsection. She examined Shirley's left hand, then her right, looking carefully at each finger while Mike followed her movements with his light. "Mike, please ask the nurse to give me five Q-tips and some tissue sample containers."

Mike turned and looked out the door toward the others, who were watching intently and had heard Michelle's request. The nurse had already extracted the requested supplies and handed them to Mike, who handed them to Michelle. She swabbed a few of the woman's fingers, then placed the Q-tips in the sample dishes.

"Ask the nurse for a sterile knife or file."

Before Mike had turned to ask, Esmerelda was already searching another drawer. She tore open a paper packet and extracted a file with a curved hook at one end, and handed it to Mike.

Michelle used the hook to dig under the corpse's fingernails, then scraped the contents off into a sample container with one of the Q-tips. As she did, she resumed her dictation. "Deceased shows indications of tissue under the fingernails of the second and third fingers of her right hand. Samples are collected for later analysis. First indications are human skin. The fingernails on the third and fourth fingers on the right hand, and the fourth finger on the left hand, are broken and show indications of recent breaks." She continued up the torso toward the dead woman's head. "Neck shows redness and small lacerations on the left and right sides, with swelling and bruising. No indication of ligature. Tongue is slightly enlarged and discolored. Skull shows a significant disfigurement on the left side, consistent with the known fall." Michelle paused her narration. "Mike, help me turn her over."

"What?"

"We need to turn her over, without pushing her off the slab. I need your help."

Mike put the phone down on a countertop, then helped Michelle lift the body and turn it onto its stomach. Once done, Michelle pulled Shirley's dress up over her buttocks and halfway up her back, exposing the skin. Mike tried hard not to stare at the dead woman's lace panties.

Michelle continued her dictation. "Deceased has bruising on the lower back at approximately the 5th or 6th vertebra running horizontally the length of the torso, approximately one inch high, and scrape marks running vertically for about three inches." She continued to examine the body and dictated some more observations about the skin and hair, but nothing that Mike considered important. Having read hundreds of coroners' reports, he had a pretty good idea about what was significant.

As Mike and Michelle were turning the body back over onto its back, the door to the infirmary burst open and Karl Keller came through. "Mr. Ferguson, what's going on here?"

Everyone turned toward Keller, who was red in the face, as if he had sprinted from wherever he had been. Ferguson turned his head and took charge of the situation. "Keller, glad you got my text. It turns out that we have a medical examiner on board and she volunteered to do a quick examination of our suspected jumper."

"I didn't authorize this," Keller said, looking first at Mike and Michelle, then turning to glare at Ferguson.

Ferguson glared back. "I authorized it. We have a dead passenger and a questionable situation. Since we have a qualified expert available, I allowed her to examine the body."

Keller stood rigidly, trying to decide how much he wanted to challenge the authority of his boss. "You should have consulted with me."

"I did. I told you to meet us here, but we decided not to wait for you."

Keller frowned. Mike thought he was pissed off, but he didn't say anything right away, so Mike stepped into the silence. "I'm sure you want to make certain you don't have a homicide here, Mr. Keller. Doctor McNeill volunteered to have a look, and Mr. Ferguson facilitated for us."

"I don't think there is any need for an autopsy," Keller fumed.

"She's not doing an autopsy," Mike said calmly. "She's just doing a surface examination to rule out any immediate suspicion of foul play. If there were any indication of a homicide, I'm sure you would want to know right away, so you could conduct an appropriate investigation." Mike stared at the security chief, as if daring him to disagree with the statement.

Keller inhaled a deep breath. "Of course I want to know, but I'm quite sure there's no reason to think this is a homicide. I've already filed my report."

"I disagree," Michelle said, emerging from the cold room and peeling off her latex gloves. "I would say that we have significant indications of a possible homicide."

Everyone looked at Michelle. "Why do you think that, Doctor McNeill?" Mike prompted.

Before Michelle could speak, Keller broke in. "I said that there is no reason to suspect a homicide. It's my responsibility. I will not have some civilian taking charge of an investigation on my ship."

"I'm no civilian!" Michelle shouted, louder than she intended. Then, she regained control of her volume. "I'm a medical examiner. If you are at all interested in protecting your passengers from a killer instead of protecting your corporate bosses from embarrassment, you'll listen to what I have to say."

Keller stared at Michelle, then at Ferguson, who spoke next. "I'm sure my finest security chief wants to get to the bottom of this and not suppress any relevant evidence, don't you, Keller?"

At this point, Keller was in a tough spot, with his boss there challenging him to be a good cop. "Of course, I do," he said, clipping his words.

"Good," Michelle used her best professional voice. "Based on my external examination, I'd say that there are significant indications of a struggle. There are defensive wounds, an indication of strangulation, a laceration and bruise on her foot consistent with a struggle and inconsistent with a fall, and a large bruise on her back. I'd have to say that an accidental fall is unlikely."

"Based on ten minutes of examination?" Keller asked incredulously.

"It doesn't take long," Michelle responded calmly. "There was tissue under her fingernails and several freshly broken nails. And the bruise on her back is consistent with being pressed violently up against the balcony railing, which is inconsistent with either a jump or an accidental fall."

Ferguson said, "So, you think a homicide is more likely than an accident or a suicide?"

"Yes," Michelle said confidently. "Do we know whether she had her shoes on when she fell?"

"Why does that matter?" Keller was losing his composure.

"It's important to understanding the scratches on her foot. When you found the body, was she wearing her shoes, or were her shoes found below the balcony?"

"No," Keller conceded. "We didn't find her shoes."

"Were the shoes in her room?"

Keller clenched his fists and seemed to be biting his tongue. "We didn't find any stray shoes in the cabin. We can't know if any of the shoes in the closet were the ones she was wearing last night."

Michelle paused to think. "She was wearing silver pumps with her red dress," she said.

"How can you possibly know that?" Keller challenged.

"Because I spoke with her in the ladies' room last night and I remember."

"OK. Fine. We'll check the room to see if there are silver pumps in the closet."

"Shall we take a walk upstairs?" Ferguson suggested.

Everyone stared at the man in the wheelchair. Finally, Mike said, "Yes, let's go look inside that cabin and see what else we can find."

"We already searched the room," Keller said firmly. "There's no need for that. I'll send an officer to check on the shoes."

Ferguson waved his hand dismissively. "You were searching the room of a woman you thought jumped off her balcony. We're now searching a potential crime scene."

"Mr. Ferguson, you know as well as I do the kind of shit-show this will become if we say it's a possible . . . murder. I don't need this publicity hound coming onto my ship and creating one of his famous media circuses."

"I'm no media hound!" Mike cut in. "I prefer to keep the media out of my investigations."

"You'd never know by the way your picture is all over the newspapers and television."

Ferguson broke in, trying to get the conversation back on track. "Our first obligation here is the safety of the passengers. There might be a murderer on this ship."

"If it was a homicide, then it was probably the husband," Keller responded. "There's very little risk to the other passengers."

"Well, Karl, I'd say having an experienced homicide detective take a look can't hurt. Right?" Ferguson glared at Keller, challenging him to disagree. Keller scowled, then turned on a heel and led the way out of the infirmary.

Chapter 19 – Rejecting the Obvious

WHEN THE GROUP APPROACHED the Blooms' cabin, someone was already there, standing at the door. Karl Keller called out to him. "Mr. Marshall, how can I help you?"

Brandon Marshall turned toward the voice. His face was at first curious, but it quickly faded into concern. "Mr. Keller. I was just trying to leave a note for a friend of mine, Shirley Bloom. We had scheduled a breakfast meeting for this morning, but she didn't show up. I hope there's nothing amiss."

Keller stopped short of the door, keeping the rest of the group behind him. "How do you know Mrs. Bloom?"

"We're old friends. I was her director on Broadway many years ago, when she was an actress. Why are all of you here? There's something wrong, isn't there?"

Keller hesitated. If Brandon was actually an old friend, then he certainly would know Max Bloom. It would only be a matter of time before the director learned the truth. He decided that it would be best if Brandon didn't go around asking about Shirley. He leaned in and spoke softly. "I'm afraid that Mrs. Bloom had an . . . accident last night. She fell from her balcony. I'm afraid that she died from the fall."

Brandon's eyes bulged. He whispered, "What? But—"

"I'm very sorry, Brandon. It's tragic."

"That rat bastard!"

"Who?" Keller couldn't help himself from asking.

"Max Bloom. The bastard must have killed her!"

Keller did a double-take. "Why would you think such a thing?"

"Because I know Max, and I know he's about the only person in the world who would want to kill Shirley."

"Nobody has been killed," Keller protested. "We think it might have been a suicide."

"That's bullshit!" Brandon stood up straight and threw his left arm into the air. "She was meeting me today to talk about a role in a play on Broadway. She was really excited about it yesterday, when I spoke to her. I may not have seen her for a while, but I'm certain she wouldn't have killed herself."

Michelle stepped sideways, to get a clear view of Brandon. "We don't know anything for sure yet."

Keller shot a disapproving glare at Michelle, then turned back to Brandon. "It may have just been a terrible accident."

Brandon looked at Michelle with a confused expression. She was not wearing a crew uniform. "I'm sorry, I'm not sure who you are, but if Shirley fell from her balcony, I'd wager that Max helped her over."

Keller took Brandon by the elbow and led him away from the door and from the group waiting to enter cabin 935. "Listen, Brandon, I'll certainly take what you've said under consideration. This is a developing situation. I'll be handling it. I need you to avoid upsetting anyone by making wild accusations about one of the guests. Now, please get a hold of yourself. Leave it to me."

"Fine. Come talk to me when you know more. I'll be happy to tell you anything I know."

"Good. I will. Now, I'm sure you have places to be. I need to get back to the – situation."

Brandon walked away, without looking back. Keller returned to the group and used his master key to open the cabin door.

Keller let a uniformed officer who had joined them when they arrived on Deck 9 enter the room first. Ferguson stayed in the hallway with Michelle, since his wheelchair would hamper everyone else's ability to move around inside the small space. Millie had opted to skip the police business and keep her appointment for a massage in the ship's spa.

Michelle told the officer to look for two things: the silver heels Mrs. Bloom was wearing the night before and the large, square-cut emerald ring. The officer found the shoes in the closet, neatly arranged next to two other pairs. They did not find the ring. Michelle had noted during her examination that the ring was missing from Shirley's finger.

Mike suggested that Keller should interview the guests in the adjoining staterooms, to see if anyone heard anything the night before. Keller bristled and said he had already determined the names of the guests in those rooms and was tracking them down, but both couples had left the ship.

"What about key card swipes?" Mike asked.

"We haven't pulled that data. It probably won't matter."

Mike stared at him. "There are substantial indications here of a homicide. We need to know whether anyone besides Shirley Bloom accessed the room before her time of death."

"If she opened the door and let someone in, there wouldn't be a card swipe."

"True," Mike agreed, "but I'm most interested in knowing whether the husband's key card shows an entry between midnight and the time he showed up with me, a little past one."

"You think the husband? I thought you were his friend."

Mike shrugged. "We always suspect the husband when a woman dies. You saw how that director guy reacted. We know that there was trouble in the marriage and we know there was a pre-nup that restricted the husband's ability to get a portion of the marital property in the event of a divorce. But, I'm guessing, not in the event of her death."

"How can you possibly know that?" Keller blurted out.

Mike smiled. "I'd say it is elementary, my dear Keller, but the truth is that Mrs. Bloom told Michelle. So, the husband had an obvious motive. I doubt that he'd be dumb enough to use his key card to swipe into the room if he went there to kill her, but you never know. People are dumb. People don't always understand that every key swipe is recorded. So, we should check."

Keller pursed his lips. "You're right – if there is any reason to suspect a homicide. I will check the records, but like you said, it's not likely to show us anything."

"Thanks. I assume nobody else would have a key to open their door, except maybe the cabin attendant and your security boys, right?"

"That's about right. There are a few other officials on the ship who have master keys, like Marjorie Barnes and her senior staff, but not many."

"What about the missing ring?" Mike asked, trying to draw

the man into the investigation, rather than working against him. "I saw that ring on her finger. It was impressive. She might have taken it off if she was getting ready for bed, but it would be in here. If we find that ring in somebody else's possession, it will be significant."

"Well, it's a big ship. We can't search every stateroom looking for it."

Mike pondered it for a moment. "Can you alert your cleaning crews to be on the lookout for it when they clean the rooms?"

"I'm not going to have the cabin attendants search our guests' rooms," Keller said, as if quite offended by the suggestion.

"Well, think about it," Mike retorted. "In the meantime, are there any security cameras that monitor this hallway?"

"Normally, yes," Keller said with a grimace. "But, at the moment, no. Did you feel that storm we passed through early yesterday morning?"

"Uh huh," Mike confirmed.

"Well, we took a lightning hit that fried our server. We have cameras all over the ship, but we have no recording ability. The casino has its own cameras and servers, but the rest of the ship is offline. The security team is monitoring the system in real time, but there are nearly a hundred cameras. We're focused on the Promenade, not the hallways. There are only so many screens we can watch live."

Mike's head dropped with disappointment. "OK, well, you should interview every other guest on this floor to see if anyone saw someone in the vicinity of this room."

Keller stiffened and glared at Mike. "Detective, I appreciate your insight, but I am not going to disturb our guests with that kind of interrogation, and I'm not going to alert anyone that there is a murder investigation happening. These people are on vacation, they're not suspects."

"Are you telling me that keeping a lid on the facts so the other guests aren't upset is more important to you than finding a killer?"

"We don't know that there *is* any killer. We don't know that there has been a murder. That's all speculation."

"So, you have an alternate theory that can explain the marks on the body and the tissue under the victim's fingernails?"

"It's not my job to explain every scratch on every passenger's body. It's my job to keep the guests secure and feeling safe. Causing a panic is not something I'm going to allow. And neither is Mr. Ferguson."

Mike just stared. As he thought about it, he realized that Keller's job description did not include tracking down a murderer. It was limited to breaking up drunken bar fights and catching guests shoplifting watches. He wasn't a cop, he was a babysitter. "Alright, well, we'll see how the investigation develops. Can you tell me whether there was any indication of the furniture on the balcony being jostled or moved around?"

"I don't know," Keller answered, seemingly annoyed by the question. "Marjorie was out there with one of my officers last night. They were working out the angle of the fall to verify that she had come from this balcony. You'll have to talk to her about the state of the furniture."

"When can I talk to her?"

"Really, Detective, I assure you that I can handle this investigation without your assistance." Keller turned to walk over to his officer and whispered something to him that Mike couldn't hear. Mike motioned to Michelle to come inside so they could talk.

"These guys are not going to find anything useful. Is there

anything specific you think we should be looking for, besides the shoes and the ring?"

"Yes," Michelle said excitedly. "The marks on her neck could have been made by a scarf or a nylon. We should be looking for something like that out of place, especially near the balcony."

"Let's look around ourselves for that," Mike suggested. "The boys here might look right past it." Mike walked slowly in the direction of the balcony door, scanning the floor for something out of place that could have been used to strangle Mrs. Bloom. The theory was that someone had entered the room, surprised Mrs. Bloom, caught her around the neck with something, then struggled with her, ramming her back against the balcony railing and stepping on her bare foot before pushing her over. There were only a few feet between the edge of the bed and the sliding glass door. Michelle got down on her hands and knees to inspect the floor under the bed.

"What are you doing?" Keller shouted at Michelle.

"I'm looking for something that could have been used to strangle the victim."

"Please let my officers take care of that."

Michelle stood up. As she did, she pulled on the blanket covering the bed and saw a glimpse of something blue and white fall on the carpet. She put her shoe on it and pulled it toward her. As it moved, she saw that it was a man's necktie, certainly Max Bloom's.

"Officer?" Michelle called out politely, "can you please collect this necktie – carefully – and put it in an evidence bag?"

The officer, a tall South Asian young man, took a step toward her and saw the item she was pointing at on the floor. He looked at Keller for guidance. Keller frowned, but then nodded his agreement. The officer pulled a plastic bag from his pocket and used it to pick up the tie, then inverted it into the bag and handed the bag to Keller.

"I don't have any lab facilities here, of course," Michelle said, "but you should mark that and hold onto it for later analysis. There may be hair or tissue samples on it."

"I know how to handle evidence, Doctor," Keller said tersely.

A few minutes later – much sooner than Mike would have approved of had it been his crime scene – Keller announced that they were finished and ordered his officer to leave the cabin.

Michelle, who was standing between the bed and the balcony, called out to Keller. "Do you need me to provide you with a written report, or is the audio recording of my examination sufficient? Where can I send it?"

"I'll take care of any reporting, if you please." He clenched his jaw together so tightly that his temple throbbed.

"OK, then," Mike said, motioning for Michelle to join him on his way out. "Thank you, Mr. Keller, I'm sure that you can handle everything from here. But if you need any assistance, or if you'd like to consult with me as you move forward, I am very happy to give you any help I can."

"Thank you for the offer," Keller said quickly, "but I'm sure we can handle it."

Without another word, Mike and Michelle left the room and stopped in the hallway next to Ferguson. Mike asked him, "Did you follow everything that was going on inside?"

"Yep. I think you need to give Keller some space now and let him do his job. I'm glad you and Doctor McNeill were here for this."

"Do you want me to participate in the interrogation of the husband? That's the obvious next step."

"No, Mike," Ferguson said, using his first name for the first time since they had been reunited. "I'm sure you would do a better job than Keller, but this is his ship. I'll let you know what happens. You go try to enjoy your cruise, and don't worry. We've got it."

Mike gave Ferguson a firm handshake, as did Michelle, and then they left him and adjourned to their own cabin. Once inside and out of the prying earshot of the chief of security, Mike asked the question he had been thinking about since they left the morgue. "How sure are you about the substance you removed from under the victim's fingernails?"

"It was skin, Mike. Very little doubt about it. Almost certainly Caucasian, although I'd need to run some tests to say for sure. You were following along with my dictation. She had bruises across her back at about the height of the balcony railing – although, again, I would need to take some specific measurements to be absolutely sure. The bruising is consistent with making violent contact with the wooden railing. Those are not bruises caused by falling accidentally, unless she fell over backwards after being thrown – or she was somehow propelled toward the railing."

Michelle paused to make sure that Mike was not going to disagree with her. He didn't. "The woman was in a struggle for her life before she went over that rail. If Keller doesn't realize that, then he's an idiot."

"He's no idiot," Mike mused, "but his job is to keep the guests calm and happy, not to create a panic by suggesting that there's a murderer on the ship. So, I'm not sure solving the crime and catching the killer are his highest priorities."

Michelle walked to their open balcony door and looked out over the water at the island beyond. "And I'm curious about her ring. You remember it, right? It was huge. She had a visible tan line and an indentation; she must have always worn it. I can't say for sure whether she was wearing it last night, but she did wear it on her ring finger. She was wearing all her other jewelry, including her wedding band, and she had not removed her makeup before she went over the balcony. It's odd that she would have taken off the ring but nothing else, although it's possible the ring was the first thing she took off, and then she was surprised."

"Can you tell whether it was the fall that killed her, or whether she was conscious when she fell?"

"No. Without a full autopsy, I can't tell."

Mike didn't bother to suggest that there might not be a killer. "The obvious first suspect is still the husband. I walked with him toward the room last night when I was coming to bed, but he could have killed her, left to go establish an alibi, and then come back. He was a bit rumpled when I saw him. I guess he could have been in a struggle."

"He didn't establish much of an alibi," Michelle observed.

"Yeah, well, he may not be a master criminal. What I don't get is why he would remove the ring."

"I know," Michelle said softly, looking down at the carpet. "I don't suppose it's possible for us to just forget about this and let Keller handle it from here, huh?"

"I'll be happy to do that – if he actually conducts an investigation."

"You think he'll try to sweep it all under the rug?"

"It wouldn't surprise me," Mike said glumly. "But, for now, let's go meet Jason and Rachel for lunch, and then go to the beach, like we planned. I'll give Ferguson a call later. Until then, we have a vacation to enjoy, right?"

Michelle shrugged, but then smiled. "Right. Let's at least try."

Chapter 20 – Primary Suspect

OVER LUNCH, RACHEL AND JASON told Mike and Michelle about their jet ski tour of the island, which was spectacular. "We even went out to a coral reef and got to snorkel around," Rachel recounted excitedly. "We saw a lionfish, which was scary and also beautiful."

After the tour, they went to an escape room near the dock, but that was evidently not as wonderful. Jason solved the puzzle in ten minutes, which deprived the rest of the group of the fun and thrills of working against the 60-minute clock. Jason was rather proud of himself, but Rachel called him a fuddy-duddy. She showed Michelle her selfies with their jet ski guide and with the other members of their escape room group.

Mike and Michelle gave Jason and Rachel a rundown on the undeniably exciting events of the night before, and on Michelle's examination of Shirley Bloom's body.

"You could have told me this morning, before we left the ship," Jason observed, seeming a bit annoyed with Mike.

"Sure, but if I had told you, and told you about our plan to have Michelle examine the body, you would have stayed with me and blown off your jet-ski tour."

"Maybe not," Jason responded quickly, looking at Rachel.

"And there was no reason for you and Rachel to miss out," Mike continued, ignoring Jason's protest.

"It was fun," Rachel agreed, "and it would have been awful to miss it. You're on vacation, Jason."

"OK. Fine. I'll admit that it's *possible* that I might have tried to come along with you, and that would have messed up our morning. So, I guess you probably made the right call, Mike."

Mike flashed a stern look. "A simple 'You were right, Mike,' is just too hard for you to say, eh, partner?"

"Best you're going to get," Jason responded with a grin.

They talked over the case and speculated about possible hypotheses as they rode in a cab from the Dockyard along the south coast of the island, toward the world-famous Horseshoe Bay beach. They staked out a bit of pink sand, dipped into the soft surf, walked along the expansive stretch of smooth tidal flats, and watched the hordes of beach-going tourists. Rachel joined in a game of beach volleyball with a group of Millennials, then spent half an hour helping three children work on a huge sand castle. Jason joined in, while Mike and Michelle yelled encouragement.

After two delightful hours in the sunshine, they packed up and walked down to the end of the curved beach. Since it was low tide, they were able to walk through huge, jagged rocks and around the point to the next stretch of beach that lay beyond. This was a private beach owned by the Elbow Beach resort, but nobody was asking them for ID. They strolled along, past a thatch-covered bar and a low-slung building housing bathrooms and changing rooms. They finally climbed up a set of wooden stairs, to a parking lot where hotel guests parked their motorbikes.

As they contemplated the climb farther up the hill to the main hotel building, a cab pulled up to discharge its passengers. When the sliding door of the mini-van opened, Mike was surprised to see Max Bloom emerge, wearing sunglasses, shorts, and a floral Hawaiian shirt and carrying a canvas beach bag. Right behind him was a leggy blonde. Mike recognized her as one of the actresses from the ship's theater company. Max did not notice Mike's group waiting to grab the taxi as he and the blonde hurried away toward the beach.

"I guess the period of mourning is over," Jason said, turning to Mike with a raised eyebrow.

"I guess so," Michelle replied. "As if there wasn't already enough evidence pointing toward him."

Rachel said, "I'm pretty sure that was Vicki Nelson. She sang that great song from *Wicked* during the musical revue."

They rode back to the Dockyard, admiring the spectacular views from the roadway, which was elevated a good two hundred feet above the beaches. They cleared security back onto the ship and went to their cabins to shower and change for dinner. Jason was assigned to use Rachel's onboard Wi-Fi account and send a message to Detective Steve Berkowitz back at the precinct in New York. They needed to get some background on Max and Shirley Bloom.

Rachel and Michelle had made plans to participate in a digital scavenger hunt. The event involved taking pictures with different people and places around the ship. It was made for Rachel, the Queen of Selfies. Mike bowed out and sent Ferguson a text message asking him to meet in Shangri-La at 5:30. When he emerged from the tiny shower, he checked his phone and saw a reply acknowledging the meeting.

Ferguson was already in the bar when Mike arrived. April, the bartender, was leaning down to set a tumbler on the table next to his wheelchair. Mike recognized the dark liquid as the Zacapa 23 rum that Ferguson had introduced him to on the first day of the cruise. Mike waved to April, who quickly returned to the bar and fetched Mike a similar glass. Before long, Jason's imposing figure appeared, silhouetted at first in the double doors leading into the room. Once they were all situated and April had come around with a rum for Jason, Ferguson gave them the rundown on the afternoon's events.

Karl Keller had run a report on Max's card swipes from the prior day, which showed his whereabouts any time he bought a drink or opened his stateroom door. The report showed him in the Clipper Bar at 11:45, then opening his door at 12:11. Shirley was spotted dead on the lifeboat at 12:20. During questioning, Max stuck to his alibi: that he took a walk on the deck and was asleep in a deck chair at the time of the "incident," as Ferguson called it. Max said he returned to his cabin a little after 1:00, which was when he ran into Mike in the hallway.

"C'mon, Ferguson, you can say the word 'murder.'"

"It's not a homicide, Stoneman, it's an investigation. Don't push that. Keller is right that there is a mandatory reporting obligation if there is a serious crime on a ship at sea. We'd have to inform the Bermudian authorities and it would be a PR nightmare."

"Fine," Mike said, sipping his Zacapa. "The guy has a piss-poor alibi and a first-class motive. Did he have any explanation for why he can't remember going to his room shortly before the – incident?"

"He says he has no idea how his room key was recorded opening the door at twelve-eleven, and in fact, when he got to the stateroom we moved him to last night, he couldn't find his key.

"But I tell you what, Stoneman, he was holding something back. He admits he had his card in the Clipper Bar, where he got a drink twenty-six minutes before the swipe on his cabin door. He says he can't remember whether he got the card back from the waiter, but we checked in the bar and the card wasn't turned in. That happens all the time – a guest gives up their key card when ordering something, and then they don't get it back, or they leave it on their table. So, it's possible that he left his card in the bar and somebody who was with him, and who knew what room he was in, took it. But the cards don't have the room numbers on them, so finding a random key card isn't going to allow someone to immediately go open his door. The hypothetical other person would need to know the number."

"So," Jason cut in, "if he arranged for somebody else to go pay a visit to his wife in their room, he could have given up his card."

"Sure," Mike said, "that would be a reasonable theory, but if he were sending someone off to kill his wife, wouldn't he go somewhere very public, like to the casino, where lots of people and cameras would see him and give him a solid alibi? Why arrange for a hit on his wife, and then go off by himself? You have to know you're going to be the prime suspect. If you're not going to set up a decent alibi, why not just do it yourself?"

"So we're back to him as the prime suspect," Jason said.

Ferguson drained his glass and set it down heavily on the

marble-topped table with a loud clank. "Gentlemen, the man is certainly a suspect, but that's all he is. The incident may still have been a suicide, or an accident. We have some suspicions, but that's all we have."

"I don't suppose the key cards have GPS trackers in them?" Mike posed the question, although he was pretty certain what the answer would be.

Ferguson shook his head. "No. The company is considering various systems that will allow interactive activities on board based on a chip that the guests wear, but we're not there yet."

"I figured it wouldn't be that easy. What did the guests in the adjoining cabins have to say?"

"We haven't spoken to them yet. We weren't able to catch them in their rooms or anywhere else private enough, so we're waiting until we can."

Mike scowled. "You know as well as I do that we should talk to them as quickly as possible. Don't we know where they're eating dinner, based on their reservations?"

"In theory we do, but guests often don't keep their meal reservations, especially when we're in port. So we can't really be sure enough to stake them out."

"You could if you thought it was important," Mike groused.

"Can it, Stoneman. I'm helping you here. Don't start giving me shit about details. Keller's still in charge, and it's his officers who would be doing it. I've already pushed him."

"What about their card swipes?" Jason suggested, changing the subject quickly. "When they use their key cards, don't you know where they are?"

"The system is not set up for real-time tracking," Ferguson explained. "We can run a report, or someone can literally watch the computer screen, but we don't have a way to flag a particular card and have an alarm go off when the card has activity."

"I'm surprised your system is so limited," Mike said.

"We're not a prison. Folks here are on vacation, so we're not normally trying to track them so closely."

"Fair enough," Mike conceded. "Well, I'll be really interested to know what they heard. But whether they can confirm sounds of a struggle or not, based on Michelle's observations and what we know about Shirley and her state of mind last night, I'll give you twenty-to-one against her going over that balcony voluntarily."

Ferguson said nothing.

"So why did you let Max leave the ship?" Mike asked. "He's certainly the prime suspect, but you let him walk off and go to the beach. What if he disappears?"

Ferguson shrugged. "We'll know if he doesn't get back on the ship when we sail for New York on Sunday afternoon. Where is he going to go? It's a small island. He's not under arrest."

"Maybe he should be," Jason said.

"Well, Detective Dickson, you don't have the authority to arrest him, and Keller has decided that he doesn't need to be confined. Like you said, if he's a murderer, he's not a mastermind. We're not worried that he pre-planned to have a private boat meet him in Bermuda and whisk him away to a secret hideout. Besides, if he bolts, then he's a fugitive and he's not our problem anymore. We'll know he's guilty and there won't be any more investigation needed until we all get back to New York. That's not a bad outcome. If he did kill his wife for her money, there's little chance that other passengers are in danger."

Mike thought about Ferguson's statement. He was right. This wasn't a police investigation, where they were worried about the suspect getting away. Keller would have to turn a suspect over to the police as soon as they made port if there was evidence of a crime. If Max flew the coop, they would be able to stand down and forget about it. Not the way a cop would handle it within his own jurisdiction, but under the circumstances, not a terrible result.

"Fair enough. Just do me a favor and text me if you need me or Jason to assist."

Ferguson shook a finger at Mike, scolding him for trying to be a detective instead of a passenger. "You're on vacation, Stoneman. Forget about this and try to have a good time."

"Old habits are hard to break, as you know," Mike said in response. "But I'll do my best."

Rachel and Michelle walked quickly down the Promenade on Deck 5, dodging shoppers pawing through piles of discounted t-shirts and purses. The little tables and chairs set up outside the Irish pub, the pizza shop, and the pastry and coffee kiosk were all filled to capacity, further shrinking the available walking space.

"What's next, after the theater?" Rachel called over her shoulder to the trailing Michelle.

"I'm not sure. I can't read the list of clues and walk at the same time. Let's get to the theater and figure it out from there. How's it look from up there?" Michelle laughed, referring to Rachel's eye level, which was nearly a foot higher than hers.

"The crow's nest reports land, ho!" she mocked and pointed to their left, where a curving walkway snaked around one of the ship's four banks of elevators. Michelle struggled to keep up with Rachel's pace as she charged forward until they both saw the sign for the Epic Theater. As they approached the large double doors leading to the auditorium, they could see a bank of photographic lights illuminating two women dressed in elaborate costumes. The women were smiling and posing for selfie photos with two young men, who were obviously thrilled to be standing next to the buxom, attractive ladies.

Michelle and Rachel came to a stop ten yards away, behind two other women whom they recognized as another team of participants in the ship's digital scavenger hunt. There were two other teams waiting their turn further ahead in the impromptu line.

They chatted with Mildred and Charlene, who were sisters from North Carolina, as they waited. Rachel helpfully explained that the clue "swimming with the whales" was a reference to the children's pool, which contained a water slide in the shape of a whale. The clue "bedazzled dancers in their natural habitat" had been pretty easy.

Michelle and Rachel recognized both dancers from their backstage tour on the first day of the cruise. On the left, Donna wore a yellow ensemble with a low-cut sequined unitard, cut high on her hips to expose her entire leg, which was encased in dark nylons. Rachel remembered her as being blonde, but today she was wearing a dark wig – unless the blonde hair had been the wig. She had yellow feathers popping up from behind her head and was dripping with jewelry that seemed to be mostly diamonds, or more likely zirconia.

Next to Donna, Darci was bedecked in a green outfit that similarly emphasized her long legs. Her sequins sparkled in the bright lights, along with a necklace, earrings, and rings composed of green stones. She had a green tint to her eyeshadow and green peacock feathers above her short spikey hairdo. Both Donna and Darci were smiling and mugging for the photos.

When it was finally Rachel and Michelle's turn, one of the ship's assistant cruise directors motioned them forward, trying to keep the growing line of scavenger hunters organized. Rachel greeted the actresses by name and complimented their costumes. The ladies were happily surprised to see Rachel.

"They call us 'Double D' when we go out together," Donna commented, drawing a roll of Darci's eyes. "They think it's an insult, but I kinda like it." Darci did not echo Donna's enthusiasm regarding the nickname.

Donna asked Rachel how her cruise was going. They chatted for a minute and then posed for their selfie, with Rachel between the two gorgeous dancers. Michelle marveled at her young friend. Without makeup or costume, she managed to hold her own with just her smile. Michelle chose to remain in the background. With a growing line of scavenger hunt teams waiting for their turn, Rachel exchanged hugs with Donna and Darci. Then she and Michelle hurried off to their next "treasure" stop.

Chapter 21 – Turf Wars

OVER DINNER, MIKE AND JASON recounted to Michelle and Rachel the information they had gathered from Ferguson. Max Bloom was not at their dinner table, leaving the four of them free to chat. They all agreed, having spent some time with Shirley Bloom, that she had not killed herself.

Although Rachel was more interested in enjoying her vacation than chasing down clues in a murder investigation, she got caught up in the excitement of the adventure and didn't put up much of a fuss when Mike suggested that they split up and take care of a few assignments after dinner. They planned to leave the ship later to browse the exhibits by Bermudian artisans in a small park adjacent to the pier, which shut down at 10:00. Then there was a local singer performing at the Frog & Onion pub until midnight. They were going to enjoy this trip, no matter what. But first, they had a few hours.

Rachel briefly lobbied to stay on the ship and watch the

performance of *Chicago*. She wanted to see what parts her new theater friends, Donna and Darci, would be playing. But, the rest of the group was content to plan on seeing the show on the final night of the cruise on Monday.

Jason went to the ship's internet café with Rachel to check his email. Since they were an hour ahead of New York time, he was hoping to have a return email from Steve Berkowitz. He was happily surprised to find two messages. Berkowitz was able to determine that Max had been divorced twice before he married the former Shirley Epstein, née Lester. Shirley's prior husband had died a few years before she married Max.

Max had been a talent agent with the William Morris agency for ten years. About a year ago, he left the agency to open his own shop. He had a website and several social media accounts extolling his virtues as an agent and featuring photos of his clients. Berkowitz had not yet been able to make contact with any of the clients or with any Broadway producers or executives who could give him any color on Max's personality.

The report on Shirley's family was more interesting. Her first husband, Harold Epstein, had been a partner in a big New York law firm. When he died of cancer, Shirley inherited his substantial fortune. She also had money she inherited from her father. She had two kids from the first marriage.

Berkowitz had contacted Shirley's daughter, Whitney, who told him she had insisted that Shirley have a prenuptial agreement that would limit Max's ability to receive any money if he divorced her. The daughter thought Max was a con man who wanted to use Shirley and her money to finance his shady Broadway angles. She confirmed what Shirley had told Michelle about Max getting no payout if he initiated a divorce. But, if Shirley died, then Max would inherit half the estate. Epic Cruise

Lines had not notified Whitney about her mother's death. After she recovered from the shock, she told Berkowitz she was sure Max killed Shirley for her money, even though Whitney didn't have any specific evidence to back up her suspicions.

Mike's assignment was to find Ferguson and find out what other information Keller had gathered from the witnesses. He texted his old friend, who replied that he was inside the Epic Theater. Mike and Michelle arrived as the crowd was filing out after "Ernie the Magnificent" finished his family-friendly magic show.

When the stream of exiting cruisers thinned out, they swam upstream until they arrived in the nearly deserted theater space. Ferguson was seated in his usual wheelchair-accessible spot. Millie was next to him, examining the ship's activity sheet. Mike stood over Ferguson's chair, while Michelle took a seat in the row in front of Millie.

"I had a thought," Mike said, as soon as he arrived. "I know you want me to give Keller some space, but I'm concerned that he's not being diligent about this case."

"I'm not going to hover over him while he does his job."

Mike squatted down, then took a seat on the step next to Ferguson's chair. "I know, it's just that I'm certain that it's critically important for somebody to interview the waiter from the Clipper Bar. We know that Max got a drink shortly before he claims to have lost his key card. The waiter who served him might have seen who was there – who might have taken the card, if in fact someone other than Max used it to open that cabin door at 12:11. This could be a vital detail, and the longer we wait, the less likely it will be that the waiter will remember. I'm worried that Keller will sit on this and not conduct an interview until it's too late."

Ferguson frowned, but said nothing. Then, Millie tapped his arm to get his attention. "Darling, it's twenty after eight now. We wanted to get seats by the piano for when that nice singer starts his set at nine o'clock, remember?"

"Yes, I do," Ferguson said, turning back to Mike. "Well, Stoneman, it turns out that we're already planning on going to the Clipper Bar, so I won't stop you from coming along."

"And we can try to talk to the waiter?" Mike prompted as he struggled to his feet.

"We're both off duty," Ferguson protested.

"Yeah, I know, but it will only take a minute. One of Keller's guys may have already talked to him, in which case we can leave him alone. But, if nobody has questioned him yet, then we're leaving a big hole in the investigation."

Ferguson didn't respond, but he grabbed his left wheel and turned his chair so Millie could help push him forward toward the exit door.

When they cleared the last row of seats, Mike insisted on pushing the wheelchair. He filled in his old colleague on his most recent case – the one that caused him to be in need of a vacation. While they talked in cop-speak, Millie and Michelle lagged behind again.

"What are Mike's plans for retirement?" Millie asked.

"I'm not sure. He's never talked about it. I suppose he's getting close to the point that he could do it, but I'm not sure what he would do with himself. I think he's in denial that he's turning fifty."

"Oh my, I remember when my Edwin turned fifty. He lost ten

pounds and started working out for the first time in his life."

Michelle dodged a group of teens, all of whom were holding ice cream cones. "Well, Mike has already been working out because of his physical therapy after his shoulder surgery. But I'm sure he'll find something else to focus on in order to avoid thinking about getting older. Say, I'm planning a small birthday celebration for Mike. Why don't you and Edwin join us? I'm sure Mike wouldn't mind. We're having a late dinner on Monday, after we see the *Chicago* performance at seven o'clock."

"I'm sure that would be wonderful. I'll let Edwin know."

Michelle knew Mike would not want a big fuss made over his birthday, but she was sure having his old mentor there would please him.

They arrived at the Clipper Bar and found a table in a corner. Within a minute, a tall waiter, wearing a gold nameplate identifying him as "Carlos," came over. He was Black, with a mostly bald head ringed by a halo of well-trimmed gray. He looked elegant in his white uniform. Mike didn't waste any time before asking if Carlos had been working the night before. He confirmed that the Clipper Bar was his normal assignment in the evenings.

"Was anybody else serving guests last night around midnight?"

Carlos hesitated, obviously wondering where the question was coming from. "No, sir. I am the only one serving the guests, aside from the bartender, who handles the guests at the bar. Did I serve you yesterday?"

"No," Mike quickly responded, "but I need to know if you recall serving a large man and his wife, who was wearing a red dress, a little before midnight. He might have ordered a Rusty Nail."

Carlos became obviously nervous and said he needed to take care of some other customers, but that he would come back to answer the question in a few minutes.

Mike turned to Ferguson. "Is that behavior normal?"

"Well, he does have responsibilities as a server. He's not supposed to spend a lot of time talking to the guests. He might also be uncomfortable talking to an unknown guest like you about that kind of thing, and he probably doesn't know who I am. I'll introduce myself when he comes back and see if that helps."

Before Carlos returned, Mike spotted one of the ship's security officers approaching their group. The slender woman, wearing a well-fitted uniform that was only subtly different from the standard crew uniforms, walked up to Ferguson. "I'm sorry to bother you, Mr. Ferguson, sir, but Chief Keller asked me to let you know that he's on his way here and that you should not speak to anyone on the staff until he arrives."

Ferguson looked up at her, assessing the situation, then replied, "I understand, Officer Miranda." Ferguson shrugged at Mike. Miranda stood against the wall, watching the group from an appropriate distance. Mike assumed she was there to make sure Ferguson didn't violate Keller's directive.

They didn't have to wait long before Karl Keller arrived, wearing casual clothes, as if he were off duty. He strode purposefully up to the little group of chairs and stopped, glaring down at Ferguson and Mike with his arms folded across his chest. "Is it true that you tried to interview Carlos?"

"Yes, that's right," Ferguson replied evenly.

"Without consulting me first?" Keller was struggling to control his temper and his tone of voice.

"Actually, I was expecting him to tell me he had already been interviewed by one of your officers, Karl. I was going to ask him that question and leave it at that, so no, I didn't try to reach out to you first. It was a spur-of-the-moment decision." Ferguson stared up at Keller expectantly. "So, has your team interviewed Carlos yet?"

"That's not the point," Keller replied, quickly losing his composure. "You are not in charge here. This is *my* ship and my team is on this. If you have a suggestion, you come to me."

Mike didn't want to be responsible for causing a rift between his old friend and his current colleague, so he broke in. "Listen, Mr. Keller, this is my fault. I had a thought that somebody should talk to the waiter before he forgot about what happened last night. I mentioned it to Ferguson here, and I pushed him to come over and find out whether the interview had happened yet. If you want to be pissed off at somebody, be pissed at me."

Keller turned to Mike and continued fuming. "I am going to get to you, Detective."

As Keller turned back to Ferguson, Mike stood up and stepped toward the security chief. "Get to me now, OK? But first, tell us that your guys already spoke to Carlos."

"That's not the point here," Keller snapped.

"Yes, it actually is," Mike shot right back, without giving Keller a chance to say anything else. "Have you spoken to him or not?"

Keller stared at Mike, then glanced around the bar, where most of the guests had stopped their conversations and were staring at the confrontation. Since Keller was not in uniform, they had no reason to think this was official business of any kind, but it was a show they didn't want to miss.

Keller lowered his hand, which was raised and pointing at Mike. He gave a weak smile and sank down into the empty chair next to Millie, then lowered his voice. "No, we haven't interviewed Carlos yet."

"Why not?" Mike said in an equally soft voice, as the rest of the patrons in the bar returned to their own drinks and conversation. "He's a key witness. If he remembers what happened to Max's key card, or whether there was anyone else there who might have taken it, that would be pretty damned important, don't you think?"

"Detective Stoneman, you are treating this as a homicide investigation, which it is not. We will talk to Carlos when it's appropriate."

"It's appropriate to do it right now. He's right over there. Let's get him over here and talk to him. It could be vitally important."

Ferguson jumped back into the fray. "Keller, the man's right. If you haven't spoken to him yet, then let's just do it and stop worrying about whose turf is whose and whose dick is bigger."

Millie's face reddened at the language.

Keller scowled at Ferguson, then rose and took a few strides away to speak quietly with Officer Miranda. She quickly walked in the direction of the bar. Keller turned back to Mike and Ferguson. "Officer Miranda is going to make arrangements for another waiter to come help out here so we can pull Carlos away to talk with him. I'll take care of it myself. We would have done it tomorrow when he was off-duty, it's not like this was something I hadn't already thought about. I've got it under control. Now, you should be enjoying your cruise and leaving the security to me." Keller turned as if to leave, but then spun back around and pointed a finger at Ferguson. "And I'm going to be placing a call to corporate, Mr. Ferguson, to make sure that your superiors are aware of your actions." He turned again and stalked away.

"Is that a real threat?" Mike asked.

"I doubt it," Ferguson said, but he frowned.

"I hope I haven't gotten you into any trouble."

"Me either," Michelle spoke up, putting out a hand to touch Ferguson's jacket sleeve. "We can take any responsibility."

"Don't worry about it," Ferguson said. His facial expression belied his nonchalance.

Mike, Jason, Michelle, and Rachel left the ship that evening and walked to an overlook called Sunset Point, next to an elaborate miniature golf course. It was the western-most point on the island and had an unobstructed view as the sun sank spectacularly into the Atlantic. They browsed the artisan's exhibits in the park under the stars, then strolled to the iconic Frog & Onion pub. They sang along with the local guitar player, who was so impressed by Rachel's enthusiastic participation that he invited her to come up and sing a duet. She never hesitated. Encouraged by Ferguson's efforts to get him to drink the aged rum on the ship, Mike tried the pub's own special "Frog Grog," a rum so black that it resembled molasses. It was smooth and sweet.

When the guitar player took a break, Rachel pulled out her phone and showed off the photos she and Michelle had taken during the digital scavenger hunt. She had pictures of herself and Michelle with a white-uniformed crew member, with Donna and Darci, the two bedazzled showgirls from the entertainment troupe, and with a hunky lifeguard by the main pool, among other shots.

"How did you find the showgirls?" Jason asked.

"It was actually pretty easy. They had them stationed outside the main theater, just waiting for scavenger hunters. They weren't the stars of the show, of course. The girls in the chorus, so to speak, are the ones who have to do the meet and greet with the guests. They were really nice, though. We actually met them during our tour on Wednesday, do you remember?"

Rachel scrolled to the photo with the actresses. "The one on the left is Donna Sher. She's from Georgia. She told me that she's in line to play Velma Kelly in the *Chicago* production soon. The other one is Darci van der Meer. She's just starting out and this is her first big gig, and she's the understudy for Roxie Hart." Rachel lamented how it could have been her standing in that gorgeous costume, if she had pursued her dancing and acting career.

When the music stopped, shortly before midnight, they meandered back to the *Colossus of the Ocean*. The ship was illuminated by lights on the dock, as if it were a jewel in a display case.

When they said good night as the elevator stopped on Deck 9, Mike and Michelle both noticed how Jason and Rachel locked into a passionate kiss before the doors closed. Michelle took Mike's arm as they walked toward their cabin. "They seem very happy together, don't you think?"

Mike squeezed his arm around her hand. "Yeah. Young and in love is a wonderful thing."

"Just like us," Michelle said, looking up into Mike's blue-gray eyes.

"We're not so young. At least, I'm not. You're still a baby, of course."

Michelle leaned her head against Mike's shoulder. "I tell you what. When we get to our cabin, I'll give you an examination to see how young you still are. I know some special tests we can run."

Mike slipped his right arm around Michelle's waist and pulled her close. "Doctor, I like the way you think."

Chapter 22 – A Chill in the Air

Saturday, May 11

THE SUN WAS ABSENT the following morning when Mike walked out onto the balcony. While the sky had been azure and the temperatures warm since their arrival, this day was overcast, with a hint of drizzle. It was also much cooler, and the wind was whipping the waves in the harbor into whitecaps.

"I'm not sure the snorkeling trip today is going to be a good idea," Mike observed.

Sure enough, when he opened their cabin door on their way out to breakfast, there was a small envelope tucked into the Epic Cruise Lines emblem on the outside of their door, advising them that their excursion had been canceled due to bad weather. Michelle immediately asked Mike to hand over the ship's daily activities newsletter. Even if shore excursions were not available, there were dozens of things to do without disembarking.

Over breakfast, Rachel and Michelle debated the virtues of various activity options onboard against indoor options out on the island, including the Crystal Caves on the far east end and the Maritime Museum in the Dockyard area.

"There's a salsa dancing class this afternoon," she said, perusing the activity sheet. "It says it's with members of the theater company. Maybe one of your new friends will be there."

"Oooh," Rachel said, grabbing Jason's arm, "you'll come take the dance class with me, won't you, Jay?"

Mike raised an eyebrow. "Jay?"

"Rachel likes to call me that. Don't get any ideas," Jason said seriously.

"I'm an idea guy. It's what I do," Mike replied playfully.

Jason scowled, then turned to Rachel. "If Mike and I are not tied up, I'll be happy to come along and watch you dance."

"What do you mean watch? And what do you mean tied up?"

Jason looked at Mike. "Are we working this case today, or not?"

Mike reached for his orange juice before responding. "I want to touch base with Ferguson and find out what he learned last night from Keller about the waiter. I also want to find out if they interviewed the people in the adjoining cabins. Depending on what we get from that, we'll have to decide whether there are any leads that need to be chased that we don't trust Keller and his team to handle."

Michelle nodded. It had been her insistence on seeing the dead body, and her belief that the death was a homicide, that got Mike involved, so she could hardly object now. "Well, since we have no snorkeling trip today, I guess this is as good a time as any. Maybe you'll wrap it up before dinner and we can relax for the rest of the trip."

Michelle reached into her purse, then exclaimed, "Oh, rats!"

"What?"

"I left my room key in my other purse – the one I had last night. Mike, can I borrow yours?"

Rachel said, "Don't worry. You can get a new key from the customer service desk on Deck 5. I'll walk down there with you while the boys do their thing."

Mike sent Ferguson a text and arranged to meet at 11:00 in the Shangri-La Lounge. April the bartender was not yet on duty, so they had the space to themselves. Ferguson put on his poker face when he saw Mike and Jason enter.

Mike took a seat opposite Ferguson next to the six-foot windows that overlooked the back of the ship, toward the open ocean. Jason grabbed a stool at the empty bar and let Mike do the talking. "What's the latest scoop on our investigation?"

Ferguson sighed. Mike, for the first time, saw the age on his old mentor, weighing him down. "Stoneman, you and your partner need to stand down."

"What do you mean?"

The older man's face hardened. "This is a business. I work for the company, and the company is in the business of keeping guests happy and fostering a reputation for safe, comfortable ships. We don't need reports about a murder investigation, and we don't need our guests feeling interrogated instead of pampered. Whatever happened, happened at sea. You have no jurisdiction and you're not authorized to conduct any investigations on this vessel."

"That's quite a change of attitude since yesterday."

Ferguson wheeled his chair closer to Mike. "I let you get me all caught up in pretending I'm a detective again. I guess I miss it. But the truth is that I'm not a cop anymore, and on this ship, neither are you. The ship's security staff has it under control. So go back to being a guest and enjoy yourself. Forget about Shirley Bloom. If you cause an unnecessary panic or disrupt the ship's operations, the captain has the authority to eject you both here in Bermuda and send you home in an airplane."

Mike listened intently but quietly while Ferguson spoke. He thought he could read between the lines. "Is that the official corporate directive?"

"It is."

"That weasel, Keller, got the corporate brass to come down on you, didn't he?" Ferguson stared out the window and said nothing. Mike continued, figuring that he was going to have to take some guesses. "The suits decided that the truth would be bad for business, and now it's your job to rein me in and keep me from making waves, is that how it is?"

Ferguson remained silent.

"OK, I get it. You need to have plausible deniability. You can't tell me anything, and you can't help me. You have to be able to say you told me to stand down and threatened to make me walk the plank if I don't comply. You've told me. Message delivered. I'm guessing that they threatened your job if you contribute to anything that hurts the bottom line. Keller probably figures he'll move up in the organization if you're out, so he's going to do anything he can to make you look bad."

Ferguson inclined his head, but said nothing.

"That sucks, but I get it. Whatever happens from here is totally on me. If I do anything to continue an investigation, I'm doing it against your instructions and potentially illegally. I wouldn't be surprised if Keller could toss me in the brig if he finds me harassing a guest, eh?"

"He absolutely has that authority, and he's the kind of man who would do it," Ferguson replied.

"You've delivered that message also. You're a real hard-ass, Ferguson. But before I go off and put on my swim trunks, I need to confirm something. I know you can't help me, so do me a favor and cough or something if I get anything wrong." Ferguson stared out the window. "I'm assuming that if I try to talk to Carlos, he's going to stonewall me, because he's been warned that if he talks to me he'll be fired." Ferguson sat passively. "Yeah, that's what I'd do if I were an asshole."

Ferguson cracked a brief smile, but remained silent.

"Thanks. In the spirit of deniability, I will tell you that I fully understand and I intend to drop the whole thing. Right, Jason?"

"Sure," Jason jumped down from his stool and walked toward his partner. "Nothing would make Rachel happier."

Mike stood up. "I plan to use my unlimited drink package to its fullest, and enjoy this wonderful ship without giving another thought to whether Max Bloom murdered his wife. You can tell your bosses, and your underling, Keller, I said exactly that."

"I will."

Mike and Jason walked out of the lounge, without a backward glance.

Chapter 23 – Gentle Persuasion

MIKE AND JASON AGREED that they needed to talk to Max. The problem was finding him and isolating him. Mike knew that the cruise line kept close track of which passengers were aboard and which had disembarked, but they had no way to access the system. Jason suggested that, since the weather was bad and he had no wife to pull him into a sightseeing trip, they should work on the assumption that Max was somewhere on the ship.

"We should split up and try to find him."

The group concluded that it was as good an activity as any on a gloomy day. They set up a group text message thread and set out to search places on the ship where they might spot Max. The vessel was huge, of course, and there was no guarantee of success, but they all agreed it was worth the effort. Rachel said it was like the scavenger hunt, but with only one objective.

The plan was to meet back in the Spinnaker Buffet at 1:00 p.m. if they all struck out. Michelle drew the short straw and was assigned to watch the gangway, in case Max exited the ship or came back on board. Since so many passengers would pass through the security area, it was an obvious observation point, but it was a dull assignment. She stopped by the ship's library to get some reading material. A novel titled *Honeymoon Cruise Murder*, by Dawn Brookes, caught her eye. It seemed like the appropriate read. Book in hand, she headed down to the second deck.

Jason and Rachel started on the Promenade level and worked their way up. Mike started on the pool deck and worked down. It would have been easier if they knew what cabin Max had been reassigned to, but Ferguson had not clued them in, and the ship's customer service staff was not going to give up the information. After ninety minutes of futility, the group had covered nearly every public area of the ship except for the gym, which they all agreed was the one place Max definitely would not be.

At 1:00 p.m., Mike, Jason, and Rachel met for lunch to compare notes. Michelle was missing. A few minutes later, they all got a text message. Michelle had spotted Max coming back onto the ship and had followed him to his new stateroom on Deck 12. She was staking out the hallway, and asked Mike to bring her a bowl of yogurt and fruit.

When the group re-formed in a lounge area next to the elevators on Deck 12 with their lunches, Michelle assured them that Max had not left his room. The cabin was tucked into the extreme front of the ship, and there was only the one hallway leading to the elevators and stairs. Unless Max had left through the crew-only door at the end of the hallway, he was still in his room.

"What's the plan?" Jason asked.

"We want to isolate him somewhere," Mike said. "Any ideas?"

Michelle held up her new book. "What about the library? It's one floor down from here on this side of the ship. When I was there before, it was pretty empty. There's a little reading room in the back with some game tables, but I doubt it will be very busy."

"Good idea. He doesn't know that we've been involved here. I was there when he first found out his wife was dead, but that's only because I was in the hallway at the time. Since then, he's only been interrogated by Keller's guys. Let's hope he still views us as friendly co-passengers and not cops."

They waited in padded chairs in the elevator lobby area, and ate the food they brought down from the buffet. When their plates were stacked up on the little glass table between them, Max Bloom finally lumbered around the corner on his way to the elevator.

"Mister Bloom!" Mike called out, walking toward him with an outstretched hand. Jason stood up and followed Mike, who grabbed Max's hand with a robust shake. "We're all so sorry about your wife. How are you holding up?"

"Um, thank you," Max stammered, "I'm doing fine."

"That's good. That's good. Listen, there's something I need to talk to you about, do you mind coming down one flight with me? It's a little confidential and I know somewhere private we can go."

Max was confused and flustered. He looked around at the space, which was empty except for Mike and his friends. "Um, sure, I guess."

"Great!" Mike grabbed him by the arm and led him to the stairs. The rest of the group followed closely behind. Upon reaching the floor below, Michelle showed them the way to the library. They walked through a small room lined with shelves of books and entered the little game room in the back. There were three square tables with chess boards inlaid into the surfaces. Racks of board games lined the far wall. The room was deserted, and although it had no door, it felt private and quiet.

"Mister Bloom, I have to tell you that I've spoken to the ship's security chief, and there are some serious suspicions that you might have had something to do with your wife's death. Have they told you about all the evidence that points toward you?"

Max reached for a chair and sat down heavily. "They spoke to me, but they didn't tell me anything."

"I'm not surprised. Look, you know I'm a cop. I feel like I should help you out and make sure nobody violates your rights."

"Thanks, Detective Stoneman. I appreciate that." Max seemed to relax a bit and sat back in his chair.

"No problem. So let me tell you what you're facing here. They have a record of your key card being used to open your cabin door shortly after midnight. Did they tell you that?"

"Not exactly," Max said nervously. "They asked me if I went to my room between midnight and twelve-fifteen. I told them I didn't, but they didn't seem to believe me. Then they wanted to know where my key card was. I told them that when I got to the new cabin they arranged for me, I couldn't find it. I'm not sure if I left it in my old cabin, or what. I told the security guy that maybe somebody stole my card."

"Sure," Mike soothed, trying to win the man's trust. "So, I'm sure you told them where you went after you left the Clipper Bar that night, right?"

"Sure I did. I went for a walk on the deck, and I got to the back of the ship and I sat down in a lounge chair. I was a little tipsy, and I fell asleep. When I woke up, I went back to my room.

That's when I bumped into you in the hallway."

"I remember," Mike said, as if he were Max's biggest supporter. "I can vouch for that." He paused to let Max feel better before changing the subject. "When I was talking to that Keller guy, he mentioned that they were looking for something. It's the big emerald ring your wife was wearing on her right hand. She showed it to us at dinner. The security guy says it's missing. Did he ask you about that?"

"He did, but I told him I have no idea."

"The thing is," Mike said, "he thinks you might have grabbed the ring. I told him that was crazy, because as the surviving spouse, the ring would belong to you anyway. So why would you steal it, right?"

Max leaned forward. "It's actually even more absurd than that. You see, the ring was mine to begin with. I gave it to her on our first anniversary. It belonged to my mother . . . I'm actually really upset that it's missing. I want it back."

"That makes sense," Mike said agreeably. "You have any idea where it might be?"

"None. I guess it's possible that Shirley threw it into the ocean, just so I wouldn't get it back. She never liked my mother. Maybe that's what happened. She was leaning out to throw my ring into the sea like the Heart of the Ocean from *Titanic*, then she lost her balance and fell."

"Seems unlikely," Mike said.

"Yeah, well, maybe. But I tell you what, if I were them, I'd be talking to that weird maid we've got."

"You mean Elisabeth?"

"Yeah. That's it. She's peculiar. We kept finding things moved around in our room. It had to be her, right? Why would she move my cufflinks or my comb? We were worried that she was going to steal something."

"I know what you mean," Mike agreed. "Did you have really strange towel animals in your room, too?"

"Yeah!" Max said excitedly, as if they were sharing an inside joke. "They were the worst."

Rachel couldn't help herself. She had to say something. "I'm sure they weren't as bad as all that."

"Oh, they absolutely were," Michelle replied. Then widened her eyes, as if prompting Mike to continue the interview.

"Well, I agree that somebody should be talking to Elisabeth. It's a real shame you don't have a better alibi. It would help if you had some explanation for what happened to your key card. That's a bit of a loose end for you. Can you think of anyone else who was with you in the Clipper Bar who could have taken it?"

Max hesitated. Mike was certain he had been asked the same question by Keller, or one of his officers. Max knew this was an important issue for his alibi. Certainly, if the truthful answer was no, he would instantly say so. The fact that he was hesitating suggested that he was thinking not about the answer, but about whether to tell Mike the truth. Mike tried to help the process along. "Max, if there was anybody else there, it could be the key to you getting off this ship without being in handcuffs. You need to tell me, so I can help you."

"There was a waiter there," Max offered.

"Yes, we know, but he was working in the Clipper Bar the whole time until two o'clock. There were dozens of witnesses who saw him there continuously and records of him swiping his crew card to document drinks that were being purchased. So, we can be pretty certain he wasn't using your key card to open your stateroom at twelve-eleven. Was there anyone else?" Mike didn't really know about Carlos' card swipes, or whether there were such witnesses, but it seemed likely.

"I – I can't remember," Max finally said. "Listen, Detective, I appreciate you trying to help, but I really need to be going. I'm not worried about Mr. Keller and his boys coming after me. I had nothing to do with my wife's tragic accident."

"So, you think it was an accident, and not suicide?"

Max, who had managed to assume a standing posture, turned toward Mike. "If I had to guess, I'd say so. I've been thinking of it that way unless proven otherwise."

"Fair enough," Mike responded. "By the way, have you been in touch with your wife's kids to let them know what happened?"

Max had taken two steps toward the exit, but stopped cold. "No. I don't have any internet access here."

"Actually, Max, your cell phone will work in Bermuda. It will cost you ten bucks or so, but you could make a call."

Max paused again for a few seconds. "Thanks, Detective, I'll make sure I do that." He then continued his trek to the exit and disappeared around the corner, leaving the rest of the group in the game room in silence.

Jason spoke first. "There *was* someone else there. He's holding back."

"You saw that, too?" Mike said, not really as a question.

"Saw what?" Rachel asked, sincerely confused. Jason explained what he and Mike both picked up on. "Ohhhh," she let out slowly. "What does it mean?"

Mike looked at Jason, then back at Rachel. "I don't know yet, but it means that we have more work to do."

"We do," Jason agreed. "And it means that Max is still very much the most likely suspect."

Chapter 24 – Heart to Heart

DESPITE THE GLOOMY WEATHER, Michelle suggested that they spend some more time out on the island, just because they could. The group of four walked through the Maritime Museum, which included exhibits depicting the origins of the island country and the many, many ships that were wrecked on the surrounding coral reefs. They marveled at the huge mural depicting island life in a colorful, happy display. After standing on the parapet of the fortification and looking out over the angry waves of the Atlantic, they adjourned back to the ship.

As they cleared through the security and identity check, they speculated about whether Max Bloom would sail north with them the next afternoon. Mike bet Jason a Zacapa 23 on Max bolting; Jason thought he was not creative enough, even if he was guilty. Half an hour later, while the women attended a sushi-making class that the men chose to skip, Mike and Jason sat at the bar in Shangri-La watching April pour them their fine aged rum. They decided that, since they were both on the unlimited drink plan, there was no point waiting for Sunday to settle up.

The international feed of ESPN was running on the television above the bar. Jason glanced up when he saw a headline and a photo: "New York Quarterback Jimmy Rydell Arrested."

"Hey, Mike, look. There's your favorite quarterback." He pointed at the screen.

Mike dropped his head. "Oh, Lord, what did the idiot do this time?"

"I don't know. We have no volume. I'm sure it's not any worse than when he shot himself in the leg in that Manhattan nightclub. You guys picked a real winner there." Jason jabbed Mike in the arm good-naturedly.

"Jimmy Freaking Rydell," Mike muttered. "Biggest mistake the team ever made. Damn, I thought we could get away from him out here in the middle of the Atlantic."

As they sipped and looked out at the still-gloomy water, Jason uncharacteristically initiated the conversation. "What do you think of Rachel?" he asked with no lead-in.

"What do you mean?" Mike said, being immediately careful with such a question.

"I mean, do you like her?"

"Sure. She's fun, she's upbeat, she seems pretty smart, and she's beautiful. What's not to like?"

"I'm serious, Mike. I really like her, but I'm not sure I know her that well. I'm interested in your assessment. Am I making a big mistake getting so into her? I mean, I know you're no expert on relationships, but I'd like to know what you think."

Mike stared at his partner as he slowly took a sip of the smooth, black rum. "Is this going to be a serious talk? Maybe we should get some good scotch."

Jason reached out and pushed against Mike's shoulder softly, knocking him slightly off balance. "We have this," he said, holding up his Zacapa. "I don't think I need to get drunk to have this conversation. I see you and Michelle, and you have a pretty good thing going. But you're both, well, older. It's not like you need to get married so you can start a family, so you're both cool with just being together, which is nice. But . . ."

"But what?"

"Well, Mike, I just – I don't want to wait until I'm fifty."

"I'm not fifty," Mike snapped back.

"I thought you were."

"Not until Monday."

"*This* Monday?" Jason asked. "I didn't know you were having a birthday on the cruise."

"Well, it was a last-minute thing, as you may recall. Besides, I don't like to make a big deal about birthdays. I'm old enough. I don't need to get any older."

"Well, we should at least mark the occasion. I mean, a half-century. Man!" Jason gave a half-bow toward his elder.

"I'd prefer if you forgot about it. I'm not feeling celebratory, if truth be told. I don't feel nearly old enough to be fifty. I've still got plenty of good years in me. Plus, Michelle makes me feel, well, younger. So, what was it that you didn't want to wait for?"

Jason held up his glass, gazing through the beveled edge at Mike. "To be in love. To find a person I want to spend my life with. I mean, I know it's rough on cops and their wives and families. Look at you. I know you never got married and had kids because you were worried that it would be too hard to be a cop and a husband and a father. You never wanted to have anybody at home waiting for you while you stayed out all night on a stakeout. You got to be the dour cop and the *culo de piedra*. It works for you. It's your personality. I'm just not sure it's what I want. I don't want to be single and looking for love at fifty."

"Where's all this coming from?" Mike asked. Jason had never before in their time as partners expressed any of these feelings.

"It's a lot of things. It's partly this cruise, I think. There are a ton of kids, and Rachel is so great with them. She's so maternal, even with me sometimes. I know she totally wants to be a mother. And watching the Max and Shirley Bloom train wreck makes me see how bad it can be when it's not the right two people together. But how do you know who's the right person? How do you know when you've met that one perfect soul?"

"You're asking the wrong guy, Jason. I've never been able to figure it out. Even with Michelle, we've known each other for years. It was only last summer that I got up the balls to ask her out. That makes me the world's most oblivious man. She was right there the whole time, and I never saw it – or never did anything about it."

"Yeah, I know. But you've seen a lot. You've seen a lot of other detectives who have families, right? Do you think it's a terrible idea or can it work?"

Mike thought about it. "There are some guys who can do it. Take Berkowitz. He's a great family man, and he seems to love it and doesn't let his job get in the way. He's found a good balance, and he's still a good cop."

"Yeah, but look at Mason. He's a mess. It's like he's you twenty years younger."

"Gee, thanks," Mike said glumly, but then cracked a little smile.

"And then there's . . . Darren Curran," Jason said, hesitating. "I mean, look what happened to him because he got injured and felt like he needed to take care of his family. I know he made some bad choices, but, you know, he probably would have made different ones if he had been single."

"You're probably right. But I can also tell you that the man would not have traded Marie and those kids for the world. There's more than one path to follow. You need to figure out what you want. What I think doesn't mean much. I can only tell you that I have no regrets."

"That's just it, Mike. I'm starting to think that I'm going to have regrets in twenty years. I'm not knocking your career. You have had an outstanding run as a detective. You're at the top of the heap, professionally. I'd love to get to where you are in the department, but I'm not sure I'm willing to sacrifice everything to get there."

"It wasn't a sacrifice for me. But if you think it will be for you, then you've already answered your own question. Rachel is a special woman. She's as vivacious as anyone I know, except maybe Helene DiVito Rosen." Mike smiled.

Jason let out a guffaw that almost made him spill his drink. "Now *there's* a model I would not take out for a test drive."

"Don't judge, kid, it takes all kinds to make up the universe."

"I hear you. But there are some lines I won't ever cross."

"Well, that's fine. I'm guessing you probably wouldn't be her type anyway." Both men laughed at the thought. "But let's get back to Rachel. She's wonderful. You two are great together. If you think she's *the one* for you, then you should do something about it. If that means you're going to have to make some tough choices about your future career and your future life, that comes with the territory. I'll tell you this, Jason," Mike leaned toward the bigger man for privacy, despite the fact that April was the only other person in the room.

"I made some choices like that a long time ago. I made peace with them and I always told myself I would never regret making them. You have to play the cards you're dealt and make the decisions you make and never have regrets. Regrets can eat you up. I never thought that I was any good at love and women, so I stopped trying. I convinced myself I was good with that, and I was – until I started seeing Michelle. Now, I have some second thoughts and wish I'd made that move a lot sooner. But I'm out of time. You're right – I'm never going to be a father. Is that what you want? To have kids?"

"I don't know," Jason said, leaning back away from Mike. "I think so. Sometimes I'm sure of it. Sometimes it scares the shit out of me. I wonder if I could handle being a cop and worrying about what might happen to me. I worry about being too careful. I worry about how hard it would be on a wife and kid if I got killed, which we both know could happen."

Mike took a sip of his rum. "I've been going through that with Michelle since we started dating last summer. I was mortified that she got put in danger because of my – our – investigation. I never want that to happen again, but she says she's a big girl and she knows the risks. She thinks it's worth it. I still dread that it could happen again. And here we are, with a killer on the ship. It eats at me. But, my only alternative is to stop seeing her. So, decisions are a bitch."

"So, you're not going to help me, are you?"

"Nope. I know better. You need to make up your own mind. If you listen to me and the decision turns out bad, it'll be my fault. I'm not taking on that kind of pressure. But I will give you one piece of advice."

"What?"

Mike drained his glass and held it up toward April, motioning for a refill. Then he turned back to Jason. "Decide what your heart wants. Then give it some time. If you still want the same thing after some time has passed, make your decision then. A lot can change, and big decisions should be made slowly."

"Spoken like a true procrastinator," Jason said with a smile.

"The best," Mike said, laughing. "But it's still good advice."

"OK. I'll take it. There's no rush."

"As long as she agrees with that thought process."

"I guess that's something I need to figure out."

"Well, if she sings that Beyoncé song to you again, that'll be a clue." They both laughed. April laughed with them, although it was not clear that the bartender knew what he was laughing at.

Chapter 25 – The Hounds and the Fox

Sunday, May 12

O N SUNDAY MORNING, Rachel suggested that they have brunch in the main dining room, rather than eating in the Spinnaker Buffet. Since they had no particular plans for the morning, everyone agreed. Mike had worked up an appetite in the gym, where he had run through all the strengthening exercises for his shoulder and managed half an hour on the elliptical machine. He was feeling virtuous about his workout and ordered the eggs benedict, asking the waiter to put the Hollandaise sauce on the side.

As they ate and chatted, watching the gentle waves out on Bermuda's Great Sound, Jason suddenly sat up straighter and motioned to his right. Mike saw Max Bloom ambling down the aisle between tables, heading for the exit. "The guy is easy to spot in a crowd," Jason observed.

"Yeah," Mike said, "it would be a piece of cake to tail him and see if he does anything suspicious."

Michelle asked, "Is that what you'd do if we were in New York instead of on a ship in Bermuda?"

"I would," Mike said, looking at Jason for affirmation. Jason nodded his agreement.

"Fine. Rachel and I were going to check out the Dolphin Quest, over by the Frog & Onion. I've always wanted to swim with dolphins. How about we all meet up at two o'clock at the pub for a last drink on the island before we sail at four? Unless you want to come with us."

Rachel looked at Jason with eyes that were both pleading and warning. "We'll meet you at two, for sure," Jason said, standing up and tossing his napkin on the table. He and Mike rushed off, leaving the women behind. They figured that Max would never take the stairs, and they were not surprised to find him waiting for a car in the elevator lobby. Mike motioned to Jason to take the stairs, while Mike waited for Max to get into the next elevator going up. Then he dashed to the waiting area to watch where the car stopped. From a surveillance perspective, the glass-enclosed elevators made it simple to track someone riding up or down.

Mike hopped into the next car on the same side of the ship. The one in which Max was riding had stopped on Deck 6. He texted Jason to check whether Max had gotten off on 6, and rode up until his car stopped on 8. When the adjoining car arrived next to his, Mike could see through the glass wall that Max was not inside the compartment. He exited, pulling out his cell phone and immediately seeing the reply from Jason, who was following Max across Deck 6, heading aft. Mike chuckled at Jason's use of the nautical terminology, as he walked along Deck 8 toward the back of the ship. He could tell what direction he was walking by the little fish on the carpet; they were swimming in the opposite direction, as if Mike were fighting his way upstream.

Mike and Jason spent the next half hour leap-frogging their surveillance of Max Bloom, taking turns in case he noticed one of them. But Max was not particularly vigilant. After stopping at a café kiosk for a latte, he spent a short time in a lounge chair on the pool deck, watching the ladies parade by in their bikinis. While Mike was watching from a position next to the railing that overlooked the pool on the next deck up, he saw a woman walk by wearing black yoga pants and a gray t-shirt that was cut off to reveal her flat stomach. She had short, dark hair held back with a pink sweatband. The dark stains on her t-shirt suggested that she was coming from a workout in the gym, which was nearby on the same deck. Mike could not see her face.

The woman stopped and spoke to Max, who sat up in his chair. It seemed that they were having a serious conversation. After a minute, the woman leaned down and gave Max a lingering kiss on the mouth. He wished that he and Jason had voice communication. He quickly grabbed his phone and tapped a text to Jason to follow the woman in the black yoga pants.

As soon as the woman walked away, Max checked his wristwatch, then quickly got up and walked toward the nearest bank of elevators. Jason was positioned near the door leading in toward the elevators, and he would not miss Max – unless he was already following the girl in the sweaty gray t-shirt. Mike rushed down a winding set of narrow stairs to the pool deck, then walked as quickly as the crowded space would allow to the elevator lobby. By then it was empty except for a couple with a baby in a stroller.

Mike's phone buzzed; Jason said he had Max on Deck 4. He

had missed the girl. Mike took the stairs down, where he found Jason standing between the stairs and the elevators.

Jason gestured toward the big double doors leading into the Epic Theater. "He went inside."

"Any other exit out of there?" Mike asked, pretty much knowing the answer.

"The doors on the upper level on Five," Jason said. "And the performers' side exits behind the stage. Remember, we used one of them on our tour on Wednesday."

"Yeah, I recall," Mike said absently, thinking about several things at once. "You think he's in there with that blonde actress we saw him with at the beach? What did Rachel say her name was?"

"Vicki Nelson. Could be," Jason said. "You want to risk going inside? We'll see him if he's in there, but he'll also likely make us as tailing him."

Before they had time to make a decision, one of the theater doors opened. Jason immediately walked across the elevator lobby to separate from Mike, then watched through the empty glass elevator shaft as Max and Vicki Nelson exited, arm-in-arm. They were talking to each other and neither would have noticed Jason or Mike unless they were lying on the ground in front of them. She was definitely the same woman they had seen Max exit a cab with at Elbow Beach on Friday.

Max and Vicki walked to the stairs, then separated. Max went to the elevator lobby, while Vicki took the stairs down. Mike sent Jason a text that he was going to stay with Max. Jason waited until Max disappeared inside the elevator, then rushed to the threshold of the stairway and looked down, watching the woman. She descended past the third deck and down one more flight before exiting and turning left. Jason quickly dashed down, pausing before getting to the bottom. Then, he casually walked around the corner in the same direction as his target.

A few paces down the corridor he ran into a door marked "crew only." Jason remembered from their tour that the area beyond was the crew quarters. There were no other exits.

When the two partners reunited a few minutes later, Mike reported that Max had gone back to his room. Jason relayed his observations of Vicki.

"Yeah," Mike mused. "Blondie sang a song during the musical revue the other night."

"Right," Jason said. "You think she's one of Max's clients?"

Mike didn't hesitate in responding. "She may be a client, but she's pretty clearly more than just that. I can't say that he's doing anything to take suspicion off himself."

Jason nodded. "Like Ferguson said, he's no criminal genius."

Chapter 26 – Terrible Towels

OVER DINNER SUNDAY EVENING, as they were sailing away from Bermuda, Rachel brought up the lingering question of the emerald ring. Shirley Bloom had been wearing it at dinner on the first night. What they couldn't say for sure was whether she had been wearing it the next night – the night she died – when Michelle and Rachel bumped into her in the ladies' room. Michelle was sure that she always wore a ring based on the indentations and the tan line on her finger. But, of course, the examination of the body could not conclusively determine what ring she wore on that finger each day. She might have alternated different rings.

Rachel thought it unlikely that she would wear something else. "If I owned that rock, I'd never take it off."

"There just aren't that many people who could have taken it from her cabin," Michelle insisted. "Her killer and Max – assuming that Max is not her killer – are about the only possibilities."

"What about Elisabeth?" Mike added.

"Oh, now Mike, do you really think our cabin attendant would steal something from a passenger's room?" Michelle's skepticism surprised Mike.

"I've seen a lot of criminals do a lot of stupid things, so nothing would surprise me. We know that she likes to touch stuff and move stuff around. What's to say she's not doing that to hide the fact that she has stolen something?"

Michelle pursed her lips and said, in a scolding tone, "I admit she's odd, and her towel animals are objectively awful, but that doesn't make her a thief, and certainly doesn't make her a suspect."

"I'm sure her towel animals are not as bad as you say," Rachel chided.

"You saw the pictures!" Michelle responded, a little indignant that Rachel was still questioning the point.

"It's hard to judge by a cell phone picture. I think you two are blowing it up because it's funny to talk about."

"I tell you what," Mike said, jumping in to defuse the argument, "tonight you come back to our cabin and see for yourself."

"Fine," Rachel said with a smile. "I'll be happy to be the judge."

"And it's not only the crazy towel animals," Mike said, trying to get the conversation back on track. "She's odd in other ways. She's never around. She isn't as attentive as I would expect – especially based on your guy, Sergio. Her attitude is not like anyone else in the crew that we've met. Something is off about her. It's a wonder she can keep the job, since top-shelf customer service seems to be a requirement on this ship."

Everyone agreed that the service had been outstanding from

everyone, except for Elisabeth. But as for the ring, they were all stumped. It didn't make a lot of sense that Max would take it, especially since he was going to own it after Shirley's death. If she took it off voluntarily before she went over the balcony, it would have been in the cabin and Max would have had no motive to move it or take it. So, if Elisabeth was not the thief, then that left only the killer.

"We need a whiteboard," Jason said jokingly to Mike.

"You think a list of suspects and characteristics would help?"

Jason laughed. "It couldn't hurt."

As the far eastern edge of Bermuda faded into the distance and the floating city slowly turned northwest, Edwin Ferguson sat in his chair in Karl Keller's office. They were alone and the door was shut.

"He's accounted for?" Ferguson asked.

"Yes. He never left the ship today. All passengers are present."

"So, you were wrong again."

Keller glared across his desk. "It was only a possibility. If I were as guilty as he seems to be, I'd consider flying home."

"Now what?" Ferguson pressed.

"Nothing. We have our marching orders. You have yours, so don't forget."

"I forget nothing. I'm also not going to forget that you went running to the CEO about this."

"You were ready to cause a shitstorm just because Stoneman is an old friend of yours. You have no idea how sensitive publicity is to this company. You're not a cop anymore,

Ferguson; you're an executive. If you knew the first thing about how to do your job, you'd understand."

"Don't lecture me, you corporate prick. This isn't over, and the shit could still hit the fan and blow back on you more than me." Ferguson and Keller stared at each other without speaking for several tense seconds. Then, Ferguson changed the subject. "Did you locate Rosario?"

Keller frowned. "No. He didn't swipe off the ship once in Bermuda. He's probably hiding in somebody's cabin. His cabin-mate finally spilled his guts about how the creep has been sleeping with just about every straight girl in the cast. He's a hound dog. He probably found some rich cougar and decided to blow off his dancing gig in favor of being a boy toy. The actors seem to think they're on the Fuck Boat. He's already fired for being AWOL. I don't really give a damn."

"Or, he could be dead and stuffed in a crawl space, or dumped overboard," Ferguson said. "One known murder, and one missing crew member. It's quite a coincidence."

"There's no known murder!" Keller shouted. "I don't care what the lady coroner says. The Bloom woman probably jumped. You can't tell with these rich women. Hell, maybe she was on board to fuck Rosario, found him with another woman, and decided to end it. It doesn't matter. I'm not going to turn this cruise into the Orient Express by conducting a full-blown murder investigation."

"You wouldn't know how to run a proper homicide investigation," Ferguson spat out. "You're a bureaucrat. You were an analyst at the FBI, not a field agent. I may not know how to be a corporate executive, but you don't know shit about how to be a cop. You don't want to investigate because you're afraid you might trip over something and have to report a murder to the authorities in New York. You think it will make you look bad. Well, you keep sticking your head in the sand and we'll see what happens. I'm on record as being opposed to your decision."

"Fine!" Keller shouted. "Now, take your record, go watch a show, and let me run my ship."

Ferguson pursed his lips, spun his chair around toward the door, and then sat silently with his back to Keller. Eventually, Keller rose from his desk, walked to the door, and opened it so that Ferguson could wheel himself out. Neither man spoke.

That evening, after dinner, Michelle announced that she was getting a headache and wanted to go back to the cabin, take some ibuprofen, and have some quiet time. Mike offered to come along, but Michelle said that being alone for a little while would be best for her head. She wanted to finish *Honeymoon Cruise Murder* before the end of the trip, since she had to take it back to the ship's library. She suggested that they meet up at 8:30 in the Epic Theater for the comedy show. If she felt better, they could do some dancing. She suggested that Mike take advantage of the time and go play some poker in the casino. Mike was happy to take her up on the suggestion.

Jason and Rachel had already gone off by themselves for a romantic walk around the deck at sunset, so Mike set out for the poker table. He was pleased to see Quentin Richardson already there, talking a blue streak to the other players. The table was full, so Mike put his name on the waiting list and stood nearby, watching the game. He wanted to see if he could pick up on any of the players' tendencies. Lenny Dykstra wasn't there, but any one of the other players could be a potential adversary at the final poker tournament table on Monday, so doing some scouting seemed wise.

After ten minutes, Quentin excused himself and got up from the table, heading in the direction of the restroom. Mike followed. When they were both exiting back toward the casino, Mike reached out and tapped his arm. "Say, Mr. Richardson."

"Oh, hey there, Mister Mike!" the big man bellowed, grabbing Mike's hand and giving it a thorough shake, although Mike had not actually offered it. "Say, how the hell are you doin'? I saw how you took down that Dykstra guy the other day. I watched after you knocked me out. Very nicely done! I could learn a few things from you, that's for sure."

Mike interrupted the rambling. "Mister Richardson – Quentin, right?"

"It sure is!"

"Quentin, I remember you said something to me the other day, about overhearing what the couple in the next cabin were saying."

"Oh, boy, that's so true! They were havin' a row and a half that first day."

"That's sort of what I wanted to talk to you about. You see, I know that couple – the Blooms. Were you in your cabin on Thursday night at about midnight?"

"Oh, no – that was the first full day at sea, right? Heck, the missus and I went to the late show and then closed down the disco at two o'clock. Man, that was a fun night! So, no. But, you know what? Some guy from the crew asked me about that, too. Why do ya think that is?"

Mike ignored the question. "Then you're not aware of anything that happened in the next cabin – the Blooms' cabin – that night?"

"Nope. Should I?"

"No," Mike said quickly. "What did you hear on Wednesday?"

"Woo, baby! I tell you what – those two were havin' a smack-down." Quentin stopped and lowered his always-loud voice. "She was yellin' at him and he was yellin' at her. Somethin' about wanting a divorce and him sleepin' around. Woo-boy, they were at it."

"Do you remember anything specific about what they said?"

"Well, I remember that my wife and I were talkin' about it after, how he said that he'd be better off if he killed her. Then she said that he should try it, 'cause she'd kill him first, or somethin' like that. Now, I know they was just yellin' and such, so I don't think either of them really meant it. And they musta made up, 'cause we ain't heard a peep from either of 'em since then."

Mike motioned for Quentin to walk back toward the casino. "Thanks, Quentin. I was worried about them, but I'm glad things have been quiet since Wednesday. Now, you go and have some good luck at the table when you get back. Are you planning to try again to qualify for the final table in the tournament?"

"I will, I think," he responded with a chuckle, "as long as I don't lose all my money in the cash game tonight."

Mike returned the laugh, slapped him on the back, and veered off when they got to the casino entrance. He needed to share this information with Michelle – headache or no headache.

Chapter 27 – Tryst for Two

SUNDAY NIGHT WAS A RARE NIGHT OFF for the production company. There was no musical or stage show because the ship's comic was performing two shows. The actors had duties around the ship until nine o'clock, and then were free to take a break. Max and Vicki had made plans.

Max was waiting on a wide lounger in the Solarium. It was mostly empty, save for two old guys in the hot tub on the opposite side of the space. There were also four elderly ladies playing bridge at a table at the top of the winding stairway that led up to the bar area perched above, with a view out the twenty-foot-tall front windows. The bar closed at nine and was now deserted. Max heard the clip-clop of heels approaching across the polished wooden deck before he saw Vicki. He sat up, sucking in his gut as best he could.

Vicki was wearing a multi-colored, wrap-around, strapless dress with a slit up the front running dangerously close to her crotch. Her dancer's legs peeked out from the thin fabric as she walked. Her bare shoulders were tanned and smooth. Max salivated as he struggled up from his seat and gave her a kiss on the cheek, before she locked her hands around his elbow and led him toward the sliding doors at the back of the space, toward the pool. She smelled like baby powder.

"Where are we going?" he asked.

"I know a place," she coyly replied.

"We need to be discreet, my dear. I don't want to get you in trouble."

"I know, Million. Don't you worry. I know exactly what I'm doing."

"Am I going to like it?"

"I think so. But you have to get me onto a Broadway stage, like you promised me."

"I'm all over that, my dear," Max said smoothly. "You must finish your contract first, or it would be very bad for your professional reputation. But when you're done, I will greet you with open arms in New York."

"You'd better," she cooed, snuggling up to his ample side. They walked through the doors and across the deck to the entrance leading inside to the stairs and elevators. Max was looking down at Vicki's chest. Vicki was watching where she was walking in her high heels so as not to slip. As they passed through the door, neither of them looked to their left, into the shadows where a group of empty chairs ringed a plastic table. Neither saw the silhouette perched on the edge of the sloping windows that reflected the interior light and illuminated a pair of smoldering eyes.

◆◆◆

Half an hour later, a satisfied Max Bloom waited in the elevator lobby on Deck 14. He had not imagined that the inflatable landing pad used to catch guests as they fell during flying trapeze lessons would make such an interesting trysting venue. It had taken him five full minutes of struggling to exit the squishy, semi-inflated mass. But Vicki's flexibility and athletic prowess had made it worth all the sweating. She left first, so they would not be seen together by some curious crew member who might rat her out for rolling in the big pillow with a guest.

As he waited for the elevator, mentally reliving his adventure, he was surprised to feel a small, warm hand massaging the back of his neck. "Mmmmm. I thought you didn't want to be seen together."

"There's nobody here," came a sultry voice, which did not belong to Vicki.

Max startled and leapt forward two feet, spinning around to see a pair of sparkling eyes staring up at him. A mischievous smile tugged at her lips. The color drained from Max's face as all his happy thoughts vanished. "Hey – Sweetheart – I'm surprised to see you. I, um, thought it was a problem for us to be seen together."

"It is," she said, stepping forward and sliding her palms up Max's chest, then looping them around his neck, pressing her chest into him. "But I've missed you sooooo much, Maxie. I really need to talk to you – and do some other things." She ground her hips into Max's groin.

With Vicki already departed, Max decided that there was no risk of her catching him with another woman. Besides, he was unexpectedly surprised at how well he was reacting. He wrapped his arms around her slender waist. "Well, if you're willing to take the risk, I suppose I shouldn't get in your way.

Where should we go to – talk?" He leaned in for a kiss. She beat him to it by lunging upward and hungrily enveloping his lips with hers. She probed for his tongue and pressed herself further into his body, bringing one thigh between his legs and massaging his growing interest.

When Max needed to come up for air, the elevator door opened. Three teenagers in shorts and flip-flops thundered out, requiring Max to disengage and move to the side. His new companion grabbed his hand and led him toward the stairs, saying she wanted to avoid being seen through the glass windows in the elevator.

They ended up in the cramped space behind the elevated stage next to the main pool deck. The pool was closed and covered with a rope net, to keep adventurous or drunk passengers from swimming when there was no lifeguard. They were shielded by two massive speaker towers and rested on a pile of mats, staged there for the next morning's poolside yoga class.

She gave Max an expert blow job, leaving him on the edge of his orgasm before lifting her dress and jumping on his exposed erection. She pleaded for Max to put his hand in her mouth to keep her from screaming and attracting attention to their activity.

Max leaned back and enjoyed the ride, surprised that he climaxed so quickly, despite the recent romp with Vicki. He wondered if it was the sea air, or possibly the absence of his wife. After they both recovered their clothes, she cuddled into the crook of his arm. "Oh, Maxie, I missed you."

"I feel the same way, Sweetie."

Then she looked up, with a more serious expression. "You promised me this gig was going to get me great reviews and build up my resume. But that awful director has me buried in the chorus. You have to *do something* for me, Maxie."

Her pleading eyes nearly melted Max's resolve, but he managed to pull himself out of the post-coital fog. "My dear, I know that it seems like slow movement, but it's all part of the process. Didn't Brandon install you as one of the lead understudies?"

"Sure – but it's just the understudy. We only do two shows a week, so there's never a chance for me to play the role. I killed in that role in college. I can sing circles around that bitch, Vicki."

"Patience, patience, my little shooting star. Vicki will rotate off the ship soon. When that happens, who do you think will get to step in? Hmmm? I already spoke to Brandon about it."

"You did? He never tells us anything about the schedule more than a week in advance."

"Soon, my dear. It's a business that moves slowly at times. But then, when your star takes off, it will zoom to the heavens in a blink."

"Do you promise?" She traced her long fingernail down the edge of his shirt collar, spinning his chest hairs.

"I promise." Max sat up slowly, grabbing onto a handle on the speaker. "Now, I tell you what. I will see if I can get some information from Brandon for you. I'm guessing you have somewhere you're supposed to be, right?"

She rose gracefully and took Max's offered hand, not that she needed any help. "Oh, Maxie, I can't wait until this gig is over so I can come to New York and have you all to myself."

"Sure. I'm looking forward to that as well."

"You're gonna buy me a big engagement ring, right? As big as your wife's?"

"Well, of course, but what's most important is your career. I want to make you a star first. Then we'll focus on other things."

"I want to fuck you in your marble bathtub." She flashed a wicked smile. "I don't want you to get lonely in that big apartment."

"That sounds like fun." He gave her a short kiss and sent her out of their little bivouac first, watching her lithe legs stride away across the pool deck. He stood there, staring out over the side of the ship. Something was tickling the back of his brain, but he couldn't quite zero in on it. He put it out of his mind and climbed out of the hiding place. He was hungry, and needed a drink. On a cruise ship, both needs could be easily and quickly filled.

Chapter 28 – Worst Towel Animal Ever

THAT NIGHT, MIKE AND MICHELLE attended the stand-up comedy performance, then spent an hour at the Karaoke Bar. Rachel and her Squad of sorority sisters were there with Jason. The Squad and Rachel did a group rendition of "Build Me Up, Buttercup" that brought down the house. Eventually, the four New Yorkers said goodbye to the Texas twenty-somethings and walked on slightly wobbly legs down the corridor toward Mike and Michelle's cabin on Deck 9. At the door, they all stopped while Mike swiped his key and motioned for Rachel to enter the room first.

"Like we said, you get to be the judge of the awfulness of Elisabeth's towel animal. You go first and tell us what you think." Mike pushed the door open and held it so that Rachel could go through. She walked in, snapped the light switch on the wall next to the door, and then screamed. It was a high-pitched note, loud and long, and included a genuine sense of horror.

"Oh, my God! Ohmygod! Jason!"

Michelle called into the room, "OK, they're pretty terrible, but that's a bit much." Then she stood aside as Jason went in next, responding to Rachel's cry.

A moment later, Rachel came back to the door, with Jason close behind. Rachel's face was blanched. She held her right hand out in front of her, away from her dress. Her fingers were stained red.

"Mike, you'd better go in," Jason said in his most serious cop voice. "Rachel, stay out here with Michelle."

"Why?" Michelle asked, stepping forward only to be met with Jason's outstretched hand.

"We'll need you in a minute, Doctor. First, we need to secure this crime scene."

Michelle looked confused. "Crime scene? Wow – you really are overblowing the whole towel animal thing."

Mike stepped through the door behind Jason and allowed the door to slam shut behind him. Michelle turned to Rachel, who looked only slightly better than she had the moment before. Rachel croaked out, "Th-there's a dead woman on your bed."

Inside the stateroom, Mike and Jason surveyed the situation. There was protocol to be followed. The first half of the room contained a small love seat on one wall and a desk area opposite, with a simple armless chair. Beyond the love seat, the bed took up the rest of the space up to the sliding glass door leading to the balcony. The bed was covered with a royal blue comforter. Next to the pillows lay a clump of towels, twisted and knotted together in a form neither Jason nor Mike could discern, not that the remnants of that night's towel animal was their focus.

In the middle of the bed, lying face down, was a body and a large amount of blood. The person was obviously dead. Mike deduced from the blood on Rachel's right hand that her EMT instincts had kicked in and she had touched the body in order to determine if there was any pulse. If there had been any sign of life, she would have said something.

Mike and Jason stood still, not wanting to step on any part of the floor that might contain evidence, such as a bloody footprint. There was a pool of blood on the carpet immediately under the body's legs, which were hanging limply off the bed. Another puddle had formed around the victim's head. Mike could see a small amount of spattered blood on the white towels, but nothing immediately visible on the walls or on the pillowcases.

They carefully stepped across the floor, avoiding the path directly between the body and the door. Mike circled around the bed to check the other side and ducked down to peer underneath. Then he checked the balcony, which was empty. Meanwhile, Jason checked the tiny bathroom, which was the only other place someone could be hiding in the cramped space. The killer was definitely not there.

"We should get Michelle in here," Mike said. "And Rachel, too. She shouldn't be out there in the hallway alone."

Jason agreed and carefully retraced his steps to the door. When Michelle and Rachel were inside, standing in the narrow space between the door and the bathroom, Mike requested that Michelle start a recording on her phone. Then Mike began narrating through the scene. He had no latex gloves, so he avoided touching anything, including the body. He described what he saw: a body, apparently female, approximately five feet tall, wearing black flats and nylon stockings. Her hair was straight, black, and short. She was wearing a black-and-silver dress that fell to her knees, with thin straps at the shoulders. She also appeared to be wearing a blue top with a white collar underneath the black dress. The color and style of the blue under-garment matched the uniforms worn by the ship's cabin attendants. Based on the appearance of the body from the rear, she appeared to be Elisabeth.

Mike described how they found the body, and what had happened since their arrival. He speculated about Rachel touching the body to determine if there was any sign of life. Rachel nodded her affirmation, and he added it to the record. When he was done, he told Michelle she could turn off the recording. But first, she said, "Mike, there's one other thing. The dress she's wearing. I'm pretty sure it's mine. If we look in the closet, I'm guessing we'll find it missing."

Mike raised an eyebrow and motioned for Michelle to check the closet. She verified that the dress, now punctured and stained with blood beyond recovery, was in fact hers. She ended the recording so they could talk off the record.

"Looks like she was trying on your dress," Mike said. "Didn't you say that some of your other stuff in the closet had been moved around?"

"Yes," Michelle said, haltingly. "There were things hung up in positions other than where I put them, as if somebody had taken them down and then put them back in the wrong place. I guess I'm about the same size as Elisabeth, so maybe she liked to try on other people's clothes."

"Well, I doubt that's why somebody stabbed her," Jason said, stating the obvious.

"How do you know she was stabbed?" Rachel asked.

"The amount of blood, and the gashes in the back of the dress," Jason said simply. "She wasn't shot. Somebody cut her. We'll need to examine the body more closely to see if we can figure out with what, and when, but I'm pretty sure we're looking at knife wounds."

"I agree," Mike said. "And as much as I'd love to have Michelle do a thorough examination right now, we don't have the gear. We're going to have to call Keller and get his people up here with gloves and evidence bags."

"I'm betting he won't be able to call this one a suicide," Jason quipped.

"No. Not this one. The only question is whether the intended victim was Elisabeth – or Michelle."

Michelle blanched. She hadn't thought of the implications of someone in her cabin, wearing her dress, being brutally stabbed to death.

Chapter 29 – Denial Has Limits

HALF AN HOUR LATER, they were all standing outside the stateroom while Karl Keller and two of his officers secured the space and collected evidence. Mike had volunteered to assist with the crime scene review, but he was forcefully told to stay outside. It was his cabin, and he was "too close" to the investigation to be allowed inside. Mike understood – he had to be considered a possible suspect. A woman, now confirmed to be Elisabeth, had been murdered in his stateroom, and she was wearing his companion's dress.

Mike, Michelle, Jason, and Rachel were all each other's alibis, since they were all together the whole evening, and they had been seen in the theater and in the Karaoke Bar by dozens of people. They didn't have any significant worries about being wrongfully accused. They were just frustrated at being excluded.

A few minutes later, a phalanx of ship's crew showed up. They formed a gauntlet between the cabin and the freight elevator, then whisked the body away on a gurney without anyone seeing it happen. Mike had to admire what a tight operation it had been. None of the passengers would know that a bloody murder had just happened – unless somebody from the security team spilled the beans. Or, unless Mike, Michelle, Jason, or Rachel said something.

Shortly after the body was removed, Marjorie Barnes was back in the Deck 9 hallway, once again talking to a guest about a room reassignment. She assured Mike and Michelle that this was the first time anything like this had ever happened. Mike nodded, but remembered the surgical precision of the operation he just witnessed and doubted that such choreography was a first-time event. Ms. Barnes suggested that Mike and Michelle could move into the cabin two doors down, which was vacant.

"This little section of hallway has had a rough cruise," Mike quipped.

Barnes' face morphed into a grimace of embarrassment when she remembered that Mike had been there the night Shirley Bloom died, and that he knew exactly why the room was vacant. "Well, at least now with Elisabeth gone you'll get better service from your cabin attendant," Barnes said, with relief in her voice.

"The poor woman was just murdered," Michelle said, surprised at the hotel manager's attitude. "I know she wasn't the best attendant ever, but she didn't deserve to die."

Barnes paused, but the expression on her face didn't change. "I know, but sometimes things work out for the best."

"What do you mean?" Michelle exclaimed.

"I'm sorry," Barnes said, "I've had a really stressful few days. Right now we need to figure out where you two can move to. We have a little bit of a problem. You see, the cruise is almost completely booked. We moved Max Bloom to the only balcony room I had open. I can place you in an interior room without a window two decks below."

Michelle frowned. "Not a very attractive option." Then, after a pause, "It's fine for us to move into the cabin the Blooms were in."

Barnes was surprised. "Really? Well, I mean – I assumed that you wouldn't want to move into that cabin since it's where Mrs. Bloom – died."

"I'm a medical examiner. Mike is a homicide detective. We're not squeamish."

"Very well, then." Barnes pulled out a small radio unit and walked away, speaking urgently to one of her underlings. She turned to Keller, who was standing in the doorway. "Are they clear to pack up a few things so they can move into 935?"

Keller said that Mike and Michelle could come in for five minutes to pack up the essentials they needed for the night while he watched. They would be allowed to come back the next day for the rest of their things, after the space had been thoroughly inspected and cleaned. While he was packing up his toothbrush and pajamas, Mike couldn't help but ask Keller a few questions.

"Have you checked the card swipes for tonight?"

Keller scowled. "Detective, I really can't discuss this situation with you until I have completed my preliminary investigation."

"I found a rubber doorstop on the floor inside," Mike told Keller. "It wasn't there before, so I'm assuming Elisabeth was using it to prop the door open and the killer kicked it away when he left. That make sense to you?"

"Yes, Detective, it does. But really, I can't talk to you about this now."

"I get it," Mike relented. "When can I expect you to interview me and Michelle?"

Keller snapped back, "I will let you know. In the meantime,

please keep this incident to yourselves. I am counting on your discretion here while I conduct an investigation. Agreed?"

"I understand," Mike replied and walked out the door after Michelle. A young woman in a uniform rushed up to Marjorie Barnes in the hallway and handed her an envelope. Keller collected key cards from Mike and Michelle, then Barnes handed them two new cards and walked them to the former cabin of Max and Shirley Bloom. She watched while they tested their cards and confirmed that they were working. Then she wished them "pleasant dreams," but then apologized and left them with, "I'm very sorry about this situation."

Inside their new digs, Michelle laid out her toiletries in the spotless bathroom. "Are we going to move in here for the duration?"

"I'd guess yes. They can't really expect us to go back to the room with the bloodstained carpet. Even if they change the mattress, I don't think they can replace that flooring so easily. Plus, it's an active crime scene."

"Keller has to think this is connected to Mrs. Bloom, right?"

Mike nodded. "Even an idiot has to think there's a connection, although it's not entirely clear to me what it might be." Then he snapped his fingers, as if just remembering something important. "Hey, do you still have that spare key card?"

The day before, when Michelle had left their cabin without her card, she got a replacement from the customer service desk. That left her with an extra card. Karl Keller had confiscated their old keys before they were given new ones, but he had only collected two cards.

"I think so," Michelle said, reaching into her purse. She pulled out the blue-and-white plastic card and handed it to Mike. "Do you think it's still active?"

"It might be. Keller just collected our cards, so he hadn't de-activated them already. Otherwise, he wouldn't have bothered taking them, and he hasn't had time yet. Let's go find out."

"Do you think we should?" Michelle asked, a bit pensive. "Would we be accused of tampering with the crime scene? Wouldn't that look bad for us?"

"It would, but we have rock-solid alibis and no possible motive for wanting to knock off our housekeeper. There isn't any evidence linking us to the crime, so I'm not that worried about how it's going to look."

"OK, Detective. I'm in." Michelle saluted Mike with a sly smile.

They crept out of their room into the hallway, which was deserted. It was only a few steps back to their original room. Mike used his key card to cut the tamper-proof tape on the door, then swiped the key and the door opened with a satisfying click. They slipped inside quickly and held the door so it didn't slam. Michelle asked, "What if Keller checks the card swipes and sees one just now?"

"Then he'll send somebody up here and I'll get to ask whether there were any other swipes besides Elisabeth's. I'll say I forgot my feather pillows and came back to get them. By the way, please grab my pillows."

"You're a good liar. I should remember that." Michelle gave Mike a good-natured wink. "What are we looking for?"

"I don't know," Mike said as he paced slowly around the room. He was no longer worried about trampling evidence on the carpet, since Keller's officers had been all over the space. There was no evidence left there to damage. Mike walked, making mental notes. The bed had been stripped down to the bare mattress, but there was still a faint red stain that had seeped through the many overlayers. The towel animal, whatever it was supposed to be, was gone and the cases had been stripped from the pillows. There was an acrid smell in the air.

"Let's walk back through this," Mike said, standing in the balcony doorway. "Elisabeth comes into the room to do the turn-down and leave us her towel monster. She puts the towel thing down on the bed, then goes into the closet to examine your dresses."

"Why does she put the towel down first?"

"Well, since the towel was on the bed and got some blood spatter on it, it had to have been there when she was stabbed, which means that it was there before she put on the dress. She would not have put on the dress with the towel in her hand, so if she brought it into the room ready to go, then she had to put it down first before heading for the closet."

"Makes sense," Michelle agreed. "So, she goes to the closet, takes my dress off the hanger, puts it on over her uniform, I guess just to try it on for kicks. Ewww. I can't tell you how much it creeps me out, thinking about that woman touching my clothes and putting them on."

"It is pretty creepy. Are you going to be alright for tonight?"

"I'll manage. There are a few shops onboard where I can buy a new dress for tomorrow night."

"Whatever you need to do," Mike said, hoping to change the subject soon.

"OK, so then how does the killer get into the room?" Michelle posed.

"I found a doorstop inside, and Keller seemed to think Elisabeth probably left the door propped open."

"Why would she do that?"

"I've seen the cabin doors open when the attendants are inside. I'm not sure why. Maybe it's a security thing – so that they're less likely to steal things. Or, maybe it's to let the occupants know that there's somebody inside. Of course, knowing how Elisabeth operated, if that was the protocol, she probably didn't follow it."

"Well, if the killer didn't have a key, then he must have been following Elisabeth," Michelle said.

Mike hesitated. He didn't want to upset Michelle more than she already was, but he also didn't want to ignore the obvious possibilities. "Or the killer was trying to kill you. He came by, saw the door open, and took the opportunity."

"Why would somebody be walking by looking to come in and kill me?" Michelle asked, perplexed. "Who on this ship would want to kill me at all?"

"The only person I can think of is Max Bloom," Mike said. "You were the person who pointed out that his wife's death looked like a murder, which points a finger at him. He might have a grudge against you."

"That's pretty tenuous, Detective."

"Yeah, I know. It's a very long shot. You also examined the body, so I suppose someone might think that knocking you off would prevent you from testifying. Of course, we know that killing you won't help. It actually would either get him caught or cast more suspicion on him, so it would be a stupid thing to do. But Max is not very smart, whether or not he actually killed his wife."

"OK, so let's say it's not Max. Then who would it be?"

Mike was silent. "I don't know," he finally said. He finished pacing through the whole room, then said, "The killer had to have the knife with him. There was no knife in the room that he could have used. So, the killer had to come into the room with the knife ready to kill somebody. Either you, or Elisabeth. If no one had a motive to kill you, then the killer was after her."

"So, all we need to know is why someone would want to kill Elisabeth."

Mike shook his head. "Yeah. And we'll have to trust that Mr. Keller's on that one hard."

Michelle opened the small closet next to the door to the bathroom. She frowned at her disturbed dresses, then stooped down. "As long as we're here, I'm going to get a pair of sandals to wear in the morning." Michelle then called out, "Mike, there's something here."

"What?" Mike could see Michelle now on her hands and knees, looking intently at the carpet in front of the closet.

"I think it's glitter."

"What?"

"Look – see the little sparkly flecks? There are silver and gold glitter specks here."

"I'm assuming it didn't come from you."

"No, Mike. Have you ever seen me wear glitter?"

"Maybe it was going to be a surprise for me."

Michelle couldn't help but laugh. "You are incorrigible, Detective, but I'd like you to please focus here. I can assure you that this glitter was not on the carpet before tonight. I would have noticed it when I put my shoes away. So, this is recent."

"Which means it came from Elisabeth – or from the killer," Mike said, taking a step back and surveying the rest of the carpeting in the room, looking for more glitter. He didn't find any. "What kind of clothing would have glitter like this?"

Michelle paused while she thought. "I guess it could be from some styles of shoes, or a dress, but not much that a man would wear. Maybe a sparkly bow tie?"

"What about from a watch or a bracelet?" Mike asked.

"Not likely. Of course, it could be body glitter."

"How could body glitter flake off a person and wind up on the floor?"

"I imagine any kind of scraping or brushing motion would do it," Michelle replied. "My niece, Mary, was into arts and crafts when she was young and she used to send me artwork covered in the stuff. It was impossible to keep the floor clean. Of course, body glitter might be different."

"Do you think Elisabeth might have been wearing that?"

"Doubtful, based on what I've seen of her," Michelle replied. "But I guess you can never be sure. She would have been standing here, in front of the closet, if she was taking my dress down from the hanger. I guess it could have been her. When she was attacked, it could have flaked off from her."

"Or from the killer. But what kind of man wears body glitter?"

"An actor. But why does it have to be a man?" Michelle asked. "Don't you always tell Jason not to make assumptions?"

"True," Mike agreed. "If the killer was a woman – or an actor – who was wearing body glitter, that would fit. I don't suppose we would be able to match this glitter to a particular person later, would we?"

"Even with a good lab, I doubt it. The stuff is pretty universally available at any cosmetic counter or drug store. It's unlikely we could match this particular glitter to anyone we find later who is also wearing body glitter. If it's even body glitter in the first place. But it must mean something."

"Yeah. Everything means something. The question is, what?" Neither of them had any good answer.

They trekked back to cabin 935 with Mike's feather pillows

and prepared for bed, not that there was much chance of sleep anytime soon.

Chapter 30 – Process of Elimination

WARM WIND WHIPPED ACROSS the railing along the running track on Deck 5. Vicki Nelson stopped bothering to brush her hair aside as it snapped against her cheeks and eyes. The half-moon showed dimly through the high clouds, casting a soft reflection on the distant waves. A rhythmic crash and wash rose from the hull of the great ship as it tore through the dark water, sending a salty mist into the air. There were no deck chairs in this area, and no passengers strolling along the track.

It was much more scenic on Deck 13, or on the sun deck above Deck 14. Here, the overhang of the deck above obscured much of the view of the sky. The line of yellow lifeboats, hanging at attention just above the deck rail at regular intervals, also obscured the ocean view. It was good for a morning run, but not conducive to a romantic midnight stroll. Vicki was the only person in sight.

She studied the slip of paper in her hand, buffeted by the

wind. She resolved to give it only one or two minutes and then leave. But the note had seemed both urgent and ominous. It was written in slanted cursive handwriting: "Meet me at midnight outside the crew door on Deck 5. Must talk to you about Million." It was signed only with a flourishing capital "D". Vicki consulted her watch to confirm that it was 12:01 and looked around at the empty deck. She was about to head back inside when the door marked "crew only" swung inward.

Vicki watched the woman approach. She was wearing black yoga pants and a black t-shirt with the Epic Cruise Lines logo. She walked unhurriedly, her arms at her sides, with her fists closed as if she was holding something. She smiled as she made eye contact with Vicki.

"Hi," Vicki said, loudly enough to be heard over the wind. "What's up with Max Million that couldn't wait?"

The other woman kept walking until she was close enough to lean in, whispering into Vicki's ear. "You can't have him."

Vicki pulled her head back. "What do you—"

Her voice was cut off by the intense pain in her neck. The other woman had quickly stepped around Vicki and swung her right arm over her head. A thin, white filament joined her two hands as she looped the garrote around Vicki's throat, planted a knee into Vicki's lower back, and pulled down. A thin, red line immediately appeared as Vicki gasped for breath and tried to pull away. She brought her hands to her neck and tried to claw at the line with her nails, but there was no space.

Vicki tried to scream, but managed only a gurgle. As she realized what was happening, she tried to lash out with her arms, but had no leverage. She kicked backwards with her left leg and made solid contact with her attacker's knee, drawing a grunt. The line around her neck relaxed momentarily. Vicki's left hand snapped to her neck and she dug two fingers underneath, drawing blood where she scraped the skin. Then the pressure returned, just as she sucked in a half-breath.

Pain lanced through her fingers as the thin line sliced through her skin. Blood oozed out and dripped down the front of her t-shirt. She couldn't breathe. The knee against her back pushed her hips forward, giving her no balance as she began to fall backwards. She flailed with her right arm, reaching blindly. She couldn't scream. Tears formed and clouded her eyes. The blurry outline of the Epic Cruise Lines logo floated in her field of vision. The pain dissipated.

As Vicki lost consciousness, her body slumped backwards. The other woman allowed the limp body to fall against her, continuing to hold the pressure as they both eased down toward the rust-colored lanes of the running track at the base of one of the lifeboats. The boat was an image out of the movie *Yellow Submarine* with its bulbous shape and fully-enclosed design. A door at the same level as the track read "Do not touch – crew only." As the final drops of life drained from Vicki's body, her attacker rolled to the side, then scrambled to her feet, unwinding the thin cord from her hands and tossing it over the railing for the wind to carry away.

Just then, the sound of several singing voices wafted over the whooshing of the wind and the crashing of the waves. The woman looked up and saw shadows coming around the curve in the track at the front of the ship. Enthusiastic strains from the chorus of Bon Jovi's "Livin' on a Prayer" preceded them.

The woman reached up and grabbed a latch in the ship's rail, pushing half of a gate open away from her. Then she grasped the silver handle on the door of the lifeboat, breaking the security seal as she pulled down and tugged the heavy door outward.

Bracing the open door with her back, she reached down and grabbed Vicki Nelson's limp corpse under each arm and dragged it toward the opening. A metal plate marked with the blue-and-white symbol for wheelchair access covered the small gap between the deck and the lifeboat. She hauled the body inside, between rows of seats outfitted with life jackets, then reached out and pulled the rail gate closed before carefully re-closing the lifeboat door.

The singers had recently left the Karaoke Bar. They drunkenly repeated their chorus over and over as they staggered down the running track. They never noticed that the latch on the rail gate was not fastened, or that the seal on the lifeboat door was broken. They stopped and howled at the half-moon for a few minutes, then passed by and found their way back inside the ship. After ten minutes, a single figure dressed in black emerged from the lifeboat, re-latched the rail gate, and used the crew-only door to vanish from the scene.

Chapter 31 – Multiple Personalities

Monday, May 13

WHEN THE SUNLIGHT PEEKED THROUGH the curtains, Mike and Michelle both awoke, not knowing for sure how much sleep they actually achieved. Mike opened the balcony door, stepped outside into the warm morning air, and gazed out at the sun-speckled ocean. When he turned around, he noticed something wedged under the door in a small trench that carried away unwanted water. It was reflecting the light. Mike bent down to examine it, then called for Michelle, who was in the bathroom. "Can you bring me a plastic bag?"

"I haven't got that here," Michelle called back. "I only brought my toothbrush, my make-up kit, and clothes for this morning."

"Do you have a tweezers in your make-up kit?"

"Sure."

"Get 'em."

Mike used the tweezers to extract a small gold charm and set it down on the little balcony table. It depicted the smiling and frowning masks of the theater. Michelle thought it looked like something that would hang from a charm bracelet.

"Could this have belonged to Shirley Bloom?" Mike asked.

"I doubt it," she responded quickly. "All of Shirley Bloom's jewelry was top shelf, and I never saw her wearing a bracelet, let alone one with cheap charms."

"How can you tell it's cheap?"

Michelle just cocked her head and stared.

"OK, so not Shirley's. Probably not Max's either, right?"

"No, this is definitely a woman's piece. It could have been left there by a passenger from a previous cruise."

"Sure. Maybe. It was down there in the channel under the door. It could have been there for a while without the cleaning crew finding it."

"Except that it would wash away the first time there was a storm. And there was a storm Wednesday night."

"Yeah," Mike said absently. "That would mean it was dropped there recently. If it doesn't belong to Max or Shirley, I guess it could have been somebody else who visited the room. It's a theater symbol, which could suggest somebody who knows Max and who's connected with the theater."

"What about one of the women in the ship's theater company? Are any of them clients of Max's?"

"I don't know. We can probably find out. Maybe Max had his friend, Vicki Nelson, up to his room?"

"That would make sense," Michelle agreed. "But he and Shirley were only in this room for a little more than a day. Do you think he'd do that while Shirley was still alive?"

"I don't know him well enough to answer that." Mike looked

around some more, in case there was anything else lying around, but he found nothing. He went back inside and sat down on the bed.

"You know what else would make sense?"

"Yeah," Mike said. "I don't see how, but it could belong to the killer."

"Exactly." Michelle walked to the bed and sat next to Mike. "That would make the killer a woman, and someone who would wear a theater charm on a bracelet. Does that make any sense?"

"Not really," Mike replied, "but I've seen a lot of murders where things didn't make sense. It's a possibility, so we need to consider it."

"You know what else theater folks sometimes wear?" Michelle looked up at Mike's face expectantly.

As they made eye contact, they both said, "Glitter."

Karl Keller was also up early on Monday morning, sitting in his office sending a report to the corporate office. He had to include Edwin Ferguson on his emails, since he was the corporate security VP. He wanted to keep Ferguson out of his hair, but he couldn't find a justification for not copying him on the messages.

There had been a murder on the ship. He could not avoid that conclusion. Elisabeth didn't stab herself. He wrote that his security crew would be fully investigating Elisabeth's activities to see if there were any suspects who would want to kill her. He refused to say that her death was connected to the death of Shirley Bloom, just two doors down the hallway. He was still listing her death as either an accident or a suicide. There was no hard evidence to the contrary. At least, that was his official report. He also chose not to mention the missing Ricky Rosario who, in his view, was irrelevant to Elisabeth's death.

Keller wrote that it was still too early in the investigation to have any firm suspects. There was some possibility that the killer believed the victim was Michelle McNeill. Elisabeth was wearing one of Doctor McNeill's dresses, the two women were about the same height and weight, and both had black hair. He listed Mike Stoneman as a possible suspect. Any time a woman was murdered, the husband or boyfriend was always a suspect. Max Bloom, however, was not listed as a suspect in the death of Shirley Bloom, because her death was not a homicide.

By 9:00 a.m., Keller had a message from Ferguson, who was on his way to Keller's office to talk about the prior night's "incident." Keller wasn't surprised, but he was annoyed.

"Have you searched the dead woman's room?" Ferguson said as soon as arrived in Keller's office.

"Not yet. We're going to do that this morning, but we're waiting for her cabin-mate to report for work first, so as not to call unnecessary attention to the situation."

"What are you telling the crew about Elisabeth?"

"That she is ill and is in the infirmary in isolation." Keller fixed a level stare at Ferguson. "It's standard protocol, per the corporate manual. 'If possible, do not communicate information about any death.'"

"Don't you think this situation is a bit different from the standard?"

"Sure, Mr. Ferguson, but I don't see any reason to be advertising that Elisabeth was murdered. I don't see how that helps us."

"You don't think that the rest of the staff should be alerted to the fact that there is a killer on the ship?"

"No. I don't," Keller responded. "Whoever did this was not just randomly killing cabin attendants."

"How do you know that?"

"Because it can't be a coincidence that we have two deaths, and they were both in Elisabeth's area on Deck 9. And because there is some evidence that there might be a connection."

"What's that?" Ferguson said with increased interest. "Whaddaya have?"

Keller sat back in his chair and expelled a deep breath. It wasn't going to be possible to keep the information to himself. "I checked Elisabeth's key card records for the night Mrs. Bloom . . . died." Keller paused while Ferguson listened intently. "It turns out that she was on an emergency call in room 938 at eleven-fifty on Thursday night. The guest in that room got seasick and puked on the carpet. It was an interior room, across the hall and two doors down from the Blooms. She did the standard clean-up and deodorization. She logged in completion of the clean-up at twelve thirty-two. So, she was on the floor near the Blooms' cabin at the time Mrs. Bloom took her dive off the balcony."

"So?" Ferguson said, challenging Keller to connect the dots for him.

"I'm not suggesting that Elisabeth tossed Mrs. Bloom over her rail. I guess that's a possibility, but I can't see any motive Elisabeth would have for that. She's a crappy cabin attendant, for sure, but she's been on the ship for nine months and she's never had any incident of violence."

"What if she was trying to steal that big-ass emerald ring?" Ferguson suggested. "If she was in the area, she could have gone into the room and tried to lift the ring, and then Mrs. Bloom confronted her and ended up over the rail."

"I thought of that, but there was no swipe from Elisabeth's card on the Blooms' door."

"What if she piggy-backed in after Mrs. Bloom?" Ferguson pressed. "She could have seen her coming, come in right after her, subdued her, stolen her ring, and then tossed her over the side."

"Did you ever meet Shirley Bloom?" When Ferguson shook his head, Keller continued. "She was five-nine at least, and in great shape. Elisabeth was barely five feet and weighed maybe one-ten. I don't see how she was physically capable of taking on Mrs. Bloom and hoisting her over the rail of her balcony."

"You confirmed that the people in the next room heard nothing?"

"Yes," Keller said.

"I was not informed of that," Ferguson said, annoyed.

"Well, I haven't filed my final report on the investigation yet," Keller said, looking away from his boss. "The point is that I don't think Elisabeth is likely to be a killer. But, it's possible that Elisabeth saw the killer in that hallway. It's possible the killer saw her, and decided to take her out."

"So, you've decided to admit that Shirley Bloom was murdered?"

Keller sat silently for a long moment. "I have not reached any conclusion about that. I'm just speculating about a hypothetical situation that would be consistent with the facts of both deaths. I'm not going to put anything in any reports. It's just us talking."

"Great. So, we have no video, right?"

"Right."

Ferguson scowled. "This is why I've been pushing for back-up systems for the surveillance cameras."

"Well, fine. But for now, we don't have them."

"Did you get Elisabeth's card swipes from last night?"

"Yeah, nothing unusual there. She did swipe into the room where she died at nine-forty-two."

"Any other swipes on that door until Stoneman found the body?"

"No. I'm not sure what that means. Elisabeth did some odd things."

"I don't suppose there could be any connection to the disappearance of Ricky Rosario?" Ferguson raised an eyebrow.

Keller scowled. "No. I'm sure he's off fucking somebody he values more than his job. But, it is annoying that he's unaccounted for."

"It's more than annoying. It could be related. Damn it, Keller, think like a cop instead of like a PR stooge."

"Don't tell me how to run my ship!"

"Fine. When are we going to search Elisabeth's cabin?"

Keller consulted the clock on his wall, trying to avoid losing his composure in front of Ferguson. "Her cabin-mate is scheduled for duty at nine-thirty, so it's likely that she's out of there by now. I have two officers going there in about ten minutes."

"Are you going to be there to supervise?"

"I have confidence in my people," Keller curtly responded. "If they find anything, I'll know about it soon enough."

Ferguson looked disgusted. "Keller, if I weren't stuck in this chair, I'd come over there and kick some sense into your thick head."

"It's lucky for you."

"How about this then? As your boss, I'm ordering you to bring Stoneman into this investigation. Use him as a resource. He's a good cop. You need his help."

Keller fumed silently. "I will note in my report that you gave me that order."

"Fine," Ferguson said, reaching for his wheels. "Keep me informed."

"I will do that – sir."

"The shit just hit the fan, Keller. I'd get out of the way of the spatter, if I were you." Ferguson then spun around and pushed himself toward the door to Keller's office, disappearing around the corner toward the elevator.

Keller turned to his computer and sent a message to his security officer to secure Elisabeth's cabin, but to stand by. He had an appointment for 10:00 to interview Mike Stoneman and Michelle McNeill.

Chapter 32 – Suspicion and Speculation

A T THREE MINUTES AFTER ten o'clock, Mike and Michelle arrived at Karl Keller's office. Jason and Rachel volunteered to come along, but Mike insisted that they go have some fun time. He suggested that they meet up at noon for a briefing.

Rachel sent Michelle a copy of her cell phone video from the night before at the Karaoke Bar. She had cajoled Jason into singing again and he did a soulful rendition of "Ain't No Sunshine." After the performance, she pointed the camera at the audience's enthusiastic ovation, including a video selfie that included Mike and Michelle sitting at their table. The group had gone to the Karaoke Bar immediately after the comedy show. Shortly after Jason's performance, they went to Mike and Michelle's cabin, where they found Elisabeth's body.

Keller declined when Michelle offered him a copy of the video file. He knew that every karaoke session was recorded. The marketing department used clips for the end-of-cruise "yearbook" video, sold to departing guests on the last day of the voyage. The video recording would be time-stamped. It was as air-tight as an alibi gets.

Michelle suggested that the time of death was about 1-2 hours before they arrived, based on the coagulation of the blood. She volunteered to examine the body, but Keller declined, again because she was "involved" in the case. "Besides," Keller said dismissively, "the cause of death was pretty clearly multiple stab wounds."

Michelle did not give the security chief a lecture on the value of having a professional review of the corpse as an aid to his investigation.

When Mike suggested that he would be happy to consult, Keller's response wasn't the brush-off he expected. "Actually, Detective, I was hoping that I could have a few words with you. In private."

Mike raised an eyebrow and wondered why Keller was being so uncharacteristically amenable. Keller suggested that Michelle should talk to Marjorie Barnes about getting a key to cabin 931, so she could pack up their belongings and move them to cabin 935.

"Are your guys done with their inspection of the room?" Mike asked.

"Yes. They are, and the room is being cleaned."

Mike held back from criticizing Keller for having the crime scene cleaned so soon, since it was too late to do anything about it. "It's a good idea, Michelle," Mike motioned with his eyes toward the office door.

Michelle gave a small nod, then walked toward the exit. She looked over her shoulder at Mike, saying, "Text me when you're done so we can meet up."

When she was gone, Mike turned to Keller, who preempted Mike by speaking first. "Listen, Detective, I know you think I haven't taken the Shirley Bloom situation seriously. You have to understand my position and my mandate from the company. The presumption is that the incident is an accident, or a suicide, until proven conclusively otherwise. Our job is to keep everyone calm and happy. Having rumors circulating around the ship that there's a murderer on board does not accomplish that. But, at this point, I can't deny that we have someone onboard willing to commit a brutal murder. I will take every step necessary to protect the rest of the passengers. That has to be my first priority. As much as I don't want to admit it . . . I could use some help."

Keller looked at Mike with an even gaze. Mike returned the stare, assessing whether he was being bullshitted. "You never worked homicide as a cop?"

"I was FBI," Keller said proudly. "I was a data analysis specialist. I evaluated documents and videos. I cracked cell phones and did statistical analysis to support field agents. I was good at it, and it translates well into this post. But your friend and my boss, Mr. Ferguson, suggested that working together on this would be best for everyone."

"Well, Mr. Keller, I also have one focus, and that's protecting Michelle and the rest of the passengers from this killer."

"We agree on one thing, then."

Mike's face softened. He had some sympathy for Keller's position, even if he was a sanctimonious asshole. No matter what Mike thought of him as a security officer, he realized that finding the killer was going to be easier with the man's help.

"Listen, I don't give a rat's ass about your corporate problems, but I have no interest in creating a fuss or making you look bad. I just want to catch this killer, so what do you say we forget everything that has happened between us up to now and work together to prevent any more murders?"

"OK. Like I said, I want your help, Detective. But you need to remember that you are not in charge. My staff reports to me. You need to appreciate that."

"I understand."

Keller gave Mike a briefing about Elisabeth's key card swipes on Thursday night, placing her near the Blooms' stateroom when Shirley had her unfortunate fall. "I'm open to the possibility that her death may be in some way connected to the death of Mrs. Bloom."

"I'd say it's likely," Mike agreed. Then Mike told Keller about the gold theater charm he found in room 935, and the theory that the killer might be a woman. He even told him about the glitter, admitting that he had gone back into room 931 the night before.

"You may want to ask your officer whether he or she noticed that the security tape on that door was breached."

Keller was skeptical about Mike's female killer theory, but conceded that they should not rule out any possibilities.

Then Mike proposed a plan of action. "We need to get a look in Elisabeth's cabin. See if there is anything there that makes a connection. Like, maybe, a large emerald ring."

"I've already dispatched an officer to make sure nobody goes in, now that her roommate has left for the day."

"You didn't secure the room last night?" Mike was astonished at the sloppy procedure.

"She has a roommate, as all the crew members do. We didn't want to start any rumors." Keller looked at Mike as if his explanation were entirely reasonable.

"So, maintaining secrecy about the murder was more important than preserving evidence."

"Not at all, Detective. There is little chance that her roommate would be tampering with evidence, since she doesn't know that anything has happened. Unless her roommate killed her. I judged the risk of any possible evidence tampering as very small."

Mike swallowed his comments, lest he risk having his permission to come along revoked. He just nodded, and stood up to allow Keller to lead the way toward the crew quarters. Mike took note that they walked through the same crew-only door Vicki Nelson had gone through the day before.

They walked down a narrow hallway with doorways evenly spaced along both sides, closer together than the rooms up on the guest decks. There was a security guard in full police-style uniform standing outside one of the doors. She stood aside for Keller, who swiped his master key and opened the cabin, allowing Mike to enter first. Keller followed, telling the officer she could return to her regular duties.

Inside, they spent half an hour meticulously combing through all of Elisabeth's belongings. They did not find the emerald ring. What they did find was far more puzzling – and intriguing.

Chapter 33 – A New Direction

MARJORIE BARNES was remarkably cool and calm, sitting in a straight-backed chair in a small conference area next to the customer service desk on Deck 5. When Keller advised her that they needed to speak regarding the "Elisabeth incident," she did not seem surprised or worried. Mike noted her demeanor as he watched Keller conduct the interview. Mike would not have called it an interrogation when it started. Keller was too nice.

Keller asked Barnes casually whether she had taken care of the clean-up in room 931. She confirmed that her team had removed the mattress and was in the process of scrubbing the carpet. Keller then inquired about the reassignment of cabin attendants on Deck 9. Mike was impressed by Keller's technique, making the witness comfortable and off-guard before starting to ask the tough questions. He didn't have long to wait.

"Marjorie, why don't you tell us about your relationship with Elisabeth Rodriguez?"

"Well, she was not our best attendant," Barnes began, taking a professional tone, as if reciting a performance evaluation. "The reports I've seen say that she lacked a good rapport with the guests, and that she was not visible enough. We've had complaints about her moving things inside the cabins, and not being responsive to special requests. Her floor supervisor had to discipline her several times."

"You seem to have an amazingly good knowledge of her personnel file."

"Well, she was a particularly problematic employee."

"If she was such a poor employee, why didn't we fire her a long time ago?"

Now, for the first time, Barnes squirmed a bit. "She had a family she sent her money to." She looked at Keller as if for approval, or confirmation. "She was with the company for a long time. I guess I felt sorry for her."

"How many employees have you fired this year, Marjorie?"

"I'm not sure, *Karl*," she said, emphasizing his first name. "I don't really keep track."

"You send a quarterly personnel report to the global VP of Human Resources, don't you?"

"Yes, I do."

"So, if I had you review the reports for the first quarter and estimate the number so far this quarter, what would be a general ballpark number?"

"I suppose it would be, maybe, fifteen or twenty."

"OK, well, let's assume it's at least twenty. Can you tell me how many of those twenty had worse performance ratings and worse disciplinary history than Elisabeth?"

Barnes got a sour look on her face, then said, "Probably not many."

"C'mon, Marjorie, you know as well as I do that Elisabeth had the worst reputation. It has always puzzled me why you can be such a task-master with the rest of your staff, but Elisabeth seemed to always get a break. Do you want to explain that to me?"

Barnes said nothing, then raised her chin and said, "I guess I just have a soft spot where she's concerned."

"So, that has nothing to do with the photos?"

"What photos?"

"We found some photos when we searched Elisabeth's things in her cabin," Keller said evenly, not tipping his hand.

"Really?" Barnes said. She kept a calm exterior, but Mike noticed a little crack in her voice, and that she suddenly grabbed her left index finger with her right hand and squeezed it repeatedly. "How did you break into her phone?"

"What phone do you mean?" Keller asked.

Barnes was now fully flustered. "I – I mean, I just assumed that if she had photos, then they would be on her phone, and I know it's hard to break into somebody else's phone, so, you know, I just assumed."

"Should I be looking at her phone for more pictures?"

"I don't know. I suppose there might be lots of things on her phone. It might give you some clues." Barnes was starting to sweat, and it looked like she was trying to dislocate her finger.

"We already found some clues. It seems that Elisabeth may have had more of a relationship with you than just being one of your staff."

"I don't know what you mean."

"The photos of the two of you having sex. The ones showing her snorting coke off your tits. I'm guessing that there's a video of that and the stills hidden in a book stuck in the back of

Elisabeth's underwear drawer are just screenshots. Is that about right?"

Barnes slumped in her chair and dropped her head to her chest. "Karl, you can't show those to anyone. I'll be fired. Oh, lord! And all because of that *bitch!* Oh, I can't tell you how much I hate that woman. She's been blackmailing me with that video!" Barnes dropped all pretense and spilled her guts.

Mike watched impassively, surprised that Keller had done such a good job. Perhaps he had underestimated the man. Apparently, when he wanted to conduct an investigation, he could do it well. His problem was that he was more interested in covering up crimes than solving them.

"I did have a little thing with her back around Christmas. I know I shouldn't have gone there, but she was – oh, my. Well, I don't know how the hell that little snake managed to take a video without me noticing. God! How could I have been such an idiot?

"And she was the *worst.* She knew I would fire her if not for that video. She took advantage of me. She practically taunted me. I've been sending money to her family every month. I wanted to *kill* her!"

Barnes stopped suddenly, realizing what she had said. She looked up, her face ashen. "But – but I didn't kill her! I wouldn't. I couldn't. It's – it's impossible. Oh, Lord, I wanted to, I'll admit that. But I didn't."

"Well, Marjorie, you can understand why I had to speak to you." Keller looked at her without any sign of compassion or understanding. "Where were you last night between nine o'clock and eleven-thirty?"

Barnes stared straight ahead without blinking for several seconds, holding her breath. Then, she let out a sigh and smiled. "I guess I'm lucky. We had a crew meeting last night in Shangri-

La at nine, since there weren't any guest events there until ten. As a matter of fact, Elisabeth was a no-show for the meeting, which was not that unusual for her. But the rest of the hotel staff was there. We had a change of plans for Tuesday morning's disembarkation process. We're docking an hour earlier than originally scheduled, so we had to re-configure the departure times for the guests and change the schedule for the turnaround on the guest rooms. The meeting lasted about forty-five minutes. Right after, I had a private meeting with two of my attendants."

Mike took note that Barnes had released the death grip on her finger. "I won't bore you with the details, but they had a – well, a dispute – and we went to my office to hash it out. I had my new assistant manager, Carol Shields, with me. She took notes, since we thought it might turn into a disciplinary matter. It was after eleven by the time Carol and I finished. We were so frustrated after the meeting that we decided to break the rules and go back to Shangri-La for a martini. April can tell you, we sat at the bar and he made us two rounds of drinks and then scolded us for taking up seats when there were guests standing."

Barnes looked at Keller, then over at Mike, who was calmly watching the show. "I guess it's a good thing that we broke the rules, huh?"

"So," Keller said in a more conciliatory tone, "we'll check out the alibi, but if it wasn't you, then can you think of anyone else who would want to kill Elisabeth?"

"I'm guessing half the guests on Deck 9 probably want to murder her, but I doubt any of them would act on it."

Keller actually laughed at the comment. "Fair enough. Anybody else? Did she have any disputes with any of the other attendants?"

"Not that I know about. But you really should check her phone. If she was blackmailing me, who knows who else she had dirt on?" Then Barnes' expression turned to pleading. "Karl, you won't be reporting all this, will you? You don't have to tell anyone if I'm not really a suspect, right?"

"I can't promise that, Marjorie." Keller was calm, but firm. "But I will consider what needs to be in my final report and what can be left out."

"I'd be truly grateful," Barnes said, with a gleam in her eye that Mike noticed, but kept to himself. He didn't need to get involved in whatever was going on between these two. "Can I go now?"

Keller looked at Mike, who nodded his affirmation. Barnes quickly left the room. Then, Keller said, "We need to hack into her phone."

Mike stood up, his knees creaking. "Of course, you should try to do that. It's possible that our killer's image will be there. But, in my experience, hacking into somebody's phone without their password will take some time."

"That's true. If I had the FBI lab, I could do it, but here it won't be easy."

"We don't know whether Elisabeth got a photo of the killer. But, we know that Elisabeth was in the vicinity of room 935 when Shirley Bloom was killed."

Keller frowned and picked up a pen from his desk, twirling it between his fingers as he spoke. "If she saw someone go into Shirley Bloom's stateroom that night, or come out of it, and if the person saw her and knew she was a witness, then that person would have a motive."

"I think there's more to it than that," Mike continued. "If she saw the killer, why would she fail to report to you, or to Ms.

Barnes, that she saw something suspicious that night? Why would she withhold that information? I assume your team spoke to her, to ask whether she saw or heard anything, right?"

"Right," Keller replied absently, as if thinking about something else. "We talked to all the attendants on the floor, and nobody saw or heard anything. But now that I'm thinking about it, in the report I saw, Elisabeth said she wasn't on the floor at that time. So, she lied. Why would she do that?"

"Maybe because she didn't want the killer discovered."

"You think she killed Mrs. Bloom?"

"No," Mike said, "but it's possible that she was blackmailing the killer."

Mike could see the wheels spinning in Keller's brain. "That would make sense. We know she was willing to blackmail her boss. If she saw somebody that night, she might try to blackmail them, too."

"She didn't understand," Mike said, looking Keller in the eye, "that it's a terrible idea to blackmail a killer."

"It still could have been the husband," Keller observed. "If he went to the room, killed his wife, then left, it's possible that Elisabeth saw him and tried to blackmail him. He could have decided to kill her to shut her up and stop the blackmail. That would make sense."

"It would. But somehow, I don't figure Max Bloom to be the stabbing type."

"We're going to have to talk to him again and find out if he has an alibi for last night."

"I agree," Mike said. "There's plenty of evidence pointing at Max, at least for Shirley's death. You did get the story from Quentin Richardson, from the next cabin, right?"

Keller looked confused. "We spoke to the guests in both of the adjoining rooms, and they all said they were not in their cabins at the time of Shirley Bloom's death. They had nothing to tell us."

"Your guys didn't dig hard enough." Mike then related his conversation with Richardson, in which he described the argument between Mr. and Mrs. Bloom on Wednesday afternoon.

"He really threatened to kill his wife?"

"That's what the man said. It could have been a typical argument that meant nothing, but considering that the woman was killed the next day, it seems more significant. Then, another death two doors down involving the cabin attendant who was in the area at the time of the first death? It's hard to think they aren't related."

"I have to agree," Keller said, "but I'm not ready to completely abandon the possibility."

"Hold on to that hope, but let's have another discussion with Max."

"I think I can handle that one myself," Keller said confidently. "But first, I'm going to see if there are any photos on Elisabeth's phone."

"Don't waste time on that," Mike said. "It would be great to confront Max with a picture of him coming out of his room – or going in. Or a picture of somebody else. But we can't wait. You did a good job with Ms. Barnes, but I think you need me with you when you talk to Max."

"I'll think about it."

Mike turned away. He examined a framed certificate hanging on the wall of the small office. Exceptional Service Award from Epic Cruise Lines. He wondered what administrative success had garnered Keller the honor. "I'm trying to help here. I'd be happy to conduct the interrogation myself."

"I appreciate that, Detective. I'll text you if I decide I need you."

Mike turned back toward Keller. "I'm going to try to be on vacation for a few hours. I've got a poker tournament at six o'clock, but between now and then, I'm available."

"If it was the husband, then I'll turn him over to the authorities in New York tomorrow. I'll document everything and they – you – can take it from there."

"What if it wasn't Max?"

"We'll see what's on that phone."

As Mike walked down the Promenade, he texted Michelle that he would meet her back at their cabin.

Chapter 34 – Songs and Theories

THAT AFTERNOON, MIKE AND JASON alternated between shipboard activities and trying to piece together a hypothetical series of events. As they walked with Michelle and Rachel toward their next appointment on the ship's activity calendar, Mike motioned for Jason to fall back. When the ladies were far enough ahead of them, Mike spoke softly enough not to be overheard.

"I'm still a little concerned about the prospect that Michelle might have been the target when Elisabeth was killed."

"You think that's still a possibility?"

"Could be. We know Elisabeth was blackmailing the hotel manager. We're speculating that she might have seen the killer Thursday night and tried to blackmail him, which is why she ended up dead. That makes some sense, but it's still just a plausible story. It's also plausible that the killer thinks Michelle is a threat because she examined Shirley Bloom's body. It may not make a lot of sense to try to silence her, but we have to keep that theory in play."

"Does Michelle think the same thing?"

"No, I don't think so. And I'd like to keep it that way. I think she has relaxed, now that we have an alternate theory. I don't want to let down my guard, but I can't be with her all the time. If nothing else, I'm going to be playing in the poker tournament finals later today, and I can't watch her while I'm playing."

"I'm sure she'll come watch."

"Yeah. I'm sure she will. But do me a favor and stay with her. Make sure she's safe. Don't tell her, or Rachel, that you're doing it for that reason. That will just freak them out. But do it. Be her bodyguard if I'm not there. Can you do that?"

"Sure, Mike," Jason said, without really thinking about it. It was a no-brainer. He had his partner's back, and he had Michelle's back.

At 2:00 p.m. they all sat at "their" table in the Karaoke Bar, waiting for the start of the music trivia contest, Michelle talked through the evolving theory of Elisabeth's murder.

"So, Elisabeth is cleaning up the puke in the interior room across from the Blooms' room, and she sees something. She recognizes the person who's going into, or coming out of, the cabin, but says nothing. She's had good success blackmailing the hotel manager, so she figures she can blackmail the killer. Maybe she has a photo or a video on her phone, or maybe not. That means the killer has to be a member of the crew, right?"

"That's what we figure," Jason agreed.

"Why?" Rachel asked. "Why couldn't it be some other guest?"

"You mean, besides Max?" Michelle said.

"It's hard to figure a way that's the case," Mike said, responding to both questions. "It's hard to blackmail a guest since the guest will be leaving the ship in a few days. You might get a quick payment of whatever cash the guy has on him, but once he's gone, it's hard to keep it up remotely. Plus, aside from Max, it's hard to figure a motive that some other guest has to kill Shirley."

"Do we have a good theory for why a crew member would do it?" Rachel asked the group.

"What about the ring?" Michelle looked around the table. "It could have been a simple robbery. Somebody saw her ring, saw her go into her cabin, and went in after her to steal the ring. But she fought back, and the killer ended up strangling her, then took the ring and dumped her over the balcony to make it look like a suicide. Elisabeth sees the killer come out of the room. That would fit."

"It's hard to figure a random cruise ship passenger trying to pull off a mugging like that, but I guess it's plausible," Mike conceded. "But it doesn't explain the swipe of Max's key card at twelve-eleven. Somebody who just happened to see her go into the room by herself would not have the key, and if Max went in while the killer was there, why would he not say something?"

"What if it's like *Ruthless People*?" Rachel asked. Everyone else looked confused. "You know – the movie? Danny DiVito? Bette Midler?"

"Great movie," Mike said, "but I'm not following your logic."

"What if Max went to the room and found his wife there, not dead, but roughed up by the robber, who took her ring. He figures that if he tosses her over the balcony, the police – well, the ship's security guys – will think it was a suicide, or will blame the robber. So, instead of helping her, he kills her."

"That's not the plot of *Ruthless People,*" Michelle said softly.

"Well, maybe not exactly, but it would explain how Max was there, and killed her, but somebody else stole the ring."

"That's true," Jason said, lowering his voice as their waitress came by and set down drinks, also leaving behind their four key cards, which she had collected when they gave their orders. When she hustled away, Jason continued. "We all agree that it makes no sense that Max would steal the ring, since it was his to start with, but—"

"Wait!" Mike broke into Jason's thought. "Look what just happened."

"What?" Michelle asked.

"Look at the table," Mike pointed to the small space where their drinks sat, as yet untouched. "When the waitress came and left our drinks, she put all our key cards on the table. She's always in a hurry to get to the next table, so she didn't interrupt our conversation to hand the cards back to each of us – she just dropped them."

"So?" Rachel said with a blank expression.

"So, what if that waiter in the Clipper Bar did the same thing that night? We know that Max got a drink. If Carlos laid down his card, somebody could have lifted it from the table, followed Shirley to her room, and used the card to get inside."

"But what's the motive?" Jason asked. "Still to steal the ring?"

"I guess. It's the most obvious motive."

"We still can't rule out the possibility that Max gave someone the key and paid them to knock off his wife," Michelle said.

Mike reached for his glass and took a sip. Since nobody else spoke up, he offered his take. "If that were true, then it would be most likely that he planned it before the cruise. I guess it's possible he could find somebody on the ship who would be willing to carry out a hit, but it was the second night of the cruise. He would have had to act really fast. It's possible, but more likely he would have arranged for the killer to be on board with the promise of payment when we get back to New York."

Rachel then picked up the yarn. "So, Max's hired killer goes to the room, knocks off Shirley, and decides to steal the ring while he's at it, then leaves. Elisabeth sees him and tries to blackmail him, but before he pays her off, he decides to kill her instead. That works."

Jason turned to Mike. "Is there anything about those two murders that suggests a pro?"

"Not a thing. Quite the contrary," Mike replied. "Plus, if Max was that much of a planner and hired a hitman, he would have been smart enough to establish a decent alibi while his guy was taking out his wife. It doesn't fit."

"And it doesn't explain the theater charm, or the glitter," Rachel pointed out.

"Do you have a better theory?" Michelle challenged.

"The thing that really makes the most sense is that Max killed his wife," Mike said, "which is why he doesn't have an alibi. Elisabeth saw him and tried to blackmail him, so Max had to kill her, too. It's just a coincidence that it happened in our room."

"Does Max have an alibi for the time Elisabeth was killed?" Michelle asked.

"I don't know. I told Keller that his next move has to be to interrogate Max again. If it were my investigation, I'd grill him to see if he can prove he was somewhere else. I guess I'd also try to see if the hired killer theory had any legs. He'd be in my interrogation room right now." Mike took another drink, looking frustrated.

"When does Keller plan to question Max again?" Jason

inquired.

"He's trying to hack into Elisabeth's phone first. He did work like that for the FBI, apparently. I don't think Keller is going to rush the investigation, unless he has indisputable video evidence against Max – or somebody else. Tomorrow, we'll all depart and Keller can write a report, turn it over to the NYPD, and be done with it. He said he'd text me if he needs me."

At that point, the assistant activity director stepped forward with a microphone and welcomed the assembled passengers to the music trivia contest. She explained that she would be projecting a snippet from a music video onto the screen at the back of the stage and the teams of guests would write down the song's name and artist.

When the first video came up, Mike immediately recognized the music and lyrics for "I Shot the Sheriff," the original Bob Marley version, not the Eric Clapton cover. Mike leaned over to Jason and whispered, "I killed my wife, but I didn't kill the cabin attendant."

Jason gave Mike a confused look.

"Seriously?" Mike exclaimed. "You don't get the joke? Oh, you are so freaking young!"

Michelle laughed. Rachel was as confused as Jason. Michelle reached for Mike's hand. "It's just that we're old, Mike."

Chapter 35 – Confession Time

AFTER THE MUSIC TRIVIA CONTEST ENDED, the group walked down to Deck 4. Rachel wanted to stroll through the ship's photo gallery, to see if there were any good pictures of her and Jason taken by the ship's professional photographers. To get there, they had to walk through the casino. Mike saw Lenny Dykstra back at the poker table with a group of players, sipping on a drink. As they walked past the slot machines, Michelle grabbed Mike's arm and pointed. Max Bloom was sitting at a blackjack table.

"We should talk to him," Jason said.

"Do you think Keller did that already?" Michelle asked.

"Doubtful," Mike replied slowly, the wheels turning in his head. "He looks too relaxed."

"What's the plan?" Jason asked.

"We need to isolate him somewhere," Mike said, almost to himself, "but after the last time, I doubt that he'll be all that excited to go with us."

"What if we tell him that Keller is looking for him?" Jason suggested. "He'll want to go somewhere to hide and we can tell him that we'll help."

"Why should he think we're trying to help him?" Mike mused. "We might do better if we tell him that we think we know who the killer is, but we need his help to prove it."

"A bluff?" Jason asked.

"Not really. We do need his help to establish that he's not the killer."

"Or to prove he is the killer," Jason leaned forward.

"Either way."

"Maybe we should tell Keller where Max is so he can drag the guy into an interrogation room," Rachel suggested. "Or do you still not trust him?"

"I'm not sure," Mike said. "He could be just pretending to be cooperative. And if he does question him, I'm not confident that he'll be trying that hard. I'd rather have my own shot at Max."

"What can we do to help?" Michelle interjected.

Mike thought about it, then said, "We need to get him away from that table so we can talk to him more privately. Do you think you can lure him away and out the back, toward the theater?"

Michelle didn't reply; she just took off toward the blackjack table. Mike, Jason, and Rachel circled around the slot machines, keeping eyes on Max's back as they headed to the rear exit. Mike saw Michelle lean over the large man's shoulder and say something into his ear. By the time the rest of the group reached the edge of the sports pub, which was situated between the casino and the aft elevator lobby, Michelle was walking toward them with Max trailing a few paces behind, stuffing casino chips into his trouser pocket.

Michelle passed right by Mike, flashing him a wink as she kept walking through the elevator lobby, around the corner, and through the padded doors leading to the Epic Theater. Mike and the others fell in behind Max, who was struggling to keep up with Michelle's walking pace.

When they arrived at the long corridor between the exterior doors to the theater and another set of doors leading to the audience seating area, Mike saw Michelle and Max standing in the middle of the aquamarine carpet. Max had his back to Mike. When Michelle's eyes wandered over Max's shoulder, the man spun around in surprise.

"I thought you wanted to talk privately."

"Well, it's private, but it's Mike you need to talk to." Michelle smiled and slid off to the side, taking up a position behind Mike and Jason. Rachel clutched Michelle's arm as they watched the confrontation.

"You have a problem, Max," Mike said calmly as he approached. Jason walked around behind Max, blocking any thought Max might have had about bolting toward the inner door leading into the theater.

"I don't have to talk to you," Max said, without much confidence. "Now move aside. I'm leaving."

"No, you're not," Jason used his most intimidating bad-cop voice. "We'll let you leave in a few minutes. After we have a chat."

"Like I said," Mike picked back up, "you've got a problem. We have two dead bodies on the ship, and the only person with a motive to kill them both . . . is you."

Max stood motionless, his mouth slightly open. "What do you mean? *Two* dead bodies? I don't – what?"

"So, Karl Keller hasn't questioned you again today and told

you?"

The blood drained out of Max's face. "No."

"Where were you last night between nine and eleven?"

"Last night?" Max was totally flustered and confused. "Um, wait. I don't have to answer your questions."

"That's true. You don't. But you're going to have to answer the questions when Mr. Keller asks you, and I guarantee you that he's not going to be as impartial about it as I am."

"I have a right to remain silent," Max said defiantly, recovering his equilibrium a bit.

"Yeah? And where does that right come from?"

"From the Constitution!" Max was now back at full strength.

"The constitution of what country?"

"You know damned well what country!"

"You see, Max, that's the problem. We're not in the United States. We're on a ship at sea, in international waters, and the laws of the U.S. don't apply here. This ship sails under the flag of Panama. Do you think there's a right to remain silent in Panama? The head of security has the right to interrogate you, or even torture you. He can throw you in the brig and keep you there until we get back to New York, where he can turn you over to the police. They'll charge you with at least one murder, and maybe two. Your refusal to answer the questions can and will be used against you, since you had no right to refuse. So, like I said, you've got a problem."

Max's confident and defiant expression faded quickly. "You keep talking about a second murder. I don't know anything about that."

"No? Well, let me ask you this, Max. Do you recall threatening to kill Shirley during a loud argument in your cabin on Wednesday afternoon?"

Max's face went through a cycle of confusion, concentration, and then panic. "Who told you that?"

"Max, you were yelling so loud the guests in the next room could hear you."

"Well, I – It doesn't mean anything. It was just talk."

"Maybe, Max, but it's one more piece of evidence pointing at you. So, tell me where you were last night."

Max licked his lips and stole a quick glance toward the door. "I'm not sure. I'll have to think about it."

"Think fast, Max. You see, somebody saw you go into your cabin on Thursday night at twelve-eleven, right before your wife took a dive off the balcony. And now, somebody has murdered that witness."

"Saw me? No. That's impossible. I wasn't there. Nobody could have seen me."

"Because you were asleep in a deck chair, right?"

"Yes. That's right."

"And yet, there's a swipe of your key card on your cabin door."

"It wasn't me. Somebody must have taken my key."

"Right, somebody in the Clipper Bar." Mike took a step forward. He was close enough to smell the sweat staining the fat man's collar. "So who was that, Max? Who was there with you in the Clipper Bar?" Max hesitated. He had done the same thing the last time. It only reaffirmed Mike's belief that he was hiding something. "C'mon, Max. It's not a difficult question. After your wife left to go back to the room, somebody else was there with you. Who was it?"

Max stared down at the carpet. "Nobody."

"Max, you can understand how that looks. Your wife is dead. You're going to inherit a bunch of money. And now you can spend more time with that hot blonde you've been chasing around the ship."

"I don't know what you're—"

"We saw you with Vicki, Max. Several times. You've been careless. We also know that you had a pre-nup with Shirley and you got nothing if you left her – unless she died first. So, you've got motive and opportunity. You're the prime suspect."

Max didn't say anything. He didn't try to deny that he had been in the company of Vicki Nelson.

"So, you can imagine that when the attendant who saw you in the hallway outside your cabin Thursday night shows up murdered, you're about the only person with a motive to knock her off. And now we need to determine if you had the opportunity." Mike took another half-step toward Max. Jason also stepped forward, placing his intimidating physique into Max's consciousness. "So, where were you last night?"

"I was—" Max stopped. A bead of perspiration dripped from his nose, leaving a dark spot on his shirt around his belly. The confined space and lack of air circulation in the small corridor weren't helping him. It wasn't exactly a hot box, but it served the purpose. "I was—" Then, Max Bloom collapsed onto the floor. He didn't faint; he simply sat down, his legs buckling under him as his butt hit the ground with a *thud*. "I'm gonna have to tell you the truth."

"That would be a good idea," Mike agreed. "Let's start with where you really were on Thursday night after you left the Clipper Bar."

"I was with Vicki."

"Is she one of your clients?" Mike was taking a stab, but it would make sense. Why else would a hot actress want to sleep with a load like Max?

"Yeah. She's one of my girls. I didn't want to say I was in her room when Shirley . . . died. I thought it would look pretty bad, especially since there's nobody else who can vouch for it. Besides Vicki, I mean."

Mike kept pressing. "Did you have Vicki in your stateroom on Thursday?"

"No," a confused Max replied. "We were in her cabin."

"Well, Max, it still looks pretty bad for you. You're out sleeping with a young actress, and then your wife is murdered."

"But it wasn't me! I swear!" Max was begging for the detective to believe him.

"Well, I'll withhold judgment on that, Max. Now, tell me where you were last night."

"Um, well, it was the same situation. Vicki and I were up in the rec room on Deck 14, on the big pillow under the trapeze school."

"You're shitting me!" Jason blurted out.

"Could I make that up?" Max craned his neck to make eye contact. "She's too hot to handle sometimes. She took me there because she didn't want anybody to see us. She could get in trouble for sleeping with a guest. So, we snuck up there and nobody saw us."

"What time was that?"

"I don't know exactly, maybe from about nine-thirty until about ten-thirty."

"An hour?" Jason said incredulously. "You want us to believe that you and that hottie were rolling on the trampoline for an hour?"

Max hesitated. "Well, I'm not sure. I wasn't timing it. We kinda took a little nap after, you know. So, then afterwards I went down to the Whisky Bar. You can check it out. I bought a few rounds, so I'm sure people saw me there."

Mike and Jason exchanged eyebrow shrugs. The story actually made sense, and much more so than his original alibi. The man sitting on the floor, practically having a heart attack in front of them, seemed pretty sincere.

"You know we're going to have to check out your story with Miss Nelson, right?"

"Yeah, sure," Max said confidently.

"I don't suppose you know where she is right now?"

Max gestured toward the inner door of the theater. "She's probably in rehearsal inside the theater."

"Right here?"

"Yeah. Probably." Max struggled to one knee. Mike reached out and offered his hand to help him up.

Chapter 36 – Desperately Seeking Vicki

MAX LED THE GROUP into the theater, where there was, indeed, a rehearsal in progress. Actors and dancers were on the stage, with recorded music playing in the background. Max trudged down the steps of the orchestra level, then turned and strode purposefully toward Brandon Marshall, who was standing in the middle of the row. Mike and Jason ducked into the row behind and tracked Max. Michelle and Rachel stayed in the aisle, watching.

"Brandon!" Max called out.

The director was intently watching the activity on the stage until he turned with an annoyed expression. "What is it, Max? I'm busy here."

"These men here are the police. They need to talk to Vicki."

"Great. So do I. If they find her, tell her she's up shit's creek." Brandon turned back to the stage.

"What? What do you mean?" Max stammered. "She's the lead in the show, how is she not here?"

"I wish I fucking knew! She was supposed to be here two hours ago, but she's a no-show. She had better be on her deathbed, or else I never want to see her again. I've got a show tonight and I'm running rehearsal with the understudy. Are you happy? One of your girls is getting her chance. You can go out and celebrate later – without Shirley." The two men glared at each other. "Now, if you don't mind, I've got a lot of work to do here. I'm down two cast members."

"Two?"

"Yes, two. Ricky's not one of yours, although it wouldn't surprise me if Donna or Darci somehow caused this. They were both sleeping with him."

"Together?"

"Well," Brandon hesitated, "I don't know about that part, but he certainly had his dick in each of them. I'm sure he's a poor substitute for the Big Million." Brandon turned back to his actors, leaving Max to stare at Mike, holding his hands out to his sides with the palms up in a shrug.

Mike motioned for Max to walk back toward the aisle, then escorted him back out of the theater the way they came in. "What was all that about those other actors?"

"I don't know," Max said quickly. "It doesn't matter. Just infighting among the cast. The only thing that matters is finding Vicki."

"I don't suppose you have any other ideas about where your girlfriend might be?"

"We should try her cabin," Max said, as if finding a lifeline. "Maybe she's sick."

He led the group back to the stairs, down to Deck 2, then through the crew-only door and to the crew quarters, where he knocked sharply on the door to number 239. When there was no response, he knocked again, five times, then slapped his open palm on the faux-wood surface, making a huge racket up and down the hallway.

"Seems like she's not here," Mike observed calmly.

"I can see that," Max sharply replied.

"We're going to have to take a walk up to see Mr. Keller."

"No!" Max shouted, then got control of himself and lowered his voice. "No, we can go look for her."

"I don't think so," Mike said, taking Max's arm and motioning to Jason, who took hold of the other in a firm grip. "I'm sure your alibi will hold up. We'll find Vicki. Where's she going to go on the ship, right? But we need help, and just in case your new story doesn't check out, we need Keller to know. He's the sheriff in town."

"Do we have to?"

"Yes, we do," Jason nudged Max back in the direction of the exit and the elevator lobby.

The five of them paraded up to Deck 5 to Keller's security office. Michelle and Rachel carried on a non-stop whispering discussion about the recent events as they walked. When Mike rapped on the jamb of Keller's door and the security chief saw him there with Max Bloom, he jumped from his chair and rushed forward.

"I was going to interview Mr. Bloom later today."

"Well, he's here, so we figured this would be a good time."

"I told you that I'd let you know if I needed your help, Detective. I don't recall letting you know."

"Yeah, I know. But there's been a change in circumstances."

"What's that?" Keller asked skeptically.

Over the next ten minutes, Mike and Jason briefed Keller on Max's new story about his activities on Thursday night, and that

Vicki, his new alibi, was now missing. Keller grilled Max himself until he was satisfied with the details.

Keller then picked up his desk phone and punched four numbers. He barked into the handset that he wanted a ship-wide alert for Vicki Nelson. Then he turned to the group in front of him. "Mister Bloom, I am going to personally go check Miss Nelson's cabin. If you'd like to accompany me, I can get an officer to come with us. Or you can wait in the brig, but I can't let you out of my sight under the circumstances."

"There really is a brig, eh?" Jason noted.

Mike spoke up. "Listen, Keller, you need all the officers you can spare to look for Vicki Nelson. Detective Dickson and I can act as your security detail. We'll make sure Max here doesn't wander off."

Keller scowled, but agreed. "But the ladies cannot come along."

Mike motioned for Michelle and Rachel to follow him out into the hallway. They reluctantly agreed to Keller's terms and made arrangements to meet in the Shangri-La Lounge in an hour. Michelle made Mike promise to text her if they found Vicki Nelson.

When he went back into Keller's office, Mike found Jason and the security chief in a stare-down. He wasn't sure what had happened while he was outside, but he saw the results.

Keller's shoulders slumped. He opened his mouth as if to speak, but then stopped himself. He took a deep breath, then sighed out the air before speaking. "Detective, I think I'm somewhat screwed here. If Mr. Bloom's new alibi checks out—"

"It'll check out!" Max interjected loudly.

"Yes, well, that will mean there's somebody else on board with a motive to kill Elisabeth, and I have no idea who that might be."

"Except it's likely the same person who killed Shirley Bloom," Jason said.

"I'm not conceding that point."

"Well," Mike said, "you'd better start getting used to the idea. I can't think of anything else that connects those two dots."

Keller looked ill. "If we prevent any more killings, that's the best possible outcome. I still have to explain how this happened on my watch."

Jason then piped in. "No matter what, we need to search Vicki Nelson's cabin."

"Fine," Keller said, marching toward the door without another word.

Michelle and Rachel made their way to the Shangri-La Lounge, where their favorite bartender, April, greeted them warmly and made them pina colada martinis. They sat impatiently, speculating about who the killer could be if Max's alibi proved legitimate.

After a few minutes and several sips, Rachel asked, "What did you say to Max to get him to come with you from the casino?"

Michelle flashed a sly smile. "I used the one thing that no philandering male can ignore. I told him his girlfriend had a sexually transmitted disease and I needed to talk with him in private." She took another sip from the frosted martini glass.

"Oh, you are wicked!" Rachel said, impressed. "Have you used that before?"

Michelle smiled again, and said nothing.

Chapter 37– Nowhere to Hide

K ELLER OPENED VICKI'S CABIN DOOR and went in with Mike, while Jason stayed in the hallway with Max. The space was cramped, like a two-student college dorm room, except even smaller. There was a twin-sized bed pushed up against each wall, with no more than three feet between them. A small sitting area at the far end was crammed underneath a tiny round porthole, through which a beam of late-afternoon sun lit up one wall.

Neither resident of the cabin was there, and it was not obvious which side belonged to Vicki. As they combed through the closet and drawers, a woman's voice in the hallway caught their attention.

"What's going on?" The woman burst through the door wearing a teal leotard, dance slippers, and a matching elastic headband holding back her jet-black hair. Her prominent cheekbones and the painted lips on her ebony face marked her as another actress. Mike thought she looked somewhat familiar from the performances, but he couldn't place her.

"You're Wanda, right?" Keller said. "Do you know who I am?"

"You're the security guy, right?"

"Yes. I'm Karl Keller, the head of security. We're involved in a serious investigation here and we need to talk to your cabin-mate, Vicki Nelson."

"Why? Vicki hasn't done anything." Wanda seemed quite protective.

"Cut the bullshit. I need to know if Vicki was in this room with that man out in the hallway on Thursday night, at about midnight."

"The Black guy?" Wanda asked, seeming quite interested in the idea.

"No, the fat White guy."

"I don't know," Wanda said. "But, I mean, she shouldn't get in trouble for that. C'mon, that guy is her agent, so it's not like he's just a guest, right?"

"I don't care about that," Keller said gruffly. "She's not in trouble for screwing the guest. It's something totally different. I need to know if you saw that man here on Thursday night."

"I wasn't here. We have a kind of system so that if somebody wants to have some privacy, the other one stays away. Vicki had dibs on the room on Thursday night. I got back about two, and Vicki was here alone. I don't know what happened before then."

"Did Vicki tell you who she was with that night?"

"No. And I didn't ask. But she did tell me that Max Bloom was on the cruise. She pointed him out to me."

"So, you can't say one way or the other?" Keller pressed.

"No." Wanda stood there, hands on hips.

"OK. Fine. I may need to talk to you again. Do you know where Vicki is now?"

"No. She was supposed to be at rehearsal this afternoon, but she never showed. Brandon is pissed at her. Nobody knows where she is."

"Do you have any idea where she might have gone instead of rehearsal?"

Wanda sat down on the left bed, then shook her head. "No. I don't know. She's never missed rehearsal before."

Mike asked, "Do you know whether Vicki had a charm bracelet with a theater charm on it, the one with the smiling face and frowning face?"

"No," Wanda replied quickly, "I've never seen Vicki wear a charm bracelet."

After a few more minutes of questions about Vicki's recent activities, which didn't net them any useful information, Keller and Mike left the room and allowed Wanda to close the door. They paraded back up to Keller's office on Deck 5 with Jason and Max.

"You thinking that Nelson could have killed Mrs. Bloom and left behind the charm?"

"Not anymore." Then Mike changed the subject. "What's the next step for us to find her?"

"Every officer on the ship is looking for her, so it shouldn't take long to locate her. I have people in every public venue. It's a big ship, but there aren't that many places she could be."

"So, why haven't you found the Rosario guy?"

Keller said nothing.

"Can you trace her key card swipes, like you can for a guest?" Jason asked.

"Not really. The entertainers don't use their key cards except for opening their cabin doors."

"Can you check to see when she last swiped her door key?"

Keller thought about it for a moment, then picked up the phone and called Marjorie Barnes. He requested that she check the computer records for key card swipes by Vicki Nelson. After a short wait, he grunted his understanding, then hung up. "She swiped her key card last night at nine twenty-six. That doesn't tell us much. She might have spent the rest of the night in her room, or she might have left at any time after that and not come back."

"OK. We're going to go meet up with the ladies. Will you text me when you find Miss Nelson? I assume you can handle looking after Max by yourself."

Keller said he would take care of Max, but did not promise to contact Mike.

As Mike and Jason trudged up the stairs to Deck 6, Mike tapped out a text to Ferguson. He wasn't sure how much support he could expect, but he wanted Ferguson to at least know what was happening.

When Jason and Mike arrived at Shangri-La, Rachel was practically bouncing in her chair. Before Jason even had a chance to sit down, Rachel called out, "We have something to show you."

Chapter 38 – A Photogenic Memory

RACHEL HELD OUT HER PHONE so Mike and Jason could see the photo. Michelle explained that Rachel's Squad of Texas sorority sisters showed up and joined them. The Squad girls wanted to make sure that Rachel was coming with them to see the *Chicago* performance that night. Rachel told them that Vicki Nelson was missing and that either Darci van der Meer or Donna Sher would probably be playing the role of Roxie. She mentioned that she had made friends with Darci and Donna, and they speculated about what role each might have in the shuffled cast. Rachel had shown her new friends the selfie she took with Donna and Darci during the digital scavenger hunt, and when the ladies from Texas were admiring the photo, Rachel noticed something.

"Look at Darci – the one on the right, in the green outfit," Rachel said excitedly.

Mike recognized Darci from that afternoon's trip to the Epic Theater. "She was rehearsing on the stage when we were there today."

"Yes," Rachel said.

Mike blinked. "So?" Rachel was fairly bursting with excitement, which made Mike curious and a little apprehensive. What was he missing?

"Mike, it's not about the part she's playing. The point is the ring!"

"What ring?"

"Look, Mike. See how her right arm is around my shoulder? We were trying to see if either of them was wearing a charm bracelet. We couldn't really tell, but look at her ring finger."

Mike squinted at the photo, unable to make out anything so small. Rachel grabbed the phone away from Mike and handed it to Jason. He put two fingers on the screen and spread them out to enlarge the photo, then adjusted the image to put the woman's hand in the center. He stared at the enlarged image, which was still tiny. "You think?"

"Think what?" Mike asked, feeling left out.

"We think so," Michelle replied.

"Think what?!" Mike said again, now getting annoyed.

Rachel took the phone back from Jason and stood next to Mike. She pointed to the woman's hand, and at the green ring on her finger. "We think it's Shirley Bloom's emerald ring."

Mike stared some more at the photo. "I'm not sure about that."

"Oh, Mike, you're always so skeptical!" Michelle scolded.

"Sorry. It's my nature. I'm not saying it isn't. The question is, what do we do with this?"

"We go find her!" Rachel blurted out. "That director will certainly be able to tell us where she is. Then we ask her about it."

"OK," Mike said slowly. "It certainly would be an important clue if that woman does, in fact, have Shirley Bloom's missing ring. We would need to find out where she got it, and that could lead us in some important directions. But before we confront her on this, I'd like to have a better idea of whether it really is the same ring. Where can we find a magnifying glass or something to help us get a better look at that image?"

It was Michelle who had the idea to find a person who would have a magnifying glass, and who was also an expert on jewelry. Ten minutes later, they all walked into the ship's jewelry store. There were only a few cruisers browsing the merchandise at 4:00 p.m. Jason raised his large hand and waved it in the direction of the tall blonde woman behind the counter.

Today, Helene DiVito Rosen was wearing a white tennis skirt that barely reached mid-thigh, and a halter top with a plunging neckline that no doubt had all the male customers focusing on her massive cleavage rather than the "unique" bracelets. She waved back and sauntered over to the far end of the glass display case to meet the group.

"Hello, Detective Jason Dickson!" she called out in her high-pitched Jersey accent. "Can I interest you in something nice for your lady friend?"

"Actually," Jason said, lowering his voice, "we need some help from you regarding an investigation."

She dropped her usually loud soprano to a hushed whisper. "Ohhhh! Well, I'd be happy to help you, Detective. You know I always support law enforcement. What can I do?"

Jason explained that they needed to magnify the photo on

Rachel's phone. Helene grabbed a jeweler's loupe from under the counter. Rachel produced the phone and punched up the photo, putting it down for inspection. "What are you trying to see?" their personal jeweler asked.

Rachel pointed at the green ring on Darci's right hand. "It's this ring. We think it's an emerald. I love them. Of course, I'll never have one that big."

Helene put the loupe in her eye and bent down to examine the picture. When she had raised and lowered her head a few times to find the proper focus through the magnifying glass, she stood up and looked at Jason.

"How did she get Mrs. Bloom's emerald ring?"

Mike asked, "Are you sure that's Mrs. Bloom's ring?"

"Oh sure!" she said, forgetting to hush her voice and quickly bringing a hand to her mouth. Then, in a softer tone, "Sorry. I mean, it's not like there are many square-cut eight-carat emerald rings with a full border of diamond baguettes. That's a very distinctive rock. She came in with her husband, Max, on the first day of the cruise. She said she was interested in an emerald necklace we have," she motioned to the display case behind the counter. "I remember the ring she was trying to match. I never forget a face, or a ring. I have a photogenic memory." She looked at the group, as if seeking some confirmation.

"Are you sure?" Mike asked.

"Detective Stoneman, I spoke to Mrs. Bloom for fifteen minutes. She told me a little about her husband. I have to say, just between us, that the guy seems like a bigger scumbag than my no-good dead ex-husband Nick. I'm surprised she stays with him. You know, I haven't seen her around the ship since the first day."

"Well, she's been busy," Mike said. "While we have you, can

you take a look at the photo again and tell me if the woman wearing the ring is also wearing a charm bracelet?"

After Mrs. Rosen looked again, she said, "No, I can't see a bracelet. If you need one, we have some on special today."

"I don't think we're in the market for one right now."

"Well, Detective Stoneman, if you see Mrs. Bloom – when you return her ring to her, I mean – please tell her that I still have that emerald necklace for her. OK?"

Mike promised to relay the message, preferring not to disclose that her customer would definitely not be buying that necklace.

As the group turned toward the exit, Helene motioned to Jason. "Detective Dickson. Come here for a minute."

"What is it?" he said as he turned back to the jewelry counter.

Helene handed him a business card. "Here. Take this, just in case you ever need something special for your lady. You can always call me. We should be back in Henrik's shop in New York in a month or so, I hope. She seems to like emeralds, and I can get you a good deal."

"Thanks," Jason said politely, as he turned to rejoin the others, who were already outside in the Promenade. When he caught up with Mike, Jason asked, "What's our next move?"

"We go see Karl Keller."

When they walked through the Customer Service area and rounded the corner toward the security office, Mike saw Edwin Ferguson sitting in his wheelchair outside Keller's door. The security director was standing next to Ferguson, speaking to him intently. Keller saw Mike and Jason and stopped talking.

He took two steps in their direction, saying, "That was fast."

"What was fast?" Mike responded.

"You got my text," Ferguson said as he spun his chair in their direction.

"What text?"

"I sent a text," Ferguson said, "it doesn't matter now that you're here. But if you didn't get my text, why *are* you here?"

"We have some very interesting information," Mike said, but before he could continue with an explanation, Ferguson cut him off.

"We found Vicki Nelson."

Mike immediately switched mental gears. "Where is she?"

Ferguson paused, then said, "Come into the office so we won't be overheard. And bring Doctor McNeill with you." Ferguson turned his chair and propelled himself forward, across the threshold of the security chief's office.

Mike motioned for Michelle to follow him into the cramped office. Jason and Rachel both squeezed in behind them.

"Everyone?" Keller asked, annoyed.

"Just get on with it!" Ferguson shouted.

Keller scowled, but gathered himself and spoke in a professional tone. "One of our maintenance guys found Miss Nelson's body stuffed inside a lifeboat on Deck 5."

"Body?" Mike said, surprised.

"Yes. We took the body to the morgue. It appears she was strangled, then pushed into the lifeboat. There's a door into that boat at deck level so it can be loaded for disabled and elderly passengers. The seal on the door was broken, but we wouldn't have found her except that the cleaning crew was doing routine maintenance in there today. This is obviously serious. Mr. Ferguson wants me to ask Doctor McNeill to take a look and see if she can give us an idea of the time of death."

All heads turned toward Michelle, who quickly agreed. She was glad that this time her examination would be sanctioned rather than clandestine. Keller led the group down the now-familiar route to the morgue, where three of the four storage units were now occupied.

On the walk, Mike pushed Ferguson's chair and filled him in on their discovery that another of the actresses, Darci van der Meer, apparently had the missing emerald ring. Ferguson was, obviously, quite interested in the news. Before they could have much of a discussion about the possible implications, however, they arrived at the infirmary.

Michelle pulled out the newest corpse and spent fifteen minutes examining it. This time she set her phone down on the slab and dictated into it. The cause of death was obvious to everyone who could see the body, which sported a nasty red scar nearly encircling its neck.

Michelle made her observations that strangulation was the likely cause of death and that some kind of cord or garrote was a possible murder weapon. She noted that since the body had been moved, it was more difficult to determine the exact time of death and that without a full autopsy she could only speculate. She eventually said it was likely between twelve and eighteen hours earlier.

"So," Keller said, trying to take charge, "sometime between ten o'clock last night and four o'clock this morning."

"Didn't you tell me that her last key swipe was a little after nine o'clock?" Mike said.

Keller confirmed it. "She must have left her cabin sometime after that, and then came into contact with the person who killed her."

Jason couldn't help himself. "So, this time you're not saying it was a suicide?"

Keller glared at Jason, but didn't respond.

"Do you think it could have been Max?" Michelle asked.

"Max just got through telling us that she was his alibi," Mike observed. "I don't think he'd tell us that story if he had already killed her. Plus, with her dead, he now has no alibi at all, so what motive would he have?"

Jason responded. "You always say, Mike, to never underestimate how stupid people can be."

Keller then offered his opinion. "If he was lying about being with her Thursday night, and again last night, and knew that she would not corroborate his story, then he'd be better off killing her so she wouldn't talk."

Mike shook his head. "That's what I was just saying, though. He would have had to kill her with the plan in mind that if he got the screws turned on him, he would tell us the story about her being his alibi. But at that time, he didn't know that we were going to accuse him of killing Elisabeth and that he was going to need an alibi for last night. I can't believe that he's thinking three steps ahead here and killing people off just in case."

"If not Max, then who?" Ferguson asked.

Everyone was silent for a moment. Then, Rachel said, "What about Darci van der Meer?"

Chapter 39 – Process of Elimination

KELLER LOOKED AT RACHEL like she had appeared out of thin air. "Darci van der Meer?" He was the only one in the room who had not been briefed about the emerald ring. Mike quickly filled him in.

Keller said "I very much doubt that the actress would kill Mrs. Bloom, steal her ring, and then wear it around the ship. We have more pressing issues now."

Jason was incredulous. "What do you mean? This is a critical fact and she is now a primary suspect. This has to happen immediately."

"It's possible, but Mr. Bloom is more urgent. Ms. van der Meer isn't going anywhere."

Jason clenched his teeth. A vein in his temple throbbed as if he was ready to explode, so Mike jumped in. "Do you mind if Jason chases down that angle while we go talk to Max?"

"Whatever." Keller said, waving in Jason's direction. "The main thing is that Bloom's alibi is dead, so that's going to be a big problem for him."

"I agree." Mike motioned to Jason to step outside the room. He admonished Jason to keep it together, and instructed him to send an email to Steve Berkowitz back at the precinct. Steve could run down any connections between Max Bloom and Darci. They knew that Vicki was one of Max's clients. Mike wanted to know if Darci was, also. Then, he wanted Jason to track down Darci and question her about where she got that ring – and whether she had an alibi for the times of the two murders. They arranged to meet up at 5:30, before Mike's final table in the poker tournament.

Michelle and Rachel had been hoping to slip in some pool time before the sun went down on their final day on the ship. Since Keller was not going to let them come along for the next interrogation, they left together, with a plan to meet up at 5:30 unless Mike sent a text sooner.

Ferguson looked up from his chair at Keller, who was standing a few feet away. "Karl, this situation has spiraled entirely out of control. You need to get a handle on it, and since Detective Stoneman is here and willing to lend his considerable expertise to the situation, I suggest that you take advantage of him. Any other decision would call your competence into question, in my opinion."

Mike jumped in before the two men could get into a confrontation. "Is Max in the brig?"

"No," Keller responded quickly. "I confined him to his cabin."

"So, what are we waiting for?"

Keller exchanged a glance with Ferguson, then stomped away, with Mike right behind him.

Keller turned to Mike as they rode up in the elevator. "Detective Stoneman, I want you to know that I'm not stupid.

And I'm not as much of an asshole as you probably think I am. I've never had a homicide on one of my ships, let alone three. I don't give a shit who's guilty. I care only about the safety of my passengers and the reputation of my company."

"And your own personal reputation as the head of security," Mike added. "I'm sure it doesn't look good for you when something like this happens on your watch. It could put a crimp in your plan to move up to Ferguson's position when he retires." Keller said nothing, so Mike continued. "Like I said this morning, I'm here to work with you, not against you. That work for you?"

"Fine with me."

They exited on Deck 12 and walked in silence to Max Bloom's stateroom. Keller dismissed the security officer who was standing watch in the hallway, then swiped his master key. Max was sitting on the balcony. He had two Old Fashioned glasses on the little table next to his lounge chair. One was empty, the other half-full. He swiveled his head around upon hearing the door open, then struggled out of his chair and walked back inside the room to meet Mike and Keller.

"Are you here to free me from confinement?" Max asked. Mike detected no hint of irony or sarcasm.

Mike took the lead. "We're here to ask you a few more questions, Max, in light of some new information."

"What information?"

"We'll get there," Mike said. "Why don't you sit down?" Max slumped down onto the bed, but continued to stare defiantly at Mike, emboldened by his recent alcohol consumption. "Max, you said that at the time somebody killed Elisabeth, the cabin attendant, you were with Vicki Nelson, right?"

"Yeah?" Max grunted.

"And you said that, at the time your wife went over the balcony, you were with Ms. Nelson?"

"Yes!" Max snapped.

"OK, so when was the last time you saw Vicki?"

Max furrowed his brow. "Like I told you, it was last night, at about ten-thirty."

"You haven't seen her at all since then?"

"No."

"So, you didn't meet her on Deck 5 later last night?"

"No."

"So, Max, who was it who strangled her and stuffed her body into a lifeboat on Deck 5?"

Max's defiant countenance immediately morphed into one of abject fear. The wheels in his head were clearly turning. He was wondering if this was a trick, meant to get him to admit something. He was wondering if it was true, in which case his only alibi was not only dead, but murdered. And he was considering whether he had an actual alibi for the prior night after he left the bar at midnight and went alone back to his room. He swallowed heavily, then said, softly, "Holy shit. No, I didn't know – is that true?"

"It's true, Max," Keller said. "We found her body this afternoon. You want to take a walk down to the morgue to see for yourself?"

Max sat in silence, trying to digest the significance of this news. There was only one person who might have done this, but he certainly couldn't tell the cops. It might look like he was involved. He had to talk to Darci. "I had nothing to do with it," he said. "I was with her, then I went to the bar until about midnight, then I came here and went to sleep."

"It's too bad your wife wasn't here to corroborate that," Keller said sarcastically.

"Fuck you, Keller!" Max spat out, unable to control himself. "I didn't kill my wife. An' I didn't kill Vicki. I know I'm a suspect, but I'm innocent. I didn't do it, OK?"

Mike and Keller had a stare-down with Max. Keller broke the silence. "Max, you told us you had an alibi, and now your alibi is dead. I don't think you're being straight with us. It's time for you to come clean. Is there anything else you want to tell us now, before it's too late?"

Max's eyes darted to the side, then back to Keller. "No. I got nothin' else to say."

"Fine," Keller said. "You're still confined to this cabin for the duration of the cruise. If any of my officers see you anywhere on the ship, I will put your ass in the brig. You got that?"

"Yeah, I'm already here, aren't I?"

"Max," Mike said in his compassionate, good-cop voice, "There's a killer on this ship, and he might kill again. This is about more than just you taking advantage of one of your young clients."

"Don't judge me!" Max spat out. "You have no idea how it is. These girls come to me with stars in their eyes. They expect miracles. It takes talent, hard work, and a fuckload of luck to make it on the stage. Most of 'em who have talent don't want to put in the work. Some of 'em don't even have the talent. Vicki's talented, and she works her ass off. All she needs – needed – was a break. I really liked her, and I was working *my* ass off for her."

"Fine," Mike said. "I don't know shit. But if you know anything that could help us prevent another murder and you don't tell us, then you'll be guilty of obstructing justice and being an accessory to a crime. You're not off the hook even if you didn't do it. You understand? Are you sure you have nothing else to tell us?"

"No. I got nothin' else to say." Max averted his eyes. "I'm gonna go back to my chair and my drink. Just don't turn off room service on me, OK?"

"Don't worry," Keller responded. "You can order whatever you want from room service. Just don't leave this cabin."

Mike and Keller turned and left. In the hallway, Keller said, "He's still holding something back."

"Yeah, I know," Mike agreed. "I can't imagine who he's protecting, besides himself. Do you think we should lock him up, just in case?"

"Nah," Keller said dismissively. "He's not going anywhere. He's four drinks into a bender. I'll have one of my officers check on him every half hour, but where can he go? If he's the actual killer, which I increasingly don't believe, do we think he's really going to leave his cabin and try to kill somebody else?"

"You're right. Let's see whether Jason gets any information out of Miss van der Meer."

While Mike and Karl Keller were questioning Max, Jason walked toward the Epic Theater. He had emailed Detective Steve Berkowitz, along with a lament that he was working a case with Mike, even while they were on vacation. Berkowitz replied that he should stop bitching about how tough it is to be on a cruise ship, then said he would try to get back to him before the end of the work day in New York, meaning 6:00 p.m. ship's time.

Finding Darci wasn't hard. The production company was scheduled to perform *Chicago* starting at 7:00, which was less than two hours away. He figured that she would be in the theater or nearby, since tonight was her big chance to play the lead. He was not wrong. One of the stage crew members directed him to a small room behind the stage that served as both make-up and wardrobe space. Darci was there, and she was alone. Apparently, she wanted to give herself plenty of time to prepare for her performance.

"Miss van der Meer?" he asked softly.

"Yes?" She looked up. Her makeup was already perfect and her hair, or more likely a wig, was done up in the blonde waves necessary for the Roxie Hart role.

"I'm Detective Jason Dickson, and I need to ask you a couple of questions." Jason did not feel compelled to announce his affiliation with the NYPD. Even on the cruise ship, Jason kept up his routine of dressing well. He hadn't yet changed into evening clothes, but still wore a sharp pair of gray, pleated slacks, a blue polo shirt, and black loafers. If she thought he was with the ship's security force, it was fine with him.

Darci maintained a calm face, showing no sign of alarm. "About what?"

"We're trying to find crew members who might have witnessed some events last night. This would have been between nine o'clock and eleven. Can I ask you where you were during that time frame?"

"What happened?" Darci asked innocently.

"I'd rather not say specifically. Can you tell me where you were at that time?"

Darci thought about it for only a moment before answering in an even voice, lacking any hint of embarrassment. "Well, from about nine-thirty until maybe ten-fifteen, I was having sex behind the pool stage on Deck 13."

Jason was definitely not expecting that answer. He cocked his head and hesitated before the next question. "May I ask with whom?"

"Detective Dickson, you said the reason you were asking was to determine whether I was a witness to some events. Were those events near the pool?"

"No, they weren't," Jason was compelled to answer, not having a good lie prepared.

"Well, then I guess I couldn't have witnessed them." Darci stared directly into Jason's eyes with an unwavering, yet entirely calm countenance.

"Were you there the whole time?"

"Yes, we stayed in the hot tub afterwards for quite a while. Then I went back to my cabin."

Realizing that this particular line of questioning was not likely to get him anywhere, Jason decided to switch streams. "There is one other thing. I see that you're dressed for the show tonight already, but a friend of mine spoke with you a few days ago and noticed that you were wearing a particularly attractive emerald ring. I guess that one doesn't go with the costume, eh?"

Darci hesitated, as if thinking about her answer, but her expression remained placid. "I do sometimes wear a bit of stage jewelry with some of our costumes. I think one of them might have been green, but I'm sure it wasn't a real emerald."

Jason was impressed with the young woman. If she was a complete innocent, she was remarkably unruffled under questioning. If she was hiding something, she was amazingly composed. "I will need you to tell me the name of the man you said you were with last night by the pool."

"Detective, I think that kind of information is rather private, don't you?"

"Normally, I would, but in this case the information could be quite important, so let me ask this. Was the man Max Bloom?"

Darci's eyes lit up and she sat up in her chair. "Why, yes! Do you know Maxie?"

Jason did not know what to say, or think. Max said that he was having sex with Vicki Nelson under the flying trapeze at the time when Elisabeth was murdered. He hadn't claimed it was a threesome including Darci. "Actually, yes, I know Mr. Bloom, but let me ask you one other thing. I assume you know Vicki Nelson?"

"Of course. Did they find her? Is she sick?"

"She's dead," Jason said, carefully watching Darci's face for her reaction. He saw confusion, followed quickly by shock.

"What?!" She slumped back in her chair. "I knew it had to be serious. What happened to her?"

"I'm afraid I can't really discuss it, and I would ask you to please not mention it to anyone else. The management wants to keep it quiet. But, I have to ask, did Max also have sex with Vicki last night?"

"Yes, he did," Darci said, again calmly and without any hint of shame or jealousy. She sat placidly in her chair; her eyes fixed on Jason beneath perfect lashes.

"Well, thank you for your time," Jason said, backing out of the room and closing the door behind him. He immediately kicked himself for allowing the tiny woman to fluster him. He wondered if Mike would have done any better, given her unexpected answers. She had denied having Shirley Bloom's ring, but Jason did not believe her.

He headed back to his stateroom to change his clothes before the scheduled rendezvous with Mike. On the way, he stopped by the internet café and used Rachel's Wi-Fi login to check his email. He had a message from Berkowitz. His colleague sent some cursory background information about Vicki and Darci: ages, home towns, and a brief list of stage, television, and movie credits. Probably from their websites, Jason thought. Piece of cake, but not particularly helpful. It figured that actresses would have their information readily available in case some producer or casting agent wanted to find them. The email also confirmed that both women listed their theatrical agent as Maximillian Bloom Talent.

Finally, Berkowitz's email noted that Darci van der Meer had popped up in the computer as a person of interest in a murder/suicide case from North Carolina from the previous summer. "No warrant for her arrest or anything, just wanted for questioning. Apparently, the local cops didn't consider her important enough to track down in New York."

Chapter 40 – Fatal Attraction

MAX SAT ON HIS BALCONY, drinking the third Rusty Nail of his confinement and sweating. Vicki was dead. She was his alibi. He was in trouble. But there was one other person who could give him an alibi. Could he rely on her? Would she react badly when she found out that he was fucking Vicki? Could he keep that fact from her, or would the cops tell her? Of course the cops would tell her. But what else could he do? He had to talk to Darci.

With courage provided by alcohol and desperation, Max threw on some clothes and opened his cabin door. He knew, now, that the hotel manager and the security chief could trace his key card swipes, so he grabbed his wallet from a drawer and wedged his American Express Gold card into the latching mechanism. He closed the door carefully so that it would appear to be locked, but he would be able to open it without a key swipe when he got back. He was pleased that there was no security guard in the hallway.

He walked as quickly as he could to the rear of the ship, then down the stairs to Deck 4 and around the corner into the vacant theater. He figured that Darci would be there, preparing for the upcoming show. None of the other actors would consider it unusual for him to be there, giving encouragement to his client. He was right, and one of the dancers pointed him to the make-up room. He stopped dead when he saw the hulking outline of Jason Dickson standing in the doorway, facing inside. Max ducked behind a curtain and watched until Jason closed the door and walked away. Then, once Jason had left the area, he scurried to the door and went inside without knocking.

"Maxie!" Darci said excitedly, leaping up from her chair. She ran toward him as if to give him a hug, but then stopped, realizing that she needed to protect her makeup. She gave him an air kiss, then hopped up onto the counter and crossed her slender legs. "I'm so glad you're here. I just talked to that officer. He asked me where I was last night when that little cabin attendant was killed."

"What did you tell him?"

"I told him the truth, of course; that I was with you, fucking by the pool." Darci smiled, as if having a fond memory of the event.

"You told him that?"

"Sure. It's true, and it gives you a perfect alibi. And you give me the same alibi. I told him we were in the hot tub afterwards for a while. So it's working out perfectly. Don't you see? Our plan is going so well. We're going to be so happy together when I get back to New York." Darci batted her oversized eyelashes and smiled, bringing out her natural dimples. Max was still a little tipsy, and distracted by how adorable she was in costume, but he slowly realized what she had said.

"Wait. *Our* plan? What are you talking about? And why would you need an alibi?"

"Oh, Maxie. You did it so well, giving me your key so I could take care of that shrew wife of yours, just like you said."

"Huh?" Max was genuinely confused. "I said?"

"You're so cute," Darci said, putting her index finger playfully on his nose. "You told me a dozen times how you wanted to get rid of that wife of yours and how you only needed to be free of her in order to marry me. So, we did it."

"We?"

"You and me. We're good now. We have each other's alibis, so the cops can't do anything. I took care of it. I took care of that little bitch who saw me, too. Do you believe that she tried to *blackmail* me? The nerve of her. So she got what was coming to her, and we're in the clear because we were together."

Max stood, mouth agape, watching Darci as if she were on stage.

"And I know Vicki was trying to seduce you. She thought she was so fucking special. But I knew you'd make sure it all worked out. You were so smart to set her up like that. But I knew we couldn't trust her. So, two birds, right? Now I get the starring role, just like you said I would as soon as old Vicki was out of the way. You told me what to do, and I got it done. Now I'm the star, and you're a free man, and you get the bitch's money!

"Oh, and I know you wanted to take me shopping for an engagement ring in New York, but I decided that I liked your wife's ring. It really brings out my eyes, I think. So thank you, Maxie. I love it! I'll wear it for you the next time I see you. But I think it's best if we don't try to fuck again tonight. I'll have the big cast party later after the show."

Max stared at the reflection of the back of Darci's head in the mirror and slowly absorbed the information. "I – I'm so glad you like the ring. It belonged to my mother," Max said, trying to think and talk at the same time. "Now, you go out there tonight and show everyone on this ship how hot you are and what a great singer you are. I'll make sure the world knows."

"I know you will!" Darci said, hopping back down from the counter. "We have to stay together forever now, because we did this together. I will make you sooooo happy," she purred and stroked Max's crotch with her open palm.

"We will!" he chirped in a startled, high-pitched tone. "But, you mustn't do anything that might get you in trouble with Brandon. Now, you have a great show, and I'll try to find you tomorrow to say goodbye before I get off the ship." Max backed away quickly, blowing a kiss toward Darci while he groped for the door handle. He escaped from the room and closed the door, breathing heavily.

He didn't know what to do, but he knew he needed to get his ass out of that theater. He left the way he came in, found the elevator waiting in the lobby on Deck 4, and, forgetting about the glass walls of the elevators, rode alone back up to Deck 12.

He walked slowly, in a zombie-like daze, back to his cabin. The door was still wedged open. He called room service to order a sandwich and two more Rusty Nails. He figured this would establish that he was in his room, in case anyone saw him violating his house arrest. He then paced around his balcony, trying to think.

He wasn't guilty of anything, so he shouldn't worry. He decided that he should just sit tight and keep quiet. If he told them about Darci, she would say that he was in on killing Shirley. They would believe it, since she had his key card. She must have lifted it from him in the Clipper Bar that night. If she got caught, he'd go down with her. She was crazy. She killed the maid – and Vicki. God! She killed Vicki. She'd kill him, too, if she felt threatened.

There was a knock on the door. He panicked, then realized that it was probably the waiter with his food and drinks. He ripped off his shirt and rumpled his hair, then tried to look sleepy, like he just woke up from a nap. He signed for his food and tipped the guy five dollars. The waiter would remember him. He gave an exaggerated yawn as the waiter left. Then he downed half of his next Rusty Nail in one gulp.

"All I have to do is stay calm and shut up," he mumbled to himself. "I can do this."

Chapter 41 – Variance

MIKE SAT CALMLY at the poker table in the casino. It was 6:45 and the four men and one woman who had started playing the final table of the poker tournament had been whittled down to the final three. Jason, Rachel, and Michelle sat on stools facing away from the casino bar, watching the developments at the table.

Before the game, while they grabbed a quick sandwich on the Promenade, Jason had given Mike a summary of his conversation with Darci. They agreed that there was no great rush to go back to talk to Keller, and then probably again to Max. He wasn't going anywhere, and neither was Darci. There was a free cruise at stake in the poker tournament, and Michelle was excited about the possibility of getting a do-over cruise: one without any dead bodies. So, Mike played cards, while the others watched.

Each player had started with 4,000 chips. Mike had a stack in front of him that Jason calculated to be about 6,000, out of the 20,000 total chips in play. Across from Mike, Lenny Dykstra hunched over his chips. Since his back was to Jason, there was no way to count his stack. The other player was a tall, thin guy with a goatee and a soul patch named Bruce. His wife, Terri, was sitting next to Jason and had been telling the story of how Bruce had beaten Dykstra in the preliminary round on Sunday. Dykstra must have qualified for the final table in the last preliminary round earlier that afternoon. Jason figured Bruce for about 9,000 chips, which would mean Dykstra had around 5,000.

But Rachel was anxious to get to the theater. Her Texas Squad had already left to claim front-row seats for the final performance of *Chicago*. Sue Ann had just texted Rachel, telling her that she needed to get there soon.

"C'mon, Jason. Come with me," Rachel pleaded. She was wearing her best dress, the purple number with the plunging back. He looked particularly sharp in his classic tuxedo. Michelle said he looked like a Black James Bond there in the casino, except that he needed a martini. He was obviously ready to enjoy his evening with Rachel, but not yet.

This was the last night on the ship, and Rachel wanted to have some fun. She knew that the investigation was important, and she was thrilled that she had played a part. But Mike had already said that the investigation could wait, and Mike could take care of it without Jason.

"Rachel, I'm here to support Mike. I have to stay until the game is over." Jason tried to seem sympathetic and disappointed.

"Why can't you come with me now? You've spent the whole trip with Mike."

"I have not," Jason replied, a little more defensively than he intended.

"You have! At least more time than with me. I want you to sit with us. My friends want to talk to you."

"Save me a seat," Jason suggested.

"Just come with me!"

Jason looked at Rachel, then at Michelle. He was starting to regret his agreement to watch over Michelle while Mike was unavailable. "Listen, I have to stay. He's my partner."

"And what am I?"

"Oh, come on. You have to understand—"

"I don't have to do anything!" she said, hopping off her stool. "Me and my Squad will be in the front row. You can come find us if you want to."

"Oh, Rachel—" Jason gave up as he watched Rachel saunter off toward the back of the casino.

Michelle turned to Jason and said softly, "You should go."

"You mean that if I was playing and Mike was sitting here with you, you would want Mike to leave me?"

"Yes. Mike would understand. Rachel may not, and between the two, Rachel is much more attractive."

Jason chuckled. "Well, Rachel needs to understand that there are times when she's not the most important thing."

"Maybe she should be."

Jason looked away to check out the action at the poker table.

Mike stared at Dykstra, who avoided eye contact. With the big blind level at 800, Mike had only about seven big blinds' worth of chips. Dykstra, with only about six big blinds, was in the small blind seat to Mike's left, with 400 chips on the table in front of him. Bruce, the chip leader, was in the big blind seat, with 800 chips over the betting line.

In the three-handed game, Mike was first to act and looked

down at his two hole cards – two black Queens. Mike knew from playing with Dykstra before that the ex-Met was likely to be very aggressive. Mike tried to induce a bluff by pushing out a call – the minimum bet of 800 chips.

As Mike hoped, Dykstra immediately announced himself, "All in," and pushed his stack of chips across the gold line on the table. Mike maintained his poker face. He was pleased that Lenny had fallen into his trap. He might lose, but he was pretty sure he would have the best starting hand when they flipped up their cards.

Then, to Mike's surprise, Bruce announced that he was also "All in," and pushed his stack of chips into the middle.

Mike thought about his odds for only about ten seconds. There was no second place in this tournament, only the grand prize winner. If Mike called the two all-in bets and won the hand, he would knock Lenny out, which would be satisfying in itself, and he would have a huge chip lead over Bruce. If he folded, he would be way behind whoever won the huge pot, and he would not likely have better cards again before the tournament ended. It was an easy call.

When they all turned up their cards, Mike was not surprised to see Lenny show a jack of clubs and a nine of diamonds – a total bluff. Bruce turned up an Ace and a King. When the flop hit the table with an Ace in the middle position, Mike's head dropped. Bruce's pair of Aces held up, and Bruce pulled in all the chips and won the free cruise. Mike gave Bruce a fist bump, then walked around the table to shake Lenny Dykstra's hand.

"Nice game, Lenny," Mike said. "It was an honor to play with you."

"Same to you," Lenny said, not remembering Mike's name. The former ballplayer picked up his half-consumed drink and fell into the consoling arms of his entourage.

Jason walked over to Mike. "Tough one."

Mike shook his head. "Nah. It was pretty standard. I would have done the same thing there with Ace-King. It's just normal variance. You can't get upset when you make a good play and it loses. That's probability. Now, if I had lost to Lenny, that would have hurt." Mike and Jason shared a laugh as Michelle stepped in and grabbed Mike's arm.

"I'm proud of you, Mike, even if we don't get the free cruise."

Mike then turned to Jason. "By the way, what's with the tux? You said you weren't packing your tux."

"I didn't," Jason replied sheepishly. "Rachel was disappointed that she had her purple dress, but I didn't have my tux. Sergio overheard her and arranged for a rental."

"Nice," Mike said. "Now I look like a schlub."

"No more than normal."

"Do you want to come with me to talk to Keller?"

"No. I think you can handle it. I have a more important priority." Jason winked at Michelle. "Are you coming?"

Mike waved for her to go ahead.

She and Jason then headed toward the theater. It was still a few minutes before showtime. They hurried out the rear of the casino. When they pushed through the big double-doors of the Epic Theater, they went down all the steps to the area in front of the stage.

Jason scanned the seats in the front row for Rachel. She was easy to spot in her sparkling purple dress. She was front and center, with her three friends packed in next to her. There were no empty seats in the whole row. He leaned in to give Rachel a kiss, but she turned her face and let him kiss her cheek.

"Sorry. We weren't able to save you a seat. I'll see you and

Michelle after the show," Rachel said, waving Jason out of her sight line. Michelle took his arm and led Jason to the aisle on the side of the house, then scoped out two seats in the third row. Jason took the aisle, where he could see Rachel and her friends laughing together.

"How much trouble am I in?" Jason asked, without turning his head.

"That all depends on how you handle it after the show."

"I'm going to handle it by telling her that Mike's my partner and I had to stay to support him. She has to understand that I have priorities and she has to take a back seat sometimes." Jason also planned to explain that he and Mike were worried that Michelle might still be in danger, but didn't want to say so to Michelle.

"That's your plan?" Michelle stared at him like he had announced his intention to hijack the ship.

"How should I handle it?" Jason asked as he looked over at Rachel, who was dancing in her seat with her Squad to the background music coming from the theater's speakers.

Michelle waited for him to turn his attention toward her. "What's your objective, Jason? Do you want to assert dominance and establish that you're the one in charge and she can't tell you what to do? Or do you want to apologize and acknowledge that you should have come with her in the first place?"

"Are those my only choices?"

"Pretty much," she said seriously. "Oh, you could try to skirt the line and have it both ways, but that will always fail in the long run. It's time for you to choose, Jason. Do you want a long-term relationship, where Rachel is the most important thing to you? Or is this just a fling and you don't want to relinquish any of your macho manhood on principle?"

"You're good at asking questions, Doctor. Can you give me an answer?"

"Nope. I think you're smart enough to figure it out."

"That makes one of us," Jason mumbled glumly.

Chapter 42 – Know When to Fold 'em

KARL KELLER WAS QUITE INTERESTED in Mike's report on Jason's conversation with Darci van der Meer. "So, she denies having the ring, and she says she was having sex with Max at the time of Elisabeth's murder. Where does she claim to have been when Mrs. Bloom was killed?"

"No idea," Mike replied. "I don't think Jason asked her that one."

"Why not?"

"Don't know, but Jason is a good investigator, so there's probably a reason."

"Why do you think Max didn't tell us that he had an alternate alibi?"

"I haven't figured that part out yet. Maybe he figured that if we try to pin any of the murders on him, he could always point to the possibility of another killer later."

"You think he's that smart?" Keller asked.

"I don't. But I try never to make assumptions. It's always

possible that he didn't want Vicki to know about Darci or the other way around, which would make some sense if he didn't know Vicki was dead. Either way, we need to go talk to our guy again."

Mike and Keller, along with a security officer Keller quickly enlisted, made their way to Max's stateroom. When Keller swiped them in, they found Max slumped in a lounge chair on the balcony, two empty glasses next to him on the little circular table. The sun was low in the sky, but still bathing the western-facing side of the ship with warm rays. Max appeared sunburned and drunk when he turned toward his visitors.

"Ah, mah fav'rite cops," he slurred. "Come back to h'rass an innocent man s'more?"

Mike stepped into the space between Max and the sun, casting a shadow over the man's ruddy face. "Max, we have a problem."

"Yer problem, then," Max said, squinting at Mike's silhouetted figure.

"We had a talk with Darci van der Meer." Mike stopped to watch Max's reaction, which was about what he expected. The man's eyes widened and he took in a quick breath, while his hands clenched the sides of his lounge chair. "Darci told us that last night, when Elisabeth was murdered, she was having sex with you."

This time, Max did not seem surprised. He looked embarrassed.

"You told us you were having sex with Vicki Nelson, who is now dead. Now, why would you say you were with Vicki if you were with Darci? What about it, Max? Who else but you, and maybe Darci, would have a motive to kill Vicki? How do you explain all this?"

Mike stopped talking and waited for Max, who gazed blankly out at the open ocean. He was thinking. Mike was fine with that. He figured the man was trying to come up with a story that would explain all these facts in a way that didn't incriminate him. In his state of inebriation, it might take him a while.

After a stretch of silence, Mike decided to try a bluff. "There's another thing, Max. Darci, it turns out, is in possession of an eight-carat, square-cut emerald ring with a circle of diamond baguettes. And do you know where she told us she got it?" Mike paused to let Max squirm. "She says she got it from *you*, Max. So, why did you give Darci your wife's ring? The one you said you didn't know where it was. Why did you lie to us about that, Max?"

"I don't b'lieve you," he said.

Mike nodded. It was a good answer. It could be he thought Mike was lying – which he was. It could be that Max knew Darci had the ring, but didn't believe she would tell the cops. It could be that he knew where the ring was, and Darci didn't have it. In any case, if Max was trying to hide something, it was smart to not accept Mike's bluff. Of course, if he were really innocent, he might have said, "That's impossible," or, "I didn't lie to you."

Max was now visibly sweating. Mike had seldom seen a suspect who looked more nervous about being questioned. He had one more bluff to play. "And there's one more thing, Max. Your little sex toy, Darci, told us that she has a knife with your fingerprints on it."

"She does not!" Max yelped, sitting forward in his chair, then slumping back against the nylon mesh.

"She doesn't what, Max?" Keller said, not content to let Mike have all the fun.

Max was silent. Then, he turned toward Keller. "She doesn't

have any fucking knife with my fingerprints, unless she's setting me up."

"Why would she set you up?" Mike pressed.

Max dropped his chin to his chest and started to cry. Mike let him sob softly, waiting for his next words. No need to rush the man. After a minute, Max composed himself, then raised his eyes toward his two accusers.

"OK. This has to stop. I'm being framed here by that crazy bitch, Darci. It was her. She did it. She stole my key and killed Shirley. She's batshit crazy. She thinks I love her and I'm gonna marry 'er, so she killed Shirley!"

"Why would she think you were going to marry her?" Mike asked.

Max sniffed and tried to compose himself. "Well, y'know how it is, Detective. I might've told her that I was gonna leave my wife someday. She was *hot*. I wanted to fuck her. I fucked her a lot. I prob'ly told her that maybe someday I'd marry her. OK. I'm an asshole, OK? But I didn't kill my wife! She did it. An' she took her ring. She told me. An' she killed that housekeeper too, and Vicki. She's fucking crazy."

"Is it true that you fucked her by the pool last night?"

"Yeah. I did," Max said, a bit proud of himself. "I fucked Vicki, then I fucked Darci."

"And we're supposed to believe that?"

"It's fucking true! I don't care what you believe. I'm done lyin' here." Max stood up slowly from the chair and leaned unsteadily on the balcony railing. "I'm not proud of what I did with those girls. I really was trying to get 'em jobs. I love 'em all. Some of 'em were even talented, like Vicki. Sure, I slep' with them. Were they gonna fuck me if they didn't think it was gonna help make 'em stars? Ha! I know. I can look in the mirror. An' so after a bit

I tol' 'em that I was gonna leave Shirley, and if they thought that they were my girl and that I'd marry 'em then who was I to tell 'em otherwise? But I sure didn't kill Vicki, an' I didn't kill Shirley!" Max wobbled in place, trying to focus on the two men in front of him.

Mike nodded his head and said, "Max, I believe you."

"Ya should b'cause it's the fuckin' truth!" Max slurred back.

"I do. It's actually the only story that makes sense. Why didn't you tell us about Darci taking your key card from the beginning? You were holding back like you were protecting her. That's what it looks like. You were worried we'd figure out you were both involved."

"I wasn't!" Max pleaded. "I didn't want you to know I was fucking Darci and Vicki. I knew that would make me look bad – like somebody who'd want to kill his wife. I didn't know what she'd say, so I kept quiet. But she did it. Alone!"

Mike stared Max down until he turned away. "The problem is that you have no proof, and we have no evidence tying Darci to any of the murders. She has a motive to kill Elisabeth, but only if we assume that she also killed Shirley and that Elisabeth saw her."

"She did!" Max blurted out, interrupting Mike's thought. "She said that! She said the housekeeper was blackmailin' her an' that's why she had to kill her." Max was becoming more coherent and less inebriated the longer he stood up and breathed in the sea breeze.

Mike shared a glance with Keller. Max could only know about the blackmail if he were telling the truth about his conversation with Darci – unless Max was the one being blackmailed.

"OK, Max. Let's assume that's true. Can you prove it? Do you have anything other than your own testimony that can prove it was her, and only her, and that you weren't in on it all along? You stand to gain here, Max. It looks a lot like you gave her the key, then went off to establish an alibi while she did your dirty work for you. Then, maybe, Darci got out of control. Maybe you didn't figure on her having to kill Elisabeth, but maybe you set up Vicki. Maybe you used her to establish an alibi, and then had Darci kill her, too. It's still pretty bad for you, even if you're trying to throw her under the bus now. Maybe she's guilty. But maybe you're also guilty. That's the way it looks to me."

It took Max a few moments to absorb Mike's words. Then he hung his head and mumbled, "What the fuck am I supposed to do? Huh? I have no evidence. I can't prove anything. I just know I didn't do it. And now I'm fucked." Max stumbled away from the balcony and back inside the room, collapsing face-first onto the bed.

"You think he's dead?" Keller deadpanned.

"I think he'd like to be," Mike responded. "I've seen guys go down hard because of a woman, but this is perhaps a new low. You think he's finally telling us the truth?"

"Yeah, I do." Keller looked down at the pathetic lump on the bed in front of him. "Like you said, it's the only thing that really makes sense. This guy is no cold-blooded killer. Hell, if he had tried to throw his wife over the rail she probably would have kicked the shit out of him and tossed him over instead. I don't know Darci van der Meer, though. You think there's any chance she's that much of psycho?"

"Never underestimate how crazy people can be," Mike said seriously. "We got a report back from our colleague in New York that Darci is a person of interest in connection with a murder/suicide case in North Carolina from last summer. It may be nothing, but it's suggestive."

"So, let's assume he's telling the truth. How do we get something we can use to pin this on the girl? Should we search her room?"

"That's a good start," Mike agreed, "but if she's as cool a customer as Jason told me, I kinda doubt we're going to find a bloody knife there."

"Yeah, well. One of the nice things about a ship at sea, for a killer, is that it's pretty easy to dispose of a murder weapon over any nearby railing," Keller lamented.

"Well, we should go take a look."

"And if we don't find anything?"

Mike thought for a moment before saying, "If we were in New York, I'd haul 'em both into interrogation rooms and play them off against each other. Try to get her to throw him under the bus, or maybe slip up and admit something. It would be even better to get them both in the same room. Of course, they'd both have to waive their rights."

"Not here," Keller said with a smile.

"Oh, yeah. International waters. No right to remain silent and no right to an attorney. But we don't have much time. When and where?"

"Let's go search her room. If we don't find anything, then I have an idea."

"I guess you don't need a warrant." Mike fell into step behind Keller.

Chapter 43 – He Had it Coming

MIKE AND KELLER SPENT FIFTEEN MINUTES combing through the drawers and shelves in Darci's cabin, but found only clothes, makeup, and some basic jewelry. Mike even extracted a plastic storage container from under the bed. He inspected the toes of all her shoes and unrolled every pair of socks. The place was so squeaky clean that Mike likened it to a federal safe house. No diary, no notes, no computer, no phone or camera. Mike found a charm bracelet in a large box on Darci's dresser where she kept a variety of necklaces, earrings, and rings, but he couldn't say at a glance whether there was a gap where a missing charm might have been. He bagged the bracelet and kept searching.

They didn't find the emerald ring, which puzzled them, since she certainly wasn't wearing it during her performance. Mike speculated that it might be in her dressing room.

"They only have cubbies in the wall for their stuff," Keller told him, "but it's possible she has it there."

"Where else could it be?" Mike mused.

Keller walked to the cabin's small closet and peered inside. "I guess it's too obvious that she would put it in her safe."

"Elisabeth didn't keep her secret stash in the safe."

"Probably because she knows we sometimes conduct random searches."

"Must be nice not to need a search warrant," Mike said with a tinge of jealousy.

Keller found the two safes tucked away in the back of the room's single closet. He opened the first with his master code and determined by the passport inside that it belonged to Darci's cabin-mate. Then he opened Darci's safe and rummaged around, emerging with a passport, a cell phone, and a small, heart-shaped ceramic dish with a lid.

The dish was painted with flowers and jingled as he carried it to the room's small desk for inspection. While Mike watched, Keller removed the lid, then dipped inside with a latex-covered hand and pulled out a glimmering emerald ring. It was a square with four notches, one along each side, surrounded by a meandering ribbon of white gold inset with a line of diamond baguettes. He held it up to the light, then turned it upside down and squinted at the underside.

"There's an engraving: MB."

"B for Bloom," Mike said. "I think Max said the ring had belonged to his mother, so that could fit."

Keller pulled out a plastic bag and dropped the ring inside. Then he examined the rest of the contents of the little ceramic dish. There were four other rings inside, each very different. One was a single diamond in a Tiffany setting that seemed like an engagement ring. One was a large opal. One was a complex, tri-color gold pattern of twists and loops. One was a man's square pinky ring with an onyx stone. Keller put the dish, along with the other rings, into another evidence bag and stuffed both bags into his jacket pocket.

"Shall we take these and have a discussion with Miss van der Meer after the show?" Mike asked.

"Why wait?"

Mike raised an eyebrow. "Why indeed?"

They left the cabin and walked up to the exterior area on Deck 4. Max sat glumly in a deck chair, with one hand hanging down toward his back. Keller took out a pocket knife and cut the plastic zip ties that were securing Max's ankle to the mesh of the chair and his wrist to a standpipe. They wanted Max along for the confrontation with Darci. They could have put him in the brig and brought Darci there, but Keller wanted to surprise her and not give her a chance to think about what she was going to say. They needed Max with them, and Max, for his part, was happy to oblige. He was sobering up by the minute, and he completely understood the trouble he was in. Getting a confession out of Darci was about his only hope.

Keller extracted the bag with the emerald ring from his pocket and showed it to Max. "Recognize that?"

"My mother's ring!" Max exclaimed. "Did Darci have it?"

"Looks that way. Can you tell me what the inscription is on the underside?"

"Yes. Her name was Margaret Bloom. Her initials are engraved on the bottom of the setting."

"We have a winner," Mike said. "Of course, it's possible that Max gave her the ring, if the two of them were working together."

"I wouldn't! I didn't! We weren't!" Max called out. He was definitely more coherent than twenty minutes earlier on his balcony. Mike figured he was telling the truth at this point, but there was still room for doubt.

So, the three of them walked back inside and found the side stage door of the theater. Keller pulled out a small radio unit and organized his officers. Keller had seen the show several times, and had a plan. Mike was happy to let the ship's chief of security lead this operation.

They entered the dark backstage area, which was teeming with actors and dancers scurrying to their next mark. Some were engaged in costume changes right there in the wings. A half-dozen stagehands and technicians were also moving purposefully around the crowded space. None of them took much notice of the three men.

The show was more than halfway done. They moved off to the side, where they were out of the way of the crew and could see onto the stage. Roxie Hart was singing "Me and My Baby," and she was owning it. She strutted around the stage, giving the audience all the emotion she could squeeze out of the song. Mike was impressed. He thought Darci could actually be a Broadway actress, and it would be a shame if she turned out to be a psychotic killer.

As the song continued, Mike looked across the stage to the wings on the far side. He saw two uniformed security officers standing there, blocking Darci from exiting in that direction. Once again, Mike marveled at how fast these uniformed officers could materialize, despite never being visible to the ship's passengers. He peeked around the curtain toward the audience and saw two more officers, who had taken up positions at the base of the stairs on either side of the stage.

Keller was standing closest to the edge of the curtain. He loosely held the bag containing the emerald ring, which dangled at the bottom of the plastic beneath his hand. The gems glinted under the stage lights.

Darci had finished the next-to-last stanza of her song. She turned to strut from the far side of the stage to the middle, where she would finish up. As she turned, she saw the three men, and recognized Max. She could see a green sparkle in a baggie held by the man next to him. The audience could not see her full face, which was turned with her left profile to the house. She looked directly at the three men. Mike saw a flash of defiance, or maybe resolve, for only a moment. Then she turned back toward the audience and soared into the ending of her number.

The crowd broke into waves of enthusiastic applause, while Darci soaked it in. When the clapping reached its crescendo and started to recede, Darci walked quickly off the stage – right toward Max. She was totally focused on her role, looking at the audience and smiling all the way into the wings. When she finally stepped behind the curtain, Keller held out an arm to block her from passing them.

"Excuse me!" she snapped, like the star of the show who was being inconvenienced, "I need to get ready for the next scene. I have a costume change."

"I'm sorry, Miss van der Meer," Keller said softly. "We have a situation and need to speak with you immediately. You have ten minutes before the next scene, and we just need you for one." He reached out a hand and grasped her arm above the elbow. "Let's move back away from the stage." He guided her into an alcove next to the exit door, where there was one overhead light, allowing them to see each other better.

Darci turned to Max and said, "Maxie? Is everything alright?"

"It's not. They found Vicki. She's dead."

"I *know*," Darci said with what seemed like genuine sadness.

"It's so sad. Did they figure out what happened?"

Mike watched her closely. He had thought Jason exaggerated how cool she was under questioning. Apparently not. She was behaving exactly as an innocent person would behave. Except, he thought, an innocent actress in this situation would be far more concerned about being interrupted in the middle of her performance.

"We did," Keller said. "She was murdered."

"Oh, my!" Darci brought a hand to her mouth.

"Cut the crap," Keller said sternly. "Max here has told us everything. We know that you killed Shirley Bloom – and Elisabeth Rodriguez. We found evidence that Elisabeth was trying to blackmail you because she saw you the night Mrs. Bloom was killed. And Max told us how you tried to use him to get yourself an alibi."

Again, Mike watched intently for any reaction from Darci. He saw nothing. She had a poker face he would not want to play against. While it was impressive, he again observed that it was not at all the reaction he would expect from an innocent person who was being accused of a double homicide. She was just ice. He guessed she would say later that she was in character. She was an actress. The absence of a reaction could not be deemed evidence of guilt. But Mike was sure now that Darci was their killer. He could feel it.

"Carlos, in the Clipper Bar, remembers you being there with Max. We know you took his key card. We know Elisabeth saw you go into the cabin that night. But you made one other mistake," Keller continued. "You took this." He held up the plastic bag, the emerald ring flashing brightly under the single ceiling light. "Max says he never gave you the ring. In fact, Max tells us that he never planned to actually marry you."

There was a momentary flicker in Darci's frosty shell. Mike saw her eyes dart in Max's direction. Max looked away, ashamed of himself, but effectively admitting that what Keller said was true. She then stared back at Keller, but said nothing.

"We noticed that the ring was missing the night Shirley Bloom died. Max didn't have it. We searched his room. The only way you could have it is if you took it from her the night you killed her. Did you take it off her finger before or after she was dead?"

Before Darci could make any attempt to respond, a tall woman with a long black ponytail rushed up to the group. She wore a headset with a microphone that curved around in front of her mouth, and all black clothes to be less visible around the stage area. She swooped in and grabbed Darci by the shoulder.

"Darci! You're up!" She pulled her away so fast that neither Mike nor Keller could stop her. Darci and the stage manager hurried back toward the stage.

Keller yelled, "Wait!" and rushed after them, but Darci had two steps on him, and the other woman was now between him and Darci, pushing the actress forward. The stage manager stopped; Keller crashed into her, sending them both toppling to the hardwood floor.

Mike jumped in their direction as soon as Keller moved, but he was also too slow to catch Darci, who kept walking right back onto the stage. The actor playing Amos was nearly done with "Mr. Cellophane." Darci strode to center stage and began dancing with Amos. The actor, to his credit, never missed a note and kept performing despite the highly irregular improvisation. Mike stopped short, not wanting to rush out onto the stage and knowing that Darci had nowhere to run.

Max lumbered over to where Mike was standing. Keller was

engaged in a heated but hushed discussion with the stage manager, who then gave sharp instructions through her microphone to her two assistants.

When the number ended, Amos stood downstage on his normal mark, with his arm around Roxie, as they absorbed the applause. Then, Amos turned and walked off toward the opposite side of the stage, leaving Roxie alone as the orchestra, in its elevated box to the left of the stage, struck up the music that accompanied a scene change.

A large, semi-circular portion of the stage started to spin on a turntable, changing the set into a courtroom with a judge's bench and tables for the prosecution and defense. The stage manager had given instructions to the crew to stay off the stage and not complete the set change. She was, at that moment, telling the conductor to keep the music playing until the set was fully changed, no matter how long it took. Meanwhile, one of her assistants was on the other side of the stage, frantically trying to wiggle Donna Sher into the costume Roxie was supposed to be wearing for the next scene.

Darci turned toward the men standing off-stage and extended her slender arm toward Max. "My Maxie," she said softly.

Mike motioned to the stage manager, pointing his thumb up, wanting her to turn up the volume on Roxie's microphone. He wanted whatever she said to be captured on the video that was undoubtedly being recorded for the ship's "yearbook." The woman barked into her headset and Darci's voice became much louder.

"Maxie. I love you. How could you? You love me, too." She took two steps toward Max, then stopped. "But, you don't, do you? You don't love me. You just used me. You *lied* to me!"

She took several more steps, putting her only ten feet or so from Max, who was shielded from the audience by a thick wing curtain. Darci then turned and walked toward the newly arrived courtroom furniture. She grabbed a small handgun from the prosecution's table: the murder weapon that Roxie Hart had used to kill her lover.

Mike figured it for a .22 – a Saturday Night Special, suitable for a woman's purse. Even if it were real, such a small gun wouldn't do much damage at a distance. But at close range, it could still kill. She carried the gun back to the middle of the stage and looked out over the audience.

Mike turned to Keller. "That's just a prop gun, right?"

Keller furrowed his brow and didn't immediately answer. "Probably," he finally said.

"What do you mean, *probably?* It has to be, doesn't it?"

Keller licked his lips and scratched his chin. "She's crew, which means she does have access to a firearm."

"Fuck," Mike said, "the lifeboats?"

"Right." Keller stared at the gun in Darci's hand.

"Does that gun look like the kind that the crew might have?"

Keller shook his head. "I can't tell for sure."

Then Darci did something that neither of them anticipated: She started singing. She launched into a song her character was supposed to sing later, near the end of the show, and the band followed her. Mike guessed that the musicians simply couldn't help themselves.

As Darci sang "Nowadays," she wandered around the front of the stage, holding the pistol, moving ever closer to where Max was standing. Then she stopped singing and turned toward Max.

"You should have loved me, Maxie."

The sound of the gunshot exploded around the theater, eliciting a collective gasp from the audience. Max Bloom staggered forward, grabbed onto the curtain, and then slid down to the floor, exposing his torso and head to the audience. A dark stain formed on the front of his shirt, around the left shoulder.

Mike leapt from behind the curtain and out onto the stage without thinking. He immediately squinted into the blindingly bright stage lights shining in his eyes. He held his left arm out in front of him, palm out toward Darci. The audience did not immediately react to his sudden appearance, but after a few seconds, he heard a woman's voice cry out, "Oh my God – that's Mike!" It sounded like Rachel, but he didn't have time to think about it.

"Darci!" Mike called out, "you need to think for a minute."

Mike glanced behind himself toward Keller, who had his radio up against his face, presumably giving instructions to his officers. He took a step toward Darci, very slowly. She was still holding the pistol out in front of her, pointed at Max's prone form. She did not immediately acknowledge Mike's voice.

"Darci! Darci! Look at me!" Mike called out, trying to be both loud and calm. He was happy when she turned her head. He was not excited about the fact that she was now pointing her gun at him. "Let's put down the gun now, Darci. You got Max. He's paid for what he did to you. It's over now. There's nobody else who needs to die today."

Darci stared at him and held the gun steady. "Who are you?" She asked, her voice still amplified by her body mic.

"I'm Mike," he said as calmly as he could. He realized that it had been Keller and Jason doing all the questioning that day; Mike had been there backstage, but she didn't know who he was. "I'm a friend of Rachel's." He had no idea whether that would make any sense to Darci, but it was all he could come up with so quickly.

"Rachel?" Darci said quizzically.

"Yes. You know her. She's a dancer."

Darci still held the gun straight out with an unwavering arm. She was strong, and still cool. She seemed to be thinking, so Mike kept talking. "Max is the guy who hurt you. He's the one who cheated on you and lied to you. Now he's dead. You killed him, Darci. He had it coming, right?"

Mike wracked his brain for the contents of the show, which he had seen on Broadway several years earlier. Darci was on stage and in costume, so he figured it couldn't hurt to play to that. "It was self-defense, right? You'll get Billy Flynn to take your case. He'll get you off, then you'll get to sing again, at the end of the show. So, you're OK, Roxie. You can put down the gun now – you don't want the cops to find you holding it when they get here, right?"

Darci lowered the gun slightly, now pointing it at Mike's feet. Over her shoulder, Mike saw the two security guards from the far side of the stage creeping across the hardwood toward Darci's back. Mike forced himself not to look at them so that Darci would not be tipped off. He kept talking, hoping that they would get to her quickly.

"You did great tonight, Roxie. You were the star and you shined. The audience loved you. You heard the applause, didn't you? They love you. You're finally getting to be the star. You're so much better than Vicki."

The nearest guard was almost there. Then, a female voice from the audience shouted, "Look out, Roxie!"

Darci spun around, just as the guard jumped at her. He hit her mid-rib. She twisted her body, causing the guard to spin off like a free safety missing a tackle on a running back. Before she could catch her balance, the other guard lunged, knocking her onto her back. Her right arm stretched out behind her head at the front of the stage, pointed toward the audience and only a few feet away from the footlights.

Mike sprang forward. Keller ran out from the wings. The guard who had knocked Darci down looked up. The gun had slipped out of her hand when she fell, but it was only a few inches away. They both reached for the gun, but Darci got there first, immediately followed by the guard's hand.

Another loud shot rang out through the theater as a flash expelled from the muzzle of the little pistol. The crowd gasped collectively. Mike saw a flurry of movement and heard a scream, but could not see beyond the edge of the stage because of the lights in his eyes.

He kept running until he reached Darci. He fell onto her left arm, then lunged toward her right hand, where the guard was struggling to secure the gun. Moments later, Keller arrived and jumped on the woman's legs. Once she was fully secured, Keller reached into his jacket pocket and extracted two plastic zip ties. He bound her ankles together, then the three men rolled her over and tied her wrists behind her back.

The orchestra had stopped playing. The stage crew flooded forward. An amplified voice came over the sound system, instructing the audience to please calmly evacuate the theater.

Half the house applauded, thinking that it was all part of the show, but the applause faded as the cheering guests realized that what they had just seen was not acting. Several people were taking video with their phones and pushed forward, rather than moving toward the doors in the back. Keller motioned toward his officers to clear out the theater.

The spotlights on Mike went out abruptly, allowing him to see beyond the stage. A clump of people were huddled around something on the floor in front of the first row of seats, but Mike couldn't make it out. He stood up, leaving the officer who was still hovering over Darci's back to keep her under control.

Mike ran back to where Max Bloom was lying on the floor next to the wing curtain and called out to anyone within earshot for a medic. He bent down next to Max and was happy to hear him groaning. Max had definitely been shot, but he was also definitely alive. Mike looked toward the side door next to the stage, hoping that help would burst through at any moment. Instead, it came from behind him.

"Get out of the way, Mike," he heard Michelle's voice say. She pushed his shoulder and sent him slowly tumbling to the floor. She was in full doctor mode and ignored Mike as she examined her patient, determined the site of the gunshot, and put pressure on the wound to stop the bleeding. Max groaned at the pain.

"Kinda strange for you to have a patient who's alive, huh?" Mike said.

"Like riding a bike," Michelle quipped back. She talked to Max, telling him that everything was going to be fine and keeping him from passing out, until a team of paramedics arrived and took over.

Mike stepped back, looked around, then heard someone calling his name from the direction of the seating area. He squinted in the direction of the voice and saw Rachel, still wearing the fabulous purple dress, waving her bare arm in his direction. He hurried to the edge of the stage.

"Jason got shot!" she yelled up at him. "Get one of those EMTs over here now!"

Mike spun around and ran back to where the paramedics were working on Max. He announced that he was NYPD and that someone from the audience had been shot and needed *immediate* attention. A moment later, he followed one of the EMTs down the stairs at the side of the stage and into the pit between the stage and the front row, where a clot of people was still gathered. The EMT yelled at them to move away as she pulled out her first aid pouch and knelt down next to Jason, who was lying on his back. His eyes were open. He saw Mike and smiled.

"I'm OK, Mike. It just grazed me."

The EMT examined the wound on Jason's left triceps. She yelled, "Who wrapped this up?"

Rachel leaned down and said, "I stopped the bleeding, but he's going to need some disinfectant and antibacterial treatment."

"You a tech?" the woman asked.

"Yes."

"Nice work." The EMT returned to her patient, unwrapping the multicolored silk scarf that Rachel had wrapped around the wound and tied off. Under the scarf was the white handkerchief that Jason always had in the pocket of his suit jacket. The rental tux jacket was lying in a heap underneath one of the seats in the front row. The EMT asked Jason whether he could sit up, which he did, shifting his arm into a position that was easier for the medic to attend to.

Mike pulled Rachel away a few steps, seeing that Jason was in good hands and not seriously hurt. "What happened?"

"He took the shot," she said, the emotion of the moment finally piercing her professional EMT exterior. She leaned on Mike. "I was there in the front row, watching the show. I saw you come out and I knew something was wrong."

"Was that you who shouted my name?"

"I guess," Rachel said. "When Roxie – um – Darci fell down

with the gun pointing out, Jason ran down here and jumped in front of me. He was trying to get me to move when the gun went off. He could have been killed."

"I doubt it," Mike said soothingly. "It's a small-caliber pistol. Unless he took it right in the eye or something, it wasn't going to kill him. It looks like it was a glance. I'm glad it didn't hit anybody else."

"Oh, Mike, how can you say that when Jason is injured?"

"Because he's fine," Mike said, smiling. "If I give him too much sympathy, he'll be insufferable."

Rachel couldn't help cracking a smile.

"You go stay with him. He may need someone to give him some love and attention tonight."

"I think I can handle that," Rachel said. She turned back to Jason, leaving Mike standing next to the stage and watching the surge of activity. Rachel's Squad of Texas sorority sisters was still there, all crowded around and telling Rachel how brave Jason was and how lucky she was to have such a hero.

Keller came down to the foot of the stage and squatted down to be closer to Mike's eye level. "I don't suppose you want to come back and help me write up the report on this?"

"Not a chance in the world," Mike said with a wide smile.

Chapter 44 – Endings and Beginnings

THAT NIGHT, MIKE HAD a good deal of explaining to do. The two couples were crowded around a table in the Shangri-La Lounge, where April was keeping them supplied with a steady flow of pina colada martinis and Zacapa 23. Since they had missed their planned dinner, April arranged for an array of appetizers to accompany their drinks.

Mike gave everyone a summary of his cooperative investigation with Karl Keller, Max's confession, finding the emerald ring, and the plan Keller hatched to confront Darci, with Max there, while the show was in progress and she was the most vulnerable.

"It was a pretty good idea," Jason observed. "I'm surprised he thought of it."

Mike nodded. "I'm not sure I would have come up with it on my own."

"You're too nice," Jason said, "that's why I always have to be the bad cop."

Mike kicked out a leg, grazing Jason's shin. "You're so full of shit."

When Mike was done, Michelle and Rachel each gave their individual perspectives on the evening's events. Rachel alternated between participating in the conversation and watching the six videos that had already been posted on Instagram of the amazing events on the stage of the *Colossus of the Ocean*. She advised the group that #CruiseShipShootout was trending on Twitter.

In between videos, Rachel explained that she cried out when she saw Mike, and then Jason appeared out of nowhere and jumped in front of her just as crazy Darci fired her gun. She snuggled up against Jason's right arm at the end of the story, laying her head on his shoulder. Jason's left arm was in a sling, provided by the ship's doctor. All of Rachel's Squad of new friends had been swooning over Jason's act of heroism – literally taking a bullet to protect Rachel.

Jason was remarkably reticent about giving his perspective on the events. He did not have a clear memory of the moments after a .22-caliber bullet bore a tiny hole in his tux jacket, then dug a small trench across his left triceps before embedding itself in the corduroy fabric of the seat next to Rachel's. The young woman who had been there during the show had the good sense to jump out of her seat and head for the aisle as soon as the crazy lady shot the fat guy on the stage.

Rachel's EMT training kicked in as soon as she saw Jason fall to the floor, holding his heavily bleeding arm. She would have done the same thing if it had been a total stranger who saved her life, she said. She had forced Jason to stay on the ground, even though he kept insisting that he was fine and it was just a scratch. Mike commented on how amazing it was that she managed the whole process without getting any blood on her nice dress.

At 11:00, Millie and Edwin Ferguson arrived. After praising Rachel and Michelle for their performance as first responders, Ferguson briefed the group on the hour he had spent with Karl Keller and the ship's captain, talking on a satellite phone with the head of corporate communication for Epic Cruise Lines, the company's general counsel, and the CEO.

Jason noted that the ship's customer service team had done an amazing job of taking care of him and making him feel appreciated. They all offered apologies and regrets and announced that he and his whole party would receive a free future cruise – in suites. He had declined to sign the liability waiver they pushed subtly in front of him along with his written statement about the events of the evening. They were real pros – at protecting the corporate ass.

Ferguson explained that the law of the sea applied to the incident and that there was a full waiver of liability built into their tickets of passage. But the company certainly would take good care of the hero cop who was shot by a psychotic member of the ship's crew.

Keller had done a brilliant job of deflecting blame from himself and claimed that he had taken full advantage of the assistance offered by the NYPD detectives who happened to be on the ship. He also credited Dr. McNeill, who was the first one to suspect that they had a killer on the ship. He took full responsibility, and all the credit, for tracking down the killer and preventing any more murders.

"Nice," Mike said. "He can have the glory and the publicity. I only wish it had been him out there on the stage with the psycho bitch."

"Mike!" Michelle scolded. "She's clearly mentally disturbed. She is sick. You shouldn't call her psycho, or a bitch. It is demeaning to women. Right, Rachel?"

"Uh huh," Rachel agreed.

"She's batshit crazy," Michelle added with a smile, "but she's still a woman."

Everyone laughed as April appeared with a Zacapa 23 for Ferguson and a pina colada martini for Millie. Mike had not seen them order anything, but April was good.

"Where's Max?" Mike asked.

"He's back in his stateroom, resting," Ferguson said. "The doctor patched him up. The little bullet lodged in his clavicle, but nothing's broken. He's going to be fine. But, he's pretty depressed. Think about it; he lost his wife and two mistresses on this cruise. And the publicity over this is not going to make him look good or bring him many new clients."

"What about the criminally insane portion of the stage performer population?" Jason asked.

"That's not more than twenty-five percent of the total," Rachel responded.

Mike laughed. "Is that just on this ship, or overall?" Rachel threw a balled-up napkin at him.

"One thing's certain," Michelle added, "nobody who saw the show tonight will ever forget it, and they'll all be talking about it for years."

"All publicity is good publicity, right?" Jason asked Ferguson.

"Don't fucking ask me. I'm in charge of security. I'm going to reconsider the idea of giving the performers access to those little pistols."

"How did she get that thing on the stage?" Mike asked. "I've been wondering."

Ferguson held up an open hand in frustration. "The locker where we keep the weapons is not supposed to be opened unless there's an emergency. But if you have the key, there's no alarm if somebody opens the locker. We don't know how the hell she got the key. We'll be looking into that. But she got it. I guess she figured she couldn't leave the gun in her cubby backstage, and she couldn't stuff it into her panties during the performance, so she swapped it out for the stage prop. Maybe she planned to grab it after the show and go kill Max. Maybe she just wanted it for insurance. But it was right there for her when you showed up, so she took advantage. She was a pretty cool cookie, I'll give her that."

"Yeah, we all admire her," Mike said sarcastically. "Did you find any evidence that will help us convict her of the murders?"

"Not yet. We're not sure what she used as a garrote when she killed Vicki Nelson, but there's nothing we can tie to her. She stabbed poor Elisabeth, but that knife has to be at the bottom of the Atlantic."

Rachel looked confused and leaned in toward Ferguson. "Isn't the fact that she had the ring and that she shot Max enough evidence?"

Jason took the floor with a professorial tone that anyone from their precinct would have recognized: his imitation of the way Mike spoke when he was teaching a class to detective candidates. "The problem is that she's got a story about how Max gave her the ring, as a promise to marry her. She'll say that Max killed his wife, and Elisabeth, and Vicki. She'll say that when she found out backstage that Max had lied to her, and that Max had falsely named her as the killer, she became enraged and shot him because he's a manipulative, philandering douchebag. That, of course, is pretty much true. So, that doesn't prove she killed Shirley Bloom, or the other two. A good lawyer – like maybe Billy Flynn from *Chicago* – might convince a jury that Max was the real criminal, and that Darci was an innocent dupe."

Mike asked, "I don't suppose she has made any incriminating statements since you took her into custody?"

Ferguson shook his head, while he took a sip of his rum. "She's in the brig and closed up like a clam."

"You've got a DNA sample from Shirley Bloom's murder," Michelle jumped in. "If that's a match to Darci, and it should be, then that will seal a murder conviction."

"Yeah, we're hoping," Ferguson said. "You did a good job collecting those samples. It's something our medical staff would not have done. We owe you one for that."

Michelle accepted the praise gracefully and said that any ME would have done the same. She offered to be available to testify about her examination if needed, and promised to send Karl Keller the audio recording of her exam before they left the ship.

Throughout the conversation, a stream of passengers came up to congratulate Mike and to offer sympathy to Jason. The fact that Mike had confronted the crazy actress during the *Chicago* show had spread around the ship like a viral dancing hamster video. Jason, with his arm in a sling, was quickly identified as the passenger who got shot in the melee. Everyone wanted to meet them and say they were there in the theater.

Mike, who didn't like the notoriety, weakly waved and sometimes shook hands with the well-wishers, downplaying his own role. Rachel, however, made him pose for selfies with her and her Squad from Texas on four different phones.

At a quarter to midnight, two white-clad waiters entered the lounge, pushing a chrome cart adorned with a white tablecloth and a huge silver dome. Mike was busy bantering with Ferguson and didn't notice. Michelle had been watching for them and subtly signaled where they should park their trolly. A minute later, the entire population of the Shangri-La Lounge was singing "Happy Birthday" while Mike tried not to smile.

The waiters unveiled a chocolate birthday cake with five candles. Mike blew them out quickly, and eventually acknowledged the good wishes and toasted to his 50th birthday. He was happy that there were only a few minutes left in the day. As soon as his watch reached midnight, he announced that the birthday party was over.

By 12:30, Jason said he was feeling tired. Mike thought his comment had something to do with the way Rachel was stroking his thigh. Jason stood up and came over to shake Mike's hand and give Michelle a kiss on the cheek. As he bent down toward her, Michelle whispered, "I guess you found a third option." Jason smiled and winked.

As he and Rachel were walking away, Mike called out, "Breakfast tomorrow at eight, before we disembark. We'll come up and meet you at your suite, right?"

Jason just waved his right hand over his shoulder, as Rachel – still wearing the purple dress with the plunging back – put her arm around his waist.

Not long after that, Ferguson said he and Millie were also going to call it a night. Mike and Michelle stood up with them. Mike gave April a twenty-dollar bill as an extra tip for all his good service, and then he and Michelle took a stroll on the exterior deck. They walked around the ship twice, enjoying the warm breeze. They were off the coast of Delaware and could see twinkling lights on the shore. The ship was meandering along, in no rush to cover the final few miles it needed to travel before arriving in New York harbor by morning.

They stopped at the stern, where they could see the wake created by the giant propellers. Michelle rested her head against Mike's shoulder. "I had visions of you getting shot up there on that stage."

"Yeah, me too."

"You probably would have taken the bullet in your left shoulder. I know you miss going to rehab with Terry."

Mike squeezed her closer to him with his left arm. "You want to know my one regret?"

"That you missed your chance to buy me an expensive piece of jewelry?"

"No. That I didn't get to sing you another love song in the Karaoke Bar."

Michelle looked up at him quizzically. "You call 'A Little Less Conversation' a love song?"

"Sure. Anything by Elvis is a love song."

"So, what were you going to serenade me with – if you had another chance?"

"You'll have to wait for the next cruise. They're giving us a free one, you know."

"You really want to get back on one of these ships, after what happened this time?"

"Sure. If they give us Sergio as our cabin attendant, I'm in."

Michelle laughed and they gazed out over the dark ocean without talking. The rhythmic crash and wash of the ship's journey through the waves was mesmerizing. Then, Mike said, "I love you, Michelle."

"I know," she replied, without turning her head. "And you sometimes scare the shit out of me. Which is how I know that I love you, too."

"Shall we attempt to avoid situations where either of us is in mortal peril for a few weeks, just to see what it feels like?"

"Why not?" Michelle replied, turning to Mike and looping her arms around his waist. The wind blew their hair. The moon cast jagged beams on the ocean waves. They shared a soft, lingering kiss.

Chapter 45 – Back to Reality

Tuesday, May 14

EARLY THE NEXT MORNING, Mike and Michelle were gathering up the few things in their cabin they had left to pack. The bulk of their clothes had been stuffed into their large suitcases, which they had left outside their cabin the night before to be whisked away to the port terminal as soon as they arrived. They each had a small bag they would be carrying off the ship.

As Mike wrapped up a slightly damp swimming suit in a plastic bag, there was a knock on the door. Mike figured it was their new cabin attendant, Raul, who had been extraordinarily attentive since Elisabeth's untimely removal from her position. Mike was planning to give him an extra tip, along with a compliment on the great towel eagle he had made for them the night before.

But it wasn't Raul at the door. It was Karl Keller. "I just

wanted to say good-bye," he said, shaking Mike's hand. "We've alerted the NYPD and they will be coming aboard to arrest Darci van der Meer as soon as we clear customs. I'm assuming you don't want to have anything to do with that."

"You are quite correct, sir."

"Yeah, I would feel the same. I also wanted to let you know that Marjorie Barnes has submitted her resignation."

"I guess it beats being fired," Mike said.

"Oh, there's one more thing you'll be interested in," Keller said with a Cheshire Cat grin. "Last night I sent out photos of all the rings we found in Darci's safe. Your partner forwarded me an email that mentioned an old case from North Carolina that Darci was connected to. I woke up the local detective down there this morning and sent him the photos. He recognized one of them as a loose end in his case. A husband and wife, both dead. They closed it up as a murder/suicide and blamed the husband, but the wife's kids claimed that the crime scene was missing a diamond engagement ring. They'll have to do a closer analysis, but they may need to re-open the investigation."

"I can't say I'm shocked that this wasn't Darci's first murder," Mike said a little sadly.

"Well, I hope we'll see you on board again. I know the company promised you a free cruise voucher. I want you to know that it's not a bribe to a cop. We would do it for anyone who had a murder committed in their stateroom during a cruise." He smiled wryly. "But seriously, if you come back soon, I'll still be here, so please come say hello. I'll do my best to make sure you have less excitement next time."

"I'll do that," Mike said, giving the man's hand one last shake. Before the door closed, Mike's cell phone rang. He figured it was Jason, so he didn't bother to check the caller ID before answering.

"Detective Stoneman! Dexter Peacock here, *New York Times*. I understand that there was some excitement on your cruise ship. I'm sure that you would want the story to be accurately reported. Can I have a few minutes of your time to make sure that we have the correct inside story of—"

Mike punched the END button.

"Who was that?" Michelle asked.

"Spam call."

"Well, let's get out of here." Michelle grabbed her bag and they headed off to meet Jason and Rachel at their junior suite.

When they exited the elevator on Deck 14, Edwin and Millie Ferguson were waiting to board the car. They held back when they saw Mike and Michelle. "I'm glad we found you before you disembarked, Stoneman," Ferguson said in his high-pitched voice. "You should try to speak to Keller before you leave. He has some interesting news."

"We know. He came by our cabin a few minutes ago. Say, I hope all this hasn't put you in an awkward position with the company."

Ferguson waved his hand dismissively. "Don't worry, Stoneman. Keller is taking credit for capturing Miss van der Meer and protecting the rest of the passengers. The deaths are being characterized as part of a love triangle, so future passengers should have no worries that Epic Cruise Lines is allowing random criminals aboard our ships. My job is quite secure, and I've already started pushing for upgrades to our onboard security systems. This unfortunate incident may actually lead to some positive changes."

"Glad to hear it," Mike said, reaching out to shake Ferguson's hand.

While the men were talking, Michelle spoke quietly to Millie. "Is this going to make your husband more or less ready to retire?"

"I'm hoping that all the excitement gets him over pining for the old cop days. But, with these boys, you never know. All I can say for certain is that he has a lot of energy today." She raised an eyebrow at Michelle and winked.

When the next elevator car arrived, Millie pushed the chair in and they all waved goodbye.

When Mike and Michelle arrived at the suite, Jason and Rachel were still packing. Actually, Rachel was still packing. Jason was merely watching. Mike motioned for his partner to join him out on the balcony and shut the glass door behind them.

"What happened to your blood-soaked rental tux?"

Jason laughed. "I left it outside the room last night so Sergio could return it to the rental shop. He came by this morning and told me there was no charge."

"Well, I guess they can't charge you after your suit got shot up by a deranged crew member. By the way, Jason, you have to tell me – what really happened last night, between the time Darci shot Max and the time she shot you?"

Jason hesitated only a moment. "To tell you the truth, when I saw you out there on the stage, I knew the shit was hitting the fan. I thought Darci might try to jump down off the stage, so I went down to stand between her and the audience, just to be a security barrier."

"So, you didn't leap in front of Rachel to take the bullet?"

"Well, I was there when she decided to shoot in our direction. I was trying to coax Rachel and the other ladies to move away, and I was trying to block Darci from leaping into the audience.

I knew that I was between Darci and Rachel, but I didn't really expect her to shoot. By the time she did, I just happened to be in the path of the bullet."

"Rachel thinks you're her hero. You took that bullet for her. You risked your life, she thinks."

Jason smiled. "Yeah, she mentioned that a few times last night."

"Are you going to take credit for that?"

"I will. The truth is, I was planning to apologize to her after the show for not going with her when she left the casino. I was going to tell her that she means the world to me and that I didn't want her to ever doubt that. Taking a bullet for her kind of got that message across. I'd prefer to have avoided the bleeding, however."

Mike laughed. "She's a great girl. My advice is still the same."

"I know, Mike. I appreciate that. But when I thought she was in danger, I knew I had to protect her. I've never felt that way about anyone before."

"Not even me?"

"Not even you, Mike. I have your back, and I might take a bullet for you, but I wouldn't feel the same heartache I felt last night when I thought Rachel might get hurt."

"So, you going to tell her that?"

Jason smiled. "I already have."

The End

Pina Colada Martini

1½ oz. pineapple rum

1½ oz. coconut rum

½ oz. pineapple juice

Combine in a shaker with ice,

then strain into a chilled martini glass

Garnish with pineapple chunk and a cherry

Rusty Nail

2 oz. scotch whiskey, poured over ice in an Old Fashioned glass

1 oz. Drambuie, floated on top of scotch

Thank you for reading *Lethal Voyage*. Since I started writing the Mike Stoneman Thriller series, I have taken great joy in hearing from readers about their reactions to the characters and the stories. I welcome critical comments and suggestions that can help me improve my writing. I urge every reader to please leave a review. Even a few words will go a long way and I will be grateful. Post on Amazon, Goodreads, BookBub, or any other platform that accepts reviews.

Keep reading to find a sneak preview of book #4 in the Mike Stoneman Thriller series – *Fatal Infraction*.

And please tell your friends about this book. As an independent author, I need all the word-of-mouth plugs I can get. Keep reading books by indie authors; there are a lot of great writers out there just waiting for you.

Kevin G. Chapman
November, 2020

AUTHOR'S NOTE & ACKNOWLEDGEMENTS

My wife, Sharon, and I are avid cruisers (well, before COVID-19 we were). So, it made sense to write a novel set on a cruise ship. It's a fun venue, and we've been on enough different cruise ships that I can write with confidence about the locations. We also love visiting Bermuda (you should go there!), and I enjoyed writing about some of our favorite places on the beautiful island.

On one of our cruises, we really did have the worst cabin attendant ever. (Members of the Marathon Expeditions trip will vouch for this.) Her name was Elisabeth. She moved things around inside our cabin for no reason. She was surly, when she wasn't absent. And she made the absolute worst towel animals. We have pictures. I'm not saying that she deserved to be murdered for them, but when I decided to have a cabin attendant get killed during this story, it was a natural to settle on her as the victim. So, if you were wondering, that's where Elisabeth's character came from.

The flip side is that we also had a wonderful cruise, on the *Oasis of the Seas*, where we spent considerable time in the Solarium bar with April, our favorite bartender. April was wonderful. He introduced us to Zacapa 23 and made sure that we felt welcome. He knew our names by day 2. April was the best. So, he gets a part in the story. See? Balance. The truth is that 98% of all the crew we've dealt with on cruise ships have been terrific. Tip them!

As always, I must credit my insightful wife, Sharon, for brainstorming the plot ideas and character development points in this book. Sharon has a fantastic vision for where my characters are going and she sees inconsistencies in the story that I sometimes miss. I could not write these books as well without her.

I also thank my brilliant editor, Samantha (Samanthachapmanediting.com) whose careful reads, sensitivity, and great ideas give me the editor that every author wants. The final product has been polished and improved significantly in the editing process. Just ask my beta readers. And kudos to my cover designer, Peter from bespokebookcovers.com. Peter worked with me through ten different design ideas before we finalized the current cover. Every cover designer should be so patient and helpful. Also kudos to Jiawie "Peter" Hsu from Fotolux in Princeton Junction, NJ (my local photo shop) for making me beautiful prints for my publicity posters.

My beta readers provided me with invaluable perspectives and ideas as the book was in development. Thanks so much to Joanna Joseph (who gave me really critical and objective notes!), Buzz & Beth Baradyn (Wow! How wonderful you are!), Mimi Bailey, John O'Sullivan, Amy Knarr, and the authors and readers at Critique Circle. All these folks were early readers who gave me their time and brain-power. If you want to be a beta reader for a future book, just send me a note via my website or at Kevin@KevinGChapman.com and I'll put you on the beta reader list.

Also a big shout-out to Dan Alatorre, whose books on fiction writing are terrific and whose personal encouragement and assistance have helped me tremendously. He's a mensch.

If you're a Mike Stoneman fan, join me on Facebook (Mike Stoneman Thriller Group) and send me a note to get on my newsletter distribution list or onto the Whiteboard Squad (my social media army). Find me at KevinGChapman.com.

About the Author

Kevin G. Chapman is, by profession, an attorney specializing in labor and employment law. He is a past Chair of the Labor & Employment Law Network of the Association of Corporate Counsel, leading a group of 6800 in-house employment lawyers. Kevin is a frequent speaker at Continuing Legal Education seminars and enjoys teaching management training courses.

Kevin's passion (aside from fantasy baseball, golf and tournament poker) is writing fiction. Kevin's first Novel: *Identity Crisis: A Rick LaBlonde, P.I. Mystery*, was self-published through Xlibris in 2003, and is now available via Amazon.com as a Kindle e-book. His second novel, *A Legacy of One*, published in 2016, was a finalist (short list) for the Chanticleer Book Review's Somerset Award for Literary Fiction. *A Legacy of One* is a serious book, filled with political and social commentary and a plot involving personal identity, self-determination, and the struggle to make the right life decisions.

Kevin has also written several short stories, including *Fool Me Twice*, the winner of the New Jersey Corporate Counsel Association's 2012 Legal Fiction Writing Competition, which was the genesis of Mike Stoneman. *Fool Me Twice* is available as a stand-alone short story on amazon, Google Play, Kobo, Nook, and other ebook retailers, or you can get it directly from Kevin's website. He has also written one complete screenplay (unproduced so far) and has another screenplay and two more novels currently in the works, one of which is a sci-fi space opera epic. And, of course, book #4 in the Mike Stoneman Thriller series, *Fatal Infraction* is in production for publication in 2021.

Kevin lives in Central New Jersey and is a graduate of Columbia College (class of '83, where he was a classmate of Barack Obama), and Boston University School of Law (magna cum laude '86). Readers can contact Kevin via his website at KevinGChapman.com

Other books by Kevin G. Chapman

Righteous Assassin (Mike Stoneman #1)
Deadly Enterprise (Mike Stoneman #2)
Fool Me Twice (A Mike Stoneman Short Story)

A Legacy of One

Identity Crisis: A Rick LaBlonde Mystery

coming soon:
Fatal Infraction (Mike Stoneman #4)

Connect with Kevin:
Kevin's website: https://www.KevinGChapman.com
Facebook page: Mike Stoneman Thriller Group
  https://www.amazon.com/gp/product/B08BZMDSVT
Email: Kevin@KevinGChapman.com

Book Club discussion questions for Lethal Voyage

1. Is Max Bloom a villain or did his clients know exactly what they were getting when they became involved with him?

2. Ferguson noted near the end that Max lost his wife, two mistresses, and most likely his career as an agent during the cruise. Does anybody feel sorry for Max – even a little?

3. Did the descriptions of the cruise ship and its activities give you a sense of being on the cruise as you read the story? If you've never been on a cruise ship, did reading this book make you more or less interested in taking a cruise in the future?

4. For readers who were already familiar with *Chicago*, did the references and illusions to the show enhance your enjoyment of the story? For readers who were not familiar with *Chicago*, did you feel like you were missing something?

5. Vicki and Darci: putting aside being a murderer, how did you feel about each of them? Were they justified in employing the available tactics to advance their careers?

6. In the theater before the *Chicago* performance, Michelle tells Jason that he has to choose whether to apologize to Rachel, or assert his dominance. When he asked whether those were his only options, she said they were. Was Michelle's advice to Jason correct?

7. What would you like to see happen in the future between Jason and Rachel?

8. What would you like to see happen in the future between Mike and Michelle?

9. In the beginning of the story, Edwin Ferguson, Mike's former mentor, assisted Mike's attempt to investigate Mrs. Bloom's death, while Karl Keller obstructed it. At the end of the story, did your feelings about Ferguson and Keller change? How and why?

10. Are you with Michelle or with Mike: Is "A Little Less Conversation" a love song? When it's your turn on the karaoke stage, what's your go-to song choice?

FATAL INFRACTION

A MIKE STONEMAN THRILLER (#4)

Jimmy Rydell Found Murdered

By Dexter Peacock, Sr. Correspondent
and Kristi Olson, Staff Writer

New York, NY. June 1, 2019 2:15 p.m.

Jimmy Rydell, Heisman Trophy winner and first round draft pick of
Gang Green in 2017, was found dead today, the victim of an apparent
shooting. He was reported missing on May 25. Rydell's body was
discovered this morning by Tony O'Malley, the operator of the
carousel in Central Park. Someone had left the body propped up in one
of the carousel's seats. The NYPD has not released any further details,
but sources interviewed by the *Times* confirmed that the body
appeared to have been dumped in that location after Rydell was killed
elsewhere. A spokesperson for the NYPD would say only that the
investigation is underway and that no suspects have yet been
identified.

In January of 2017, Rydell led the Mississippi State University
Bulldogs to an unexpected SEC championship. Rydell's record-setting
43 touchdown passes earned him both the Heisman Trophy and the
Davey O'Brien Award as the nation's top quarterback.

Before his first professional season, Rydell was involved in several
off-field incidents, including a fight with security officers in a New

York nightclub and an arrest for driving while intoxicated in New Jersey. He became a national figurehead when he took a knee during the singing of the National Anthem prior to the opening game of the season, despite a league directive that all players should stand. Rydell was fined, but not suspended, for the incident, and continued to display his support for the Black Lives Matter movement on and off the field. During. After a disappointing loss to Chicago, Rydell had a sensational on-camera meltdown on the sidelines where he took a swing at his head coach, Eddie Malone. Despite that incident, Rydell remained the starting quarterback until a minor knee injury knocked him out for the remainder of his rookie year. Fans were unhappy, and team management embarrassed, when Baker Mayfield, drafted by Cleveland with one of the picks the team traded away, finished second in the NFL's rookie of the year balloting

Rydell's 2018 season was similarly marred by off-field incidents, culminating with his embarrassing arrest in a Manhattan strip club after he shot himself in the foot with an unregistered gun. His season was ended prematurely again by the injury, and he was later convicted of two counts of gun-related charges, for which he was serving a period of probation and public service at the time of his death. Rydell and his supporters protested the decision to prosecute, claiming that White professional athletes in New York and elsewhere who committed similar offenses were not charged or were allowed to plead guilty to misdemeanors.

Team owner Woody Matheson said in a statement last night that the entire organization is shocked and saddened by the tragic death of their quarterback. "Despite his troubles off the field and his injuries, Jimmy Rydell was a young man of tremendous character and amazing talent, who will be missed by everyone in our locker room and front office." Matheson's son, Chip, the team's General Manager, who has been critical of Rydell's behavior and on-field performance, was unavailable for comment.

Since the end of the 2018 season, rumors have surfaced linking Rydell and two other New York players to a league-wide investigation into possible point-shaving. Rydell had declined to comment on the rumors and the league denied that there was any ongoing investigation. However, inside sources told *The New York Times* that federal agents were working on the case and that involved individuals linked to the Gallata crime family were also under investigation. Mr. Rydell's apparent murder may be connected to the sports gambling probe, although the police have so far declined to provide corroboration to such a link.

Funeral services for Jimmy Rydell will be held at St. Patrick's Cathedral on Saturday, beginning at 1:00 p.m. The team has made a donation of $100,000 in Rydell's name to the Boys and Girls Clubs of Greater New York, a charity for which Rydell did substantial fundraising work during his troubled time in New York City. Fans are urged to make donations to the organization.

* * *

MIKE STONEMAN AND JASON DICKSON sat across from each other in the small conference room, at the head of the table in the cramped space on the third floor of their precinct house on 94th Street. Captain Edward Sullivan leaned into the pock-marked wood, trying to get his face closer to the chrome speaker box positioned in the middle of the table. It had been a long call already.

Mike leaned back in his chair, a notepad on his lap. Jason sat straight up, as always, despite the sling covering his left arm. He was still healing from a gunshot wound he had received three weeks earlier onboard Epic Cruise Lines' *Colossus of the Ocean*. The other detectives were still ribbing him about not being able to take a vacation without getting into a gunfight.

Sully's face was getting redder by the minute. Jason made eye contact with Mike and shrugged, silently mouthing, "Shit show," to his partner.

"There's more press on this than on the royal wedding," Kimberly Williams said with unmasked anxiety. Williams was the head of communications for Mayor Frederick Douglass. Her job was to make sure the mayor's media profile was positive and that any public statements from city agencies, including the police department, were politically appropriate.

"I'm not concerned about the damned press!" came the angry voice of police commissioner Earl Ward. "We've got a dead athlete, a city full of freaked-out residents, and a ton of evidence that's getting stale while we sit around and argue about the optics and the publicity angles. I'm not waiting for the feds before we get our investigation going. I want Stoneman and Dickson over at Rydell's apartment building with a squad of uniforms right now!"

Sully agreed. Mike and Jason sat passively, not speaking. They pretty much knew how this was going to end, so adding their commentary would not shorten the call. After several more minutes of discussion about the pros and cons of letting the FBI take the lead in the investigation, Ward finally cut off the conversation, told Williams that he would speak to the mayor directly, and gave Sullivan the order to get his team on the case right away.

"OK, you two," Sullivan said, after punching the button to end the phone call. "Take four uniforms with you and get over to Rydell's building. When the feds arrive, try not to shoot them, OK?"

"We'll be our usual cooperative and friendly selves," Mike replied as he stood up, hearing his knees creak. He had been hoping for a relatively quiet first month back to work after his hastily planned vacation with Jason, and after the excitement of the week before that. The shootout at the Alexander Hamilton

Hotel in Brooklyn seemed like years earlier, but it had only been four weeks. He and Jason should have felt rested and refreshed after a six-day cruise to Bermuda on a luxury ship, but the cruise had ended up more like work than vacation. Sully and the rest of the detectives didn't want to hear about how exhausted they felt. They refused to believe that six days on a cruise ship with an unlimited premium drink package and a balcony cabin could have been stressful — the bullet wound in Jason's triceps notwithstanding.

As they walked out after Sullivan and headed for the stairs down to the street, Jason remarked, "At least nobody has the video of you in the Karaoke Bar."

* * *

Look for *Fatal Infraction,* book #4 in the Mike Stoneman Thriller series. Get updates and pre-order information at KevinGChapman.com.